LIGHTNING'S EDGE

LOST WORLD ODYSSEY

C. BUCK JONES

WOLFSTAR PUBLISHING

Contents

CHAPTER ONE

LIGHTNING

"That was great. I love your chicken enchiladas." Ryan picked up the last two plates from the kitchen table and set them on the counter beside the sink, where Emily, in a blue tank top and cut-off jeans, rinsed the pans and glasses before putting them in the dishwasher. The aroma of chilies and corn tortillas still filled the room.

"What do you have planned for tonight?" He put his arms around her waist and kissed the soft brown skin on her neck below the brunette ponytail. "I think we should light a fire and make out on the sofa," he whispered in her ear.

Emily shook her head, slapping him with her hair while she pushed back on the counter. "You know I've got to get ready to give my testimony at Celebrate Recovery tomorrow. Pastor Paul is counting on me, especially after you gave yours last month.

Many people, especially women, want to know how we made it through your infidelity and kept our marriage intact."

"I know." He kissed her neck again. "But you smell so good."

"Stop. Go take Toby for his walk and let me finish."

Toby, their three-year-old German shepherd, sat at the back door waiting and staring at him with his big brown puppy-dog eyes. Toby served as their watchdog and companion. Emily said she felt safe having him around, especially when Ryan traveled to his various clients scattered around the world. Last year, Toby chased a mountain lion out of the yard while Ryan was in Cincinnati. Though Emily loved the dog and spent a lot of time with him, he remained attached to Ryan, who spent the time training and walking him.

"Well, boy. It looks like me and Mrs. Jones won't have a thing going on tonight. Shall we go for a walk?" He kissed Emily's neck one more time before releasing her.

Toby yelped and turned a circle before bouncing on his front paws.

When Ryan went to the hall closet for his jacket, Emily said, "I'll be here when you get back, you know. It shouldn't take me too long to go through the testimony. Why don't you bring in some firewood when you get back?"

"I can do that." He grabbed his jacket and went to the back door. *I am the luckiest guy in the world. Who would have thought seven years ago when I cheated on her, we would still be married. That she would forgive me and even let me continue my consulting job. God did an incredible work of healing in us.*

Toby barked, letting his impatience show.

"I'm coming, boy." Stopping behind Emily, he kissed her neck again.

This time, she turned around and kissed him, holding her mouth against his before saying, "Go on, now, and let me finish."

He opened the back door and Toby ran out into the late afternoon sun. *God, I can't thank you enough for restoring my marriage and changing me.*

When he stepped out onto the back deck, Toby was standing at the edge of the yard, looking back, wanting to know which direction they would go. Though there was no fence, the mowed area around the house designated the yard. Past that, the weeds grew tall. Toby would not go beyond the yard without permission.

"Go on, boy." Ryan pointed to the left and Toby bounded into the weeds with his nose to the ground.

Ryan walked across the yard to the path that led to the creek. Toby ran a few yards ahead, pausing occasionally to look back and see where he was. When the dog got to the creek, he waded in and took a quick drink, then waited for his master to show him which direction they would go. Ryan pointed left again, and Toby started downstream.

They went down the well-traveled path that meandered along the creek bank. The willow bushes lining the path opened occasionally into meadows of long grass and aspen groves where beavers built their dams. They stopped, and he watched the brook trout rippling the surface of the pond. It had been a while since he had brought his fly rod down here. Maybe this weekend he would catch a mess of brookies. But tonight, he wanted to spend time with Emily, so he didn't want to go too far.

The sun was setting. Birds chirped and flitted in and out of the willows along the stream. Ahead of him, Toby stood at the edge of a clearing, growling with the hair on his neck on end. Ryan hurried over, wondering if Toby had spotted a bear or a lion. But when he got there, he couldn't see anything, though Toby still growled.

"It's all right, boy." He reached down and stroked Toby's neck. "Let's step out and have a closer look, then we'll head back to the house."

That's funny. The birds have stopped. He took two steps into the clearing with Toby, who remained alert with his ears up. The dog crouched like a predator beside him, ready to spring. Ryan's body tingled all over, like an electric current was flowing through him. A buzzing noise grew louder, then a blinding light flashed. He threw his arm up to shield his eyes. Pain seared his chest, burning his skin. The smell of ozone filled his nostrils. Then everything turned black.

CHAPTER TWO

THE DREAM

Ryan opened his eyes to a bright sun shining on his face. Too bright for him to see anything around him. He lay still for a moment before he tried to sit up, but his whole body tingled, like a thousand insects were crawling over his skin. Then a shadow blocked the sun, and a wet tongue licked his face, followed by a whine.

"Toby, stop."

The dog barked and continued to lick Ryan's face. He finally pushed him away, wiggled his fingers, then touched each finger to the thumb of the same hand until the tingling went away.

Toby continued to bark.

Ryan sat up; Toby came to lick his face again. The moisture evaporating off his face was cooling. *What happened? When did the sun get so bright and hot? Wasn't it sunset?* Ryan tried to remember. Looking around, all he saw was tall grass. Toby bounded in front of him, grabbed his sleeve, and pulled, wanting him to get up.

"Okay. Okay. Give me a second." Ryan moved to his hands and knees, then stood, swaying, trying to keep his balance. The ground seemed to spin under him. When the dizziness passed, all he could see was tall grass and rolling hills. *Where's the creek, the willow bushes? Am I dreaming?*

Ryan tried to raise his right hand to shade his eyes from the sun, but pain that felt like a hot knife stabbing into his shoulder prevented him from lifting it. After a few seconds, it subsided, and he lifted his arm.

Toby ran through the waist-high grass to Ryan's left, toward the top of the hill. The dog stopped, looked back, and barked, acting like he wanted Ryan to follow him up the hill.

"Okay, boy. I'm coming." He followed Toby, but stopped just below the crest of the hill, where he could look over the grass and down the other side. There he gazed upon a sea of black and brown shapes rolling toward them. The animals looked like bison, huge bison. More than he had ever seen, and they were coming fast. Then he noticed tawny shapes loping at the edge of the herd. *Are those lions?*

Toby whined and started back down the hill. "You're right, boy. We need to get out of their way." Ryan and Toby jogged along the top of the ridge that ran perpendicular to the herd's path. They trotted toward a line of trees to their left, hurrying to get out of the bison's path and hoping the lions didn't see them. They reached the tree line with the thunder of thousands of hooves reverberating through the ground behind them. Ryan watched from the cover of a large pine tree as the herd rumbled down the hill a mere quarter of a mile away.

Sweat ran down Ryan's face and back. He sat against the trunk of the pine with Toby panting beside him.

He looked at the dog. "If this is just a dream, why can't you talk?" Toby sat up and cocked his head and looked at him. He reached over to the dog, petting his neck and behind his ears. The last thing he remembered was kissing Emily. *Why can't I wake up? Why does everything feel so real? This is the worst dream ever.*

"I'm thirsty. We should head down the hill through the trees. Maybe there's a creek down there."

The hike through the forest seemed to continue forever, and the trees got thicker the farther down they went. The shade from the trees and the sinking sun turned the early heat into a penetrating chill as the wind blew harder. Ahead of them stood a fir tree with branches hanging nearly to the ground that grabbed his attention. "Well, Toby, it doesn't look like we'll find water today. That tree should give us some shelter from the wind and hide us for the night."

They sat under the boughs of the fir. Exhausted and aching, Ryan fell asleep. He dreamed of sitting at the kitchen table. Emily danced around with a pitcher of iced tea. She poured him a tall glass, then disappeared. Opening his eyes, he was still under the tree with barely any spit in his raspy throat.

Toby's head was on his lap, the dog's body heat helping to ease the chill. He had to move. His back felt locked and didn't want to bend. He leaned over and curled up next to Toby's body. It took a while for him to go back to sleep. The wind sighed through the trees of the pitch-black night. He could hear the howl of wolves or coyotes in the distance. *When I wake up, I'll be home in my bed next to Emily.*

Chapter Three

Survivor Mode

Ryan woke up with a stabbing pain in his left shoulder. He eased his arm out, trying to find Emily. She wasn't there, only the furry warmth of Toby. He sat up. *What's happening?* The darkness pressed in on him. He moved his arms and twisted his back to loosen his joints. He reached up and struck a limb.

"Ugh." Toby's cold nose pressed against his cheek. "Hi, boy," he said, petting the dog's neck, then he leaned back against the trunk of the tree. Toby lay back down with his head on Ryan's lap. *What time is it? Where am I? I was walking Toby and stepped into that clearing.*

He remembered the events of the previous day. *I thought this was a dream, but here I am under a tree with Toby. How did we get here?* He couldn't make sense of anything. It was impossible. He checked his Fitbit to see what time it was, but the battery was dead. *Great.*

Toby's head was still across his lap, locking him into the sitting position. He shifted his back to the left to get away from a knot that was poking him. He hurt all over, but eventually, the fatigue won, and he drifted back to sleep.

A cacophony of birds woke him to the gray dawn. Stiff, achy, and cold, he moved and woke Toby, who stood and nuzzled his face into Ryan's chest.

"It's okay, boy. I don't understand what's happening either." He gave the dog some reassuring pats, then rolled to his hands and knees and crawled out from under the tree. The light breeze cut right through his light jacket. It felt like twenty degrees, but he knew it was probably closer to forty since no frost covered the ground. *I wish I had worn a heavier jacket.*

Swinging his arms and stomping his feet, he continued to loosen his stiff joints. Twisting, his back popped with an audible crack that got Toby's attention. The dog stood a few yards away, sniffing a bush. The dog came back to him and looked at him with pleading eyes and whined.

"I know, boy, I'm hungry and thirsty too. Let's keep moving downhill. Eventually, we will get to some water. At least I hope so." He had been elk hunting enough to know that the streams ran through the valleys. They should find water down at the bottom of the hill.

Ryan walked a mile or more, until the slope increased, and the deadfall forced him to climb over all the fallen trees, while Toby went under or around them and waited for him on the other side. His body and mind seemed sluggish, and his head ached. Dehydration. It felt like altitude sickness. *Slow down, I can't afford to fall. It could be fatal.*

After an hour of scrambling over and through the dense forest, Ryan sat on a fallen tree to rest. Toby sat panting at his feet. "I hope we find water soon," he rasped.

They trudged on through the trees. Ryan lost track of time, but eventually the forest thinned out, and the trees changed from dense spruce and fir to ones resembling ponderosa pines with limbs uniformly spaced and long needles in clumps. He saw a clearing ahead, and when he stepped out of the trees, he was in a narrow valley. A clear stream flowed at the bottom. Toby ran ahead to the stream and waded in, drinking loudly as he lapped the water with his tongue. Ryan's legs felt too heavy to run, so he walked faster, but his feet slid out from under him when he started down the steep bank. He bounced hard on his rump, jarring his teeth. "Ugh!"

He crawled the last few feet to the clear, rocky stream and plunged his face into the cold water before drinking. The cool water tickled his parched throat as he swallowed. He drank and drank until satisfied. Then, moving a short distance up the bank, he lay back on a patch of soft green grass. The afternoon sun warmed his body and eased some of the aching. He closed his eyes and fell asleep.

When he opened his eyes, the sun was getting low. Toby lay near him with his ears erect, listening. A natural guard dog, he always stayed alert. When Ryan sat up, Toby stood. "It's getting late, boy. We need to look for a place to spend the night."

As they walked down the valley, the walls steepened into a small canyon. The stream got narrower and deeper, with large rocks and pools. Spotting a boulder with an overhanging face, he said, "That looks like a good place to shelter for the night."

Though Ryan still believed he was dreaming, he thought about survival. He had been through a couple of short survival training courses and spent plenty of time in the mountains hunting, fishing, and backpacking. As he sat under the rock face, he took inventory. He had his clothes and shoes, including a jacket, a belt, and a useless Fitbit. In his pockets, he had a wallet and a small pocket knife.

When he finished, he went into the forest and found enough small tree limbs on the ground to form a lean-to against the rock face. With his pocket knife, he cut fir boughs and laid them over the lean-to frame to create a rough shelter, then he put other boughs under it to form a bed. When he was done, he headed down to the stream for some water.

Below them, the stream split into two flows with a gravel bar between them, which made it a little wider and shallower than it was higher up. Toby ran ahead and drank from the nearest flow. When Ryan got there, he kneeled on the gravel and drank. He looked up at Toby. The dog was acting strangely. He looked at the water, barked, and plunged his nose into the stream.

"What's going on, boy?" Ryan asked, but Toby didn't respond. He watched as the dog plunged his head in again. This time he came out with a fish in his mouth.

"Good boy! You're a good dog!" Ryan waded across to where Toby stood. The dog dropped his catch on the sandbar and played with it, pawing and sniffing it as it flopped around on the gravel.

In the stream where Toby had caught the fish, Ryan noticed more of them in a small pocket along the far bank in front of him. He waded upstream, herding the fish in front of him, closer to the bank. Then, he put his hands into the water and tried to grab one, but they were too fast and too slippery. He waited with his hands in the water, staying as still as possible with the fish between him and the bank before throwing his hands out and up, launching a fish out onto the gravel.

He took his catch over to where Toby played with the first fish. "Good boy, Toby," he said as he took it from under Toby's paws. He cleaned the two trout, giving Toby the roe that had swollen the fishes' bellies. The dog gobbled up the eggs and begged for more. Ryan cut the meat from the bones, giving Toby one fish, before he gulped down the second. It tasted like sushi, but without the wasabi.

After eating, they waded back across and went up to the shelter. Ryan gathered some dry wood and pine bark along the way. When they got back to the shelter, he cut a thin stick and sharpened one end into a point. With a piece of bark and some dry grass, he tried to make a fire by spinning the point of the stick into the bark. He worked until his hands were sore but couldn't get a spark. *I wish I had paid more attention during classes. They made it look so easy.*

Sitting with his back against the boulder, he watched as the sunset turned the sky into a fiery orange and listened to the birds. "Well, Toby." He stroked the dog's neck while he lay on the ground next to him. "We found food and water. I think we should stay here for a while and regain some of our strength. It's going to be another cool night, but at least we have a decent shelter tonight. Are you ready to turn in?"

Toby tilted his head and stared at him.

Unlike the previous night, Ryan didn't go right to sleep. His mind raced. He imagined Emily frantically searching for him. When he dozed off, he dreamed of aliens transporting him into a huge spaceship hovering above his house. A robotic arm with a large hypodermic needle reached for his stomach. He woke to sharp pain and cramps in his gut. He moved, trying to relieve the pain, but had to crawl out of the shelter and stand. Walking seemed to help. After a few minutes, the cramps eased.

Toby lay at the entrance to the shelter, watching him. The bright moon lit the open areas and the black moon shadows painted a stark monochrome contrast to the surrounding scene. The moon looked too small and too bright, without the familiar dark splotches that he remembered. Eventually, the cool air forced him back into the shelter where Toby lay next to him, and he slept.

The next morning, they returned to the stream for water and more fish. Ryan walked around the perimeter of the small island and on the upstream end, he found a straight piece of wood that was about six and a half feet long and an inch and a half in diameter. Taking it back to where Toby stood smelling the fish bones, he sat on a rock and spent most of the morning whittling the smaller end of the stick to a sharp point. The wood was tough, making it difficult to cut with his small knife. When he finished the crude spear, he fished again using the same technique as before.

After eating, Ryan lay on the stream bank and soaked up the afternoon sun. He took a different route back to the shelter. Walking downstream, he looked for other places to fish. A quarter of a mile downstream, he spotted a bush among the rocks with red berries. When he got closer, he picked one and tasted it. They were raspberries. Pleased, he ate his fill, and took as many as he could carry in the pockets of his jacket.

He sat by the bush and tears welled up as he remembered picking wild raspberries along the Platte River with Emily when their son was seven years old. They took the berries home and put them on top of homemade ice cream. The sour-sweet taste reminded him of those good times. Here, all he had eaten since he came to this strange land was raw fish. He held some of the berries in his hand for Toby, who only ate a few and didn't seem impressed.

That afternoon, Ryan felt like his strength was returning. He picked up his hand drill and worked at starting a fire. This strange, idyllic land teemed with birds who woke him early every morning with their singing. There were other species of wildlife inhabiting the area. He had seen a large deer with huge antlers farther up the valley. Toby had chased rabbits and squirrels. It wasn't much different from Colorado. Ryan was shifting into survivor mode. He needed to survive if he was ever going to see Emily again.

If I could get a fire going, I could make a rabbit stick and maybe get something different to eat.

The shelter provided better protection than staying under a tree since the wind didn't go through it as easily and it held the heat in better. That night, he would have slept better if the coyotes or wolves hadn't been so noisy. They kept Toby on edge. The dog was up and down all night, growling occasionally. When Ryan finally fell into a deep sleep, he dreamed of sitting on the porch at home with Emily, drinking coffee, but Toby woke him.

Before going back to sleep, he prayed, "God, I miss Emily. Heavenly Father, help me get back home. I don't know where I am. I'm lost. A hot cup of coffee would taste so good right now. I need your help to get a fire started."

The next morning, Toby was ready to go. Ryan thought he must be hungry. Though already outside the shelter, the dog would stick his head in the entrance and bark, letting Ryan know he wanted to go.

He crawled out and donned his jacket after using it as a blanket while he slept. Then he picked up the spear and headed down to the river with Toby. As they rounded a big rock, Toby froze. His hackles raised, and he growled. Ryan glanced down at the stream. There on the island stood the biggest cat he had ever seen. It appeared to be as tall as him, with long fangs protruding from its upper jaw, extending down past its lower jaw.

My God, it's a saber-toothed tiger.

CHAPTER FOUR

SABER-TOOTH

The sight of the huge, orange, speckled cat sucked the air out of Ryan's lungs. His eyes opened wide, and his heart raced. His feet felt like he wore lead boots. He hoped the beast wouldn't see them as it sniffed around the island and licked the rocks where they had cleaned the fish. The cat raised its head and its yellow eyes looked right at him. It roared, and it leaped across the creek in one giant bound.

Ryan turned and ran. Hopeless, he knew he couldn't outrun the beast. Ten yards in front of him stood a tall pine tree. He sprinted straight toward it. He could feel the big cat's breath on his neck as he grabbed onto the first limb with one hand. His momentum swung him up into the tree. The saber-tooth couldn't stop that fast and slid under it. Ryan scrambled up the next two higher branches, holding onto his spear. He paused a moment and looked at the saber-tooth twelve feet below him at the base of the tree. Toby ran in circles and barked several yards to the cat's left. It looked at Toby, but then it looked up at Ryan. *Surely, it's too big to climb up here.*

But the big cat jumped, holding onto the tree trunk with its long claws and snapping its jaws at Ryan's feet. Grasping the branch above with his free hand, he stabbed at the cat with his spear, poking it in the nose. It roared and fell. Ryan climbed as fast as he could up the tree. Near the top, he found a pair of branches that provided a stable seat. The cat was back on the tree, rapidly closing the distance between them. From his perch, he hoped he could hold it off by poking it in the face with his spear. *God, help me hold on. I don't want to be cat food.*

The big cat held onto the tree trunk, snapping at Ryan, who poked at it, eliciting screams when he hit the animal's nose or mouth. After several minutes of being poked in the face, the saber-tooth gave up and climbed down. But it didn't leave. It paced around the tree, looking up at him and ignoring Toby's incessant barking. After thirty or forty more minutes of pacing, the cat lay down at the tree's base.

Ryan watched it, not wanting to be surprised by another attack. The cat seemed unconcerned about him and lay there licking its paws and the blood from wounds on its nose and face. Its light orange back, dappled with brown spots, rose and fell as the animal breathed. *I need to stay alert. I don't want to fall out of this tree. Hopefully, it will give up and go look for something easier to eat.*

Toby had stopped barking and sat with his ears up, eyeing the big cat, but he also appeared to be relaxed. Then the dog stood up, crouched with his ears forward, and growled. Ryan looked down at the saber-tooth. It stood at the base of the tree, looking up at him again. He tightened his grip on the spear, ready for another attack, but the cat turned and bounded off into the forest. Toby came to the tree and looked up at Ryan, who was unwilling to come down yet. He wanted to wait until he was sure the saber-tooth wouldn't be back.

About an hour later, he climbed down to the now sleeping Toby. The cat must have been far enough away from them that Toby couldn't hear it or smell it. When he reached the bottom, they headed back to the shelter.

"I don't think we can stay here any longer." Ryan grabbed his hand drill and the remaining berries. "That saber-tooth knows we are here and may come back looking for us. Let's head downstream. What do you think, Toby?"

Toby barked.

The terrain got steeper as they moved down. The birds had stopped singing during the heat of the day, and when they rested, they heard the saber-tooth roaring in the distance. "It sounds like the big cat caught his meal." Toby just looked at him. "It would be nice if you could talk to me. I can't always tell what you're thinking. But it is nice having you with me. You're a good boy."

Toby wagged his tail and licked Ryan's face.

Ryan ate a few berries and scratched behind Toby's ears before they started into the deeper canyon. The rough, boulder-filled slope slowed their progress. When they came to an opening in the trees, Ryan stood at the edge of a steep canyon with a river flowing white through the rocks below. The roar of fast water drowned out the other forest sounds.

"We can't cross that, Toby." He turned away from the river. "Let's go back up to the smaller creek and ford it before we go any farther."

Ryan picked his way back up the slope of the canyon to level ground, wishing he could navigate the slope as easily as Toby. At the top, they headed parallel to the canyon until they reached the smaller stream. It was even bigger here, and deeper than where they had stayed. They went upstream another quarter of a mile and found a spot Ryan thought he could wade. He used his spear as a staff and picked his way across the slick rocks of the creek bottom. The thigh-deep water was too deep for Toby, who had to swim while the current carried him downstream. Ryan stood in the middle of the creek and saw his dog struggling to stay close, but the current took the dog around a boulder and out of sight.

"Toby!" Ryan tried to move downstream, but the fast water and slick rock bottom prevented him from getting a better look at where Toby had gone. He needed to concentrate on his own footing. When he reached the opposite bank, he climbed out and ran downstream.

"Toby! Toby!" he called, but all he could hear was the water. *Father, help me find Toby. I don't think I can survive without him.*

He continued to call and listen as the stream dropped, plunging over waterfalls into deeper pools of the canyon. The boulder-strewn bank proved extremely challenging. He scrambled over and around the large rocks and called until he heard an answering bark. He listened and continued downstream until he saw Toby in a deep pool surrounded by rocks that stuck too high above the surface for the dog to climb. The water flowed down a three-foot drop above the pool, and below that, an eight-foot waterfall cascaded into another pool. Toby swam in the eddy along the rocks. He struggled to keep his head above the water, but barked when he saw Ryan, who made his way to the lowest of the rocks. Lying down, still an arm's length above the water, he called, "Toby, come."

Toby swam over to him and tried to climb out, but he couldn't get his front paws up far enough. Ryan reached down, grabbed his forelegs, and pulled. Toby had weighed eighty pounds at his last vet check, but now, soaking wet, he weighed more. Ryan was weak from their ordeal and struggled to pull the dog up onto the rock, but he eventually got Toby far enough out of the water that the dog could use his own legs to help pull himself up. Once on top of the rock, Toby shook and threw water everywhere. He leaned his wet body into Ryan, soaking his clothes, which had dried during the search.

Exhausted and wet, they rested in the warm sunshine to dry. After regaining some energy, Ryan sat up and said, "Toby, let's find somewhere to make a shelter and rest tonight before we move farther downstream."

They moved up the hill away from the water, where Ryan built a quick shelter between two boulders that were about four feet apart. He put branches and pine boughs over the top and pine boughs on the ground. The dark, roiling clouds to the west threatened rain. Ryan tried again, without success, to start a fire with the hand drill, though this time he got smoke before his hands and arms became too tired to continue.

That night, the wind howled, and the sky opened in a massive thunderstorm that poured sheets of rain over them. Though not completely waterproof, the shelter kept them reasonably dry. The thunder and lightning frightened Toby, who leaned against Ryan, panting. Again, the big dog's body provided some welcome warmth and reassurance.

Chapter Five

Downstream

R yan and Toby spent three days in the shelter above the stream. Toby found carcasses to scavenge from, but Ryan ate the berries he had foraged before seeing the saber-tooth. On the third day, he finally got a fire started after trying unsuccessfully every morning and evening.

The warmth from the fire reflected off the rock walls and gave them the warmest night since their arrival in this strange land. But troubled dreams filled his sleep, dreams about Emily. She believed he had run off with another woman and she would not let him back into their house. He sat up and stared at the dying embers of the fire. Tears ran down his face. He hugged himself. *Why can't I wake up? This must be a dream.*

He spent the next morning gathering wood from the hillside above for the night's fire. When he dropped the load at the shelter, he saw a curved branch about eighteen inches long that fit nicely in his hand. *If I can make a throwing stick, that means the new menu includes rabbits and squirrels. If I can hit one, I can cook it; I have fire.*

They went back up the hill to get more wood. On the way back to the shelter, Toby scared up a rabbit, but it was too quick, and it got away. Later that evening, Toby wandered off into the trees. He came prancing back into the firelight after dark, carrying the leg bone of an animal he had found. It stunk, but Toby pulled bits of flesh from it and gnawed on the bone.

"At least one of us has food. You probably need it more than I do, since you don't eat raspberries and we've caught no fish since we got here."

The next morning, he piled the firewood he gathered between the two rocks at the entrance to the shelter. Then he put more pine boughs on the roof to help keep the rain out. The rest of the morning and early afternoon was spent removing the bark and smoothing the throwing stick with his pocket knife. Once satisfied, he went up the hill to where the rocks thinned. He found a small bush he could use as a target. He stood ten paces away and threw the stick. On his first throw, he hit the bush. Surprised, he kept throwing until he could hit it with ten consecutive tries. He believed he had a good feel for how the stick flew. As the sun sank below the horizon, he started back and saw a rabbit sitting on a sun-warmed rock. *Why not try? What do I have to lose?*

His first throw nailed the rabbit, which tumbled off the rock to the grass below. He ran over and grabbed its still-kicking hind legs while putting his foot on its head and pulled the rabbit's head off, then peeled the skin and fur before he gutted it just like his father had taught him when he first learned to hunt. In Colorado, you didn't want to keep the fur on the dead rabbit because of the fleas. So, you skinned it right away and moved to clean it.

"Woo-hoo. Woo-hoo. I have meat!"

Toby heard the yell and came running. When he arrived, he started smelling the rabbit, jumping on Ryan, and whining.

"Leave it! You will get yours after I've cooked it and eaten my share."

Back at camp, he put the carcass on the boughs over the shelter and started the fire. Then he skewered the rabbit on a stick that he stuck into the ground, leaning it over the fire to roast it. The fat melted and sizzled when it dripped into the fire. His stomach growled. The aroma of the burning fat and roasting meat made him realize how long it had been since he had any real meat. Toby gave him a questioning look when his stomach rumbled, then sat by him and stared at the carcass. The dog whined and licked his lips.

"I know just how you feel, boy."

When the rabbit looked done, he tore off one of the big back legs and bit a chunk out of it. The meat was tough but delicious, and the juices ran down his chin. He pulled the other hind leg off. When he finished with the meat, he tossed the bones to Toby. After he ate the front legs and part of the back, he gave the carcass to the dog, who carried it a short distance away to eat it.

That night, with the warmth of the fire and a full belly, he slept better than any night since he had left home. He dreamed about hunting and not about Emily for a change.

They hunted every day they remained at the camp, and even though he didn't hit his target on every throw, there was plenty of game, and he had enough chances that he killed something to eat almost every day. By the third day of his new diet, he felt like he had more energy. So, they started back downstream in search of people.

It took them three days of climbing over rocks and deadfall while they descended into the canyon. The rough terrain made hunting difficult, but Ryan had brought some meat he had cooked back at camp. On the third day, the canyon opened into a broad valley and the river widened and slowed. Toby ran to the river and drank. He also caught a small fish. Later, Ryan killed a bird that looked like a grouse.

"I think we'll be okay for a little while," he said to Toby as they sat by the fire in front of their new lean-to.

The next day, after the sun was high, they went to the river. He stripped off his clothes and waded into the slow-moving water, submerging himself, and using the sand from the river bottom to remove the dust, grime, and blood from his skin. Then he rinsed out his clothes and hung them in the willows where they dried. While he waited, Toby brought him a stick, and they played fetch.

He felt like he was finally adapting to the hunter-gatherer lifestyle, but that night back at camp, his thoughts turned to home. He remembered Emily standing at the sink, kissing her neck, and holding her. *God, I want to go home. I miss her.*

Early the next morning, they headed up the hill through the trees to look for game. After an hour with no success, Toby stopped. The hair on his neck and back stood up, and he growled.

"What do you hear, boy?" After the incident with the saber-tooth, Ryan stayed alert to Toby's warnings. They continued slowly up the hill, listening. Toby moved with his ears up. Finally, Ryan heard the screams.

"That sounds like a person," he said. "With me, don't wander off." He signaled for the dog to stay close.

They crept toward the sounds. The screams that were clearly human, mixed with the screeches of an animal grew louder. As the trees ahead of them thinned, they slowed even more. When they got to the edge of a clearing, they stopped.

Chapter Six

Weeko

Weeko kneeled on the rock at the water's edge, filling the waterskin. The sun, rising just above the horizon, did not provide enough warmth to remove the chill from her body. She shivered before lifting the skin from the lake. The forest and mountains across the lake reflected in the smooth surface of the water. She turned and went up the path, through the reeds, to the village. Birds sang and flitted through the tall grass. Smoke from the village fires hung low. She could smell meat cooking.

Her village sat on the edge of the lake with several huts just a few paces from the shore, but the water was too shallow there to fill the skins. The twenty huts formed a circle, inside a brush fence, around a large central firepit. She carried the water to her hut, where Wanika, her father, stood at the door.

"Here's the water, Papa." Weeko held the skin out to her father.

"Take it to your mother," he said. "I will be in soon and we can eat before you go to gather firewood."

Inside the hut, Weeko hung the waterskin on a branch that extended from one limb that formed the hut wall. In the center of the room, a low fire burned. The smoke drifted up through an opening in the roof. Her mother kneeled at a flat rock beside the fire, slicing fruit with a stone knife.

"Bring some of the dried meat." Her mother pointed to the bag hanging near where Weeko hung the water.

Wanika came into the hut and sat beside her mother. Weeko brought the strips of dried meat and handed them to her mother, then sat beside her father. The warmth of the fire chased the chill from her body. Though the morning was cool, she knew the day would be hot while she gathered firewood. She listened to her father tell of the plans for the fall hunt. The tribe would need at least two tanka to get them through the next winter.

"Weeko," her friend Nanji said from the door. "Are you going to gather wood this morning? We can go together."

"She is," Wanika answered. "It's a good idea that you don't go alone. We have heard troubling calls from the forest lately, and game has become scarce. There may be a predator in the area."

Weeko finished her meal and hugged her parents before she left with Nanji. It would be nice having company, and between them they should finish the chore before midday. Nanji was strong, two years older than Weeko and not as thin. Soon a young hunter would take her as a wife, so her conversation centered on which of the eligible men might choose her. Weeko listened to her talk, but she wasn't interested in marriage yet.

Nanji continued to talk while they stacked dead branches in a pile at the edge of the forest. Nanji tied the branches together so they could drag them back to the village, but before she finished, Weeko screamed and pointed.

Two tanwakua had come out of the trees. Nanji had talked so much they hadn't heard them. The birds had short, stubby wings with fur-like feathers and long, bluish legs ending in three-toed, taloned feet. Their bodies were brown and black with a long black neck topped by a white and yellow head with an orange crest. Their massive orange-yellow beaks ended with a sharp hook.

"To the trees!" Weeko ran toward the forest with Nanji behind her. The birds closed the distance screeching and snapping their huge beaks. "Go get help," Weeko said. "I'll distract them."

Nanji ran into the trees and Weeko climbed into a pine tree, screaming and waving her arms. The birds circled the tree below and jumped, trying to reach her. She climbed higher to be certain she was out of reach and continued to scream, announcing her location.

While the birds screeched and jumped, circling the base of the tree, a small manetoo ran toward them, barking. The bird kicked, but the manetoo veered, and the taloned foot missed. The bird jumped after the manetoo. When it looked like the tanwakua would catch it, a giant stepped out of the trees and threw a stick, hitting the bird. It stopped and shook its head, then turned and went at the giant. When it got within twenty feet, it leaped into the air with its large, taloned feet aimed straight at him. He ducked, the talons missing him by less than a foot. He drove the spear he carried into the monster's side. It screamed and fell. The manetoo ran up and grabbed the bird's throat and held on until it stopped moving.

Weeko kept screaming, but the second terror bird went to help the first. It didn't charge the man. It didn't leap, but it moved erratically, and tried to get the man within range of its sharp beak. The bird snapped and thrust its head at him. He couldn't get a clear opening to stab the monster with the spear he had retrieved from the first bird. He was in trouble.

Just when it looked like the bird would win, the manetoo ran in from behind and grabbed the enormous bird's leg, just above the knee. The bird turned, which gave the giant the target he needed. He rammed the spear into the bird's side, burying the shaft all the way to his hands and knocking the beast over. This time, the spear pierced the bird's heart. It hit the ground with a thud, dead.

He pulled the bloody spear out and fell on his rump. The manetoo came over and nuzzled the man's face, smearing it with his blood-soaked muzzle and licking the blood off. The man put his arm around the animal's neck.

Weeko couldn't believe what she had seen. A lone hunter had killed two terror birds with the help of a small manetoo. And now, the manetoo licked the man's face like they were pack mates. She kept screaming.

Chapter Seven

Terror Birds

Ryan sat with his arm around Toby, letting the dog lick his face. "Good boy, Toby, but you can't just attack. One of these times, the beast will get you. I don't know what I would do without you."

It took him a few minutes to realize that the person up in the tree was still screaming. He got up, and they approached the tree.

"It is okay. We are friends. You can come down now." He was close enough to see that the person was a girl. She didn't respond. She just kept screaming. *I don't think she understands me.*

She continued to scream, while Toby and Ryan stood at the base of the tree and looked up at her. Then Toby turned, crouched, and growled. Ryan looked in the direction the dog was facing and saw a band of armed men running into the clearing.

The men ran into the clearing and surrounded them. They resembled the indigenous people of the Amazon he had seen in documentary films. They were short, with the tallest standing only about five feet seven inches. Their long, straight, black hair hung to their shoulders, and many had bones or sticks through their noses. All wore only breechcloths hung over a leather thong tied around their waist, and each carried a stone-tipped spear or a stone axe.

"Stay," Ryan commanded Toby, who growled and appeared to want to go after them. He laid his spear, which he had retrieved from the giant bird, on the ground and lifted his hands over his head.

The group tightened the surrounding circle until their spearpoints nearly touched him. Toby growled and whined, but he didn't break his stay. *Maybe finding people wasn't such a good idea. I hope they're not cannibals.*

The girl in the tree finally came down, still yelling. She ran to one warrior and threw her hands in the air. He wrapped his arms around her and spoke to her. Ryan couldn't understand them, but the girl pointed to the terror birds on the other side of the clearing. The girl and the warrior jabbered for a few minutes, then the man said something, and the rest of the warriors relaxed and took a step back.

The girl and the warrior walked into the circle and spoke gibberish to Ryan, who leaned down and patted Toby's head.

He figured the girl had told the man about the encounter with the birds.

"It's okay, boy," he said and stood facing the warrior. The girl reached her hand out toward Toby, saying, "Manetoo."

Toby sniffed her hand then licked it, and she came closer, petting him, and then she hugged him, repeating the word, manetoo.

The warrior stood in front of Ryan and pointed to the terror birds. "Tanwakua." Ryan assumed that was what they called them. Then he pounded his chest and said, "Wanika."

Ryan pointed to him and repeated, "Wanika." Then he pointed to the dead birds and said, "Tanwakua." The man smiled, and the other warriors raised their spears and grunted. Ryan patted his chest and said, "Ryan." Then he patted Toby's head and said, "Toby."

The warrior, Wanika, tilted his head and pointed to Toby. "Manetoo"

Ryan nodded and put his hand on Toby's head and said, "Manetoo. Toby." Then he said, "Toby. Manetoo."

Wanika smiled. "Toby. Manetoo." He turned and said something to the other warriors, and they started back into the forest. The girl took Ryan's hand and pulled him along. He stopped the girl so he could pick up his spear and throwing stick before he allowed her to lead him after the others.

They followed an ill-defined trail into the trees and up a hill for about a mile. When they came to the top, the trees opened out into a large clearing with a small lake and a stream along the western edge. About halfway down to the lakeshore sat a village of rough stick huts surrounded by a brush boma. Smoke came from the center of the village and several of the huts. The smell of burning pine drifted toward them on the gentle breeze that blew from the west.

As they neared the village, more people ran out to meet them. Most ran to the girl from the tree, chattering. Like the warriors, their only clothing was a breechcloth. When they finally entered the village, the rest of the villagers crowded around Ryan and Toby. Many reached out and pulled on his shirt. Wanika finally said something to them, and they all backed away.

Inside the boma, the huts formed a circle facing a large fire pit in the center. They led Ryan past the fire to a hut near the lake and left him there. The only place inside where he could stand fully erect was near the fire in the center. A pad of rushes to the right of the entrance, he assumed, functioned as the bed. Two crudely fashioned clay bowls sat on the rocks that surrounded the firepit.

He lay down on the rushes. *I wish I could talk to these people. How am I going to figure out how to get back home? They have their hands full just trying to survive. I don't think they can help me.*

Toby curled up beside him, and he drifted off to sleep. He woke to Toby's bark and saw the girl from the tree standing in the doorway with an armload of sticks. Toby didn't even get up when she walked in and dropped them next to the firepit, then came over to pet him softly, saying, "Manetoo." Then she stood and said more unintelligible words and left.

Ryan sat up, and a few minutes later, the girl returned with a large skin bag of water. She took his hand and pointed out at the center of the village, where they had suspended two legs from the terror birds, the tanwakua, on spits over the fire. Most of the villagers were out there. She signaled Ryan to join them.

He stood and patted his chest and said, "Ryan." He pointed to her.

She slapped her bare chest. "Weeko."

He pointed to her and said, "Weeko."

She smiled and took him out to the gathering. The smell of the roasting meat made his stomach growl and churn. His mouth watered. Women cut off slabs from the legs and distributed them to those gathered, starting with Ryan. He took a bite of the hot, greasy meat. The villagers cheered and ate their own portions. It tasted a little like chicken legs but was moister and chewier. He hadn't realized how much he needed the fat that ran down his chin, staining his shirt.

After the meal, the warriors did a dance that seemed to depict the day's events. Then, as the fire died, the villagers trickled off to their huts. He and Toby went to their hut and started a fire using a brand from the central firepit. Lying on the bed of reeds, he watched the flames dancing and the sparks floating up in the smoke. *They may not help me get home, but they can help me learn to survive in this wild place. Maybe I should stay awhile and learn.*

Chapter Eight

The Village

After the celebration of her rescue, Weeko returned to her family's hut. She couldn't stop thinking about the manetoo that obeyed the stranger. It was smaller than the ones that hunted in the north of their village. But she had never seen one brave enough to attack an adult tanwakua. The stranger called it Toby. Weeko wasn't sure if it was the animal's name or what the stranger called a manetoo in his language. She needed to learn more about both of them.

"What are you thinking about, Weeko?" Wanika sat next to her mat.

"The stranger and the little manetoo," Weeko said. "I have seen nothing like them. The animal seems to obey the man's commands."

"They are both strangers. I believe the man came through the magic." Wanika poked the fire with a stick. "I have not seen one before, but the legends speak of them. They rarely survive, so this one must have powerful magic. Powerful enough to control the manetoo. Why don't you spend time with this stranger? Teach him our language and learn about him."

"I would like that." Weeko smiled and hugged her father.

"I will send word to Wakakan about the stranger. He will want to meet him." Her father stood. "Sleep. You had a traumatic day."

The next morning, Weeko didn't wait for Nanji. She left early to gather firewood, then went to the hut where the stranger was still sleeping. She sat at the door, waiting. Toby, who slept beside the stranger, got up and came to the door. He sniffed her, then lay beside her crossed legs. Weeko put her hand on Toby's neck and ran her fingers through his fur. He leaned against her and laid his head on her lap. While she was petting Toby, she heard the stranger moving around inside the hut. The dog's ears stood up, but he stayed beside her.

The stranger stepped out and said something Weeko didn't understand. She pointed to him and said, "Ryn."

"Ry-an," he said and pointed to her. "Wee-ko."

Weeko smiled, then repeated, "Ry-an."

Toby sat up. Weeko hugged his neck, then said, "Toby."

The stranger nodded his head. "Toby."

Weeko spent the rest of the morning at the stranger's hut. They took turns naming various objects in the hut, each of them repeating the name in the other's language. After going through the objects, they did the same thing for the major parts of their bodies.

At midday, Weeko returned to her family and finished her daily chores. She smiled as she worked.

Her father came into the hut. He took a cup of water from the bag and tilted his head slightly as he watched her. "You seem happy."

"I am happy. Toby is soft, and he likes me. He lets me stroke him, and he leans against me." She sat beside her father. "I am teaching Ry-an some of our language." Then she repeated the names in the stranger's tongue for some objects in their hut.

Wanika smiled and put his hand on Weeko's shoulder. "You have done well. Soon we can communicate with this stranger."

Weeko spent the next several weeks as Ryan's language teacher, spending each morning with him and Toby. She explained village life to him and learned English as he learned their language. Ryan ate meals with her family, Wanika, her father, Niaki, her mother, and Tokea, her older brother. After the meals, Wanika and Tokea taught Ryan how to make stone weapons and tools. He became adept at knapping the flint found in the hills near the village. Niaki and Weeko showed him the edible plants and roots.

Weeko liked Ryan, but she loved Toby. Ryan showed her how to play with Toby using a stick. She could throw it and the dog would run after it and grab it in his jaws, then bring it back and drop it at her feet. He would do it repeatedly until he was tired and would lie at her feet. Weeko would run with Toby, who would chase and circle her. He would follow her into the lake and swim with her.

She spent little time with her friends. They teased her and called her Nanhin's woman. Three weeks after the stranger arrived in the village, she sat next to Ryan's hut, petting Toby. Nanji and two other girls walked by talking loudly.

"Weeko doesn't like young men. She ignores the young hunters and spends all her time with the old stranger."

Weeko stood. "I'm teaching him our ways! My father asked me to do it."

The other girls laughed, and one said, "What is Nanhin teaching you? It won't be long until none of the young men will want you."

"Shut up! You know nothing!" Tears formed in Weeko's eyes. "Go away!"

Nanji picked up a dirt clod and threw it at Weeko. Toby barked and ran toward Nanji, snarling and baring his teeth. She screamed.

Before Toby got to Nanji and the girls, the stranger came out and yelled, "Stay!" Toby stopped, still growling.

"Come," Ryan said, and Toby went to him and sat.

Wanika and a warrior came to determine the cause of all the noise. "What is happening here?"

"The manetoo tried to attack me," Nanji said.

"Only because you attacked me," Weeko said. "Toby was just protecting me like he did with the tanwakua."

Wanika looked at Nanji. "Is that true?"

"We were teasing her, and then Nanji threw a dirt clod," one girl said.

"Why were you teasing her?" Wanika said.

"She doesn't spend any time with us. It is like she is married to Nanhin," the girl said.

Wanika walked up to Ryan. "How are the lessons going?"

"I am learning your language and can take care of my own needs with the food you provide. Though I can hunt for myself if needed," Ryan said in the villager's tongue.

Wanika nodded. "Weeko, you will return to your normal chores and spend less time with Ryan and Toby. Go see your mother."

"Yes, Father." She started for her hut.

Before she left, she heard Ryan ask, "What does Nanhin mean? Many of the villagers call me that."

Wanika looked at Weeko. "Tell him what it means in his tongue."

"It means gray face. Almost none of our people have hair on their faces and if they do, it isn't gray. Few of the villagers know your name, so you are called Nanhin."

CHAPTER NINE

THE HUNT

J ust after sunup one morning, Tokea came to Ryan's hut. "Nanhin, we go to hunt the thanka today. Will you join us?"

"Yes, Tokea. I will join the hunt. When do we leave?" Ryan had learned the thankas were the bison he had seen when he first arrived.

"Soon. Bring your spear and knife and a skin of water. The hunt can last several days."

Tokea left, and Ryan gathered his gear. *This should be interesting. I wonder how close we will get to the spot where I arrived?*

He stepped out and looked at the orange ball of the sun rising in the east and felt the cool morning air. He joined the group of men gathered around the village fire. *How do they stay warm in the winter when they wear so little clothing? I have my pants, shirt, and jacket. They wear only loincloths.*

They left the village at a trot down the hill toward the plains. Even after spending weeks with these people, he soon labored to keep pace with the other men, causing the group to slow.

"Nanhin's clothes slow him down," one taunted, and the others laughed.

"Nanhin has old legs. His skin is white because his strength has left his body," said another, still laughing.

"Nanhin needs a wife to keep him warm at night and build his endurance," Tokea said.

They all laughed, but they did not leave him behind. He had earned their respect. The necklace he wore, with the tanwakua's talons that Wanika had fashioned, was a symbol of their acceptance. They ran into the denser forest, where they rested under the welcomed shade of branches of a pine and ate dried salty meat and berries. Ryan welcomed the rest and food and hoped it would provide a boost for the afternoon's run that would take them to the edge of the plain.

They stopped earlier in the afternoon than Ryan expected. They needed time to build a rough shelter and boma before hunting small game for dinner. After a meal of roasted pezi (ground hog), nuts, and warm water, they settled around the fire.

"Nanhin, when we find the thanka, they will not fear us." Wanika sat next to Ryan. "We will try to separate one or two from the herd. Once separated, they are aggressive and will charge at us, trying to return to the herd. You must be quick to get out of the way. The thanka can kill you with its head, horns, or hooves. As it runs past you, throw your spear into its side just behind the shoulder. This will bring it down."

The hunters continued telling stories, while Ryan lay on his back and looked at the stars appearing in the darkening sky. He couldn't find any of the familiar constellations: no Big Dipper, no Orion, just a dense cloud of stars. As the conversation around the fire quieted, he fell asleep.

When nature called, he woke in the middle of the night chilled. He got up and walked to the boma to relieve himself. When he returned, Tokea was up, adding wood to the fire.

"It is cold tonight. I wish we had our women to keep us warm." He smiled.

"Yes. A woman would be nice." Ryan sat by the fire to get warm. *I would like to be in bed next to Emily.*

Tokea stirred the fire. "Weeko says that Nanhin fears nothing. She said you faced the two tanwakuas without flinching. You need that courage when we find the thanka."

"Weeko was wrong. When the tanwakuas came at me, they scared me to death. I think I was too afraid to run."

"You may have been too afraid to run, but you were not too afraid to fight."

They talked for a few more minutes, then Ryan lay back down and went back to sleep.

Wanika woke him the next morning, poking him with the butt of his spear. "Wake up, Nanhin. The thankas are calling us. We must be going."

The hunters gathered up their few belongings, and they set out as the orange sun rose. They traveled along the crest of a long ridge that provided a view of the yellow grass plains below. The wind that formed waves in the long grass blew in their faces.

At midmorning, Wanika signaled a stop as they climbed another ridge. "The thanka are close," he said, sniffing the air.

They crept up the hill until they were just a few feet from the crest, where they stopped again. Here, even Ryan detected the musky scent of urine and manure. They crawled on their hands and knees to the top of the ridge where they saw the vast island of brown in the yellow sea.

After they watched the herd, Wanika explained the plan of attack. There were several young thankas about halfway down near the flank of the herd that they would try to separate from the main body.

They crawled through the tall grass to stay hidden. As they got closer to the animals, the musky scent became a stench, and the low moan Ryan had heard at the top of the ridge became a roar. At about thirty feet from the herd, Wanika stood and ran at the animals. They all joined him, shouting and shaking their spears. The thanka nearest to the hunters moved away, with the flank of the herd flexing in, but a few of them bolted and ran past the hunters, away from the herd. Wanika pointed to two young thankas. The hunters moved to form a wall between the two animals and the rest of the herd. The hunters closed in on them, forming a semicircle around them. They waved their arms, trying to look as big as possible to confuse the beasts.

As they drew closer, the young thankas panicked. The first one charged to Ryan's right and scattered the three hunters at the far end of the semicircle. They threw their spears but missed. While he watched them, the second charged straight at him. He turned just in time to see the brown battering ram approaching. He froze for a second, then stepped right, but the thanka was too close. It hit him in the chest, tossing him to the ground, then turned to charge at him again.

Ryan struggled to his feet and threw his spear into the animal's side as it ran by. Wanika's spear pierced its other flank. The thanka screamed with a sound like a crying baby, but neither wound proved immediately fatal. The young animal ran to rejoin the herd, though it was bleeding badly. Wanika gathered the hunters, and they followed from a safe distance, waiting for the injured animal to fall. An hour later, it staggered out of the herd. It stumbled and got up three times before it eventually fell and died.

The hunters ran to the body and began cleaning it. When they pulled out the heart, they gave it to Wanika. He took it in his hands and held it high, thanking the herd for the gift, then putting it to his mouth, he took a bite; the blood smeared over his face. He handed it to Ryan.

He looked at the dripping mass in his hands, not sure if he could eat it, but not wanting to insult the other hunters, he took a bite. It was tough, and he had difficulty tearing a piece off the raw organ with his teeth. The warm blood tasted metallic and ran down his chin as he chewed it. It did not turn his stomach as he feared. He guessed that he had eaten enough raw, wild game since his arrival that his stomach had become used to it.

They skinned the thanka, then tied the skin between two spears, making a sort of travois. They piled most of the meat on the hide. The rest they tied into bundles that they carried on their backs.

Once they packed the meat, they started back to the village, not wanting to remain around the carcass too long. The vultures already circled in the sky above, and they could hear the high-pitched cries of hyenas, but the loads on their backs and on the travois prevented them from moving too quickly.

Even at their slow pace, Ryan fell behind. A piercing pain in his chest became worse when he breathed deeply. It felt like he had broken or badly bruised ribs. His right knee ached with each step, and he felt it tighten and swell. When Wanika stopped for a rest, he staggered up to the rest of the party.

Tokea came up to him. "What is wrong, Nanhin?"

"I think the thanka broke some of my ribs when it hit me. It is hard to breathe, and my knee hurts."

"Sit. Let me look." He took the meat off Ryan's back and lifted his shirt. "Your chest has a nasty bruise there. I think you are right about the ribs." He looked at Ryan's knee. "Hmm, shall I get someone to help with your load?"

"Not yet. Let me rest and help me get it back on. I will keep up the best I can. It will be dark soon and then I can rest."

By the time they entered the trees, he was thirty yards behind the rest of the group, hoping they would stop. That's when he heard the roar behind him. He didn't look back to see if it was a saber-tooth or a lion, but he tried to quicken his pace. The hunters ahead of him heard it as well, and he saw them turn to see what was happening. His legs were like stiff boards, and he couldn't get any air. Before he had gone ten more yards, the beast knocked him down on his face. He tried to scream but with his mouth in the dirt, it came out as a grunt. The weight of the animal on his back forced what little air he had out of his lungs and pain shot through his body. He blacked out.

CHAPTER TEN

ZICA

When Ryan regained consciousness, he thought he was lying in a bed with his arms around Emily. Her warm skin felt great against him until he moved. The sharp pain in his side made him gasp. He sat up slowly and looked around. This wasn't home. He was back in the hut in Wanika's village.

"Nanhin. You are awake," said a native woman lying next to him, her skin reflecting the orange light of the fire. "Are you okay?"

"Who are you?" Ryan said.

"I am Zica. I am here to keep you warm and take care of your needs. Shall I get you some water?" She sat up, leaving him with a chill where her body had warmed him.

"Water? No. Where am I, and how did I get here?"

"You are back in your hut in the village. The hunters carried you in after the watonga (lion) attacked you three days ago."

He stared at her, not sure if he believed her. "I've been here three days?"

"Yes. The watonga severely injured you, and you had a fever. Wakakan had me come to you." She got out of bed. "Wanika asked me to get him if you woke up. Shall I go now?"

"Yes." Ryan looked around for his clothes but couldn't see them.

Zica left, and he continued to look around the room. Things had moved since he left with the hunters. More pots sat around the fire, and more skins covered the bed. The tightly wrapped leather sash around his ribs was the only clothing he had on. Now he wished he had let Zica bring him the water.

He got up, but had to move gingerly to minimize the pain, and found the water jar. He was drinking from it when Zica and Wanika came into the hut.

"Nanhin. You have survived. It is good to see you up," Wanika said.

Zica took his arm and led him to the bed. "Sit and rest, Nanhin," she said. Once he had settled back on the bed, she draped a hide over his shoulders.

Wanika sat on a log near the fire. "We did not know if you would live."

"What happened? The last thing I remember is hearing the roar and falling on my face."

"You trailed the rest of us as we returned. We heard the roar and turned in time to see the watonga jump on your back. We all ran back to chase him away, but he was hungry and there were two females with him. It took some time, but we finally chased them off. The big male that attacked you tried to carry you away, but the thong holding the meat to your back broke, and he took the pack instead." Then he looked at Zica. "Get us some food and fresh water while we talk."

She left and Wanika continued, "The meat on your back prevented the watonga from injuring you more severely. You had deep cuts and scratches on your legs and arms, and it shredded the odd clothing you wore. Your head also hit the ground hard." He took out a small leather pouch and handed it to Ryan. "These are the strange things you carried in your clothes and the necklace you wore."

Zica returned carrying strips of smoked meat, which he ate while Wanika talked. "After we chased the lions away, we put you on the travois with the meat and hauled you to the village. When we got here, I sent for Wakakan. He bandaged your ribs and, since you had a fever, he arranged for Zica to care for you. She is now your woman and will care for you."

"My woman. What does that mean?" Ryan asked.

"She is your wife," he said, and stood. "Rest. I hope you can join us on another hunt soon. You are very brave."

Just then, Toby ran into the hut and jumped on Ryan. "Ugh, that hurts. Get off me. Down." The dog obeyed and lay at Ryan's side where he stroked his fur.

"That is the reason we had Weeko keep Toby away. She is the only one he will allow to take him anywhere," Wanika said. "I have sent Tokea to inform Wakakan that your fever has broken.

He should be back in the village tomorrow to check on you. But tonight, if you are well enough, we will have a celebration of the hunt. Zica will help you out to the fire." He turned to leave, then turned back, and said, "It is good to see you up and around, my friend."

After he left, Ryan watched Zica as she busied herself bringing in firewood and taking the bowls and jars from the fire out to the lake. He assumed she cleaned them there. When she returned, he continued to watch her. She moved around the hut. Her breasts were full and the stretch marks on her midsection told him she had born children. She was not a young girl, but she was thin and muscular. Her skin and black hair reminded him of Emily. They attracted him to her, and he felt his natural urges stir which made him blush, especially when Weeko returned to take Toby out. *I can't go there. What would I tell Emily? But what if I can't make it back home? If I must remain here, having a wife could make life easier.* He drifted off into a dream-filled sleep.

When he woke up, Zica was sitting next to him, staring at his face. She smiled when his eyes opened. "It is good for you to rest, Nanhin," she said. "Let me get you some water. Would you like to go to the lake and bathe? I can wash your legs while we are there."

"Yes. Can you get me something to wear? I don't enjoy being so exposed."

She laughed. "Nanhin, you should not be uncomfortable. You are a brave hunter. You are very tall and even though your skin is light, you are quite attractive."

"Thank you, but it is not my custom to go around naked."

She stood. "I will bring you a loincloth." She left and returned with it and helped him stand. He leaned on her, and they walked to the lake where he sat on a rock while she gently washed his legs and arms, checking the scabs on the cuts and scratches from the lion attack.

"You are a beautiful and attentive woman, Zica," he said. "Don't you have a husband?"

"A bear killed my husband two years ago during a hunt," she said, and gently pulled him off the rock into the water where she washed his back. "My children, a son, and an infant daughter, died of the fever last winter. I was alone until Wakakan gave me to you. Now you are my husband, and you will provide for me."

"But I already have a wife at my home in Colorado."

"I do not know where this Colorado is, and she is not here. But if she were, I would share you with her. That is our way," she said. "Until then, I will care for you. I am a good wife." She took his hand and led him out of the water toward their hut. "Do you feel like attending the celebration?"

"Yes. I think I have been stuck in the hut too long. I need the distraction."

"Good. I will let Wanika know. The village will be happy to see you."

Later, as the sun set, Zica helped Ryan out to the fire, wearing his new loincloth. He sat next to Wanika, while Zica joined the other women in cutting slices from the bison roasting over the fire. His stomach growled at the smell of meat cooking.

She brought him a bowl with a large slab of bison, black and red berries, and a root, like a yam, that was roasted in the coals of the fire. Then she brought him a cup full of sweet beer that tasted like they made it from honey. It was probably more like mead than beer, but since he had never tasted mead, he couldn't be sure. The men sat around the fire telling tales of the last hunt. Ryan expected serious ribbing by those who were with him, since the bison ran him over and the lion nearly killed him, but they directed most of the jibes at the three hunters who fled from the first bison. Though they did tease both Wanika and Ryan for their poor spear throws.

As the evening wore on and everyone had their fill, the women joined the circle around the fire. Zica sat behind Ryan and leaned against his back. The younger girls continued to bring large jars of beer, filling the men's cups. The hunting tales got wilder with stories of killing the long-nosed beasts, which Ryan assumed were elephants or mammoths, saber-tooths, lions, bears, and dragons they called suzuecu. Ryan didn't believe in dragons, so he thought the stories were fables.

Since he was not a drinker, a few cups of beer were too many, and Zica had to help him stagger back to the hut before the celebration ended. She led him to the bed and helped him down, then curled around him under the pelts.

The next morning, Ryan woke with a splitting headache. His mouth was dry, and his tongue felt swollen. When he sat up, Zica pulled him back down and kissed him. He vaguely remembered being intimate with her during the night. *What have I done? Emily will never forgive me. I already hurt her once.* But he returned Zica's kiss before he got up. He gulped down the cool water from the jar beside the bed and went outside.

When he limped back into the hut, she was busy slicing a melon for breakfast. She looked up and smiled. "Did you make this knife?"

"Yes, it was my second or third attempt, but it turned out well."

"It is quite sharp, and I like the leather on the end for holding onto. When I tell the other women about this, they may have their men make them one." She continued slicing. He thought she must really like it, since she sliced three times as much melon as they could eat.

"Do you expect me to eat all of that?" he asked.

"No. I am cutting some for Wakakan. He will arrive soon."

Not long after she finished slicing, Ryan heard a commotion outside.

"Wakakan is here," Zica said. "You should go meet him. He came to see you."

His ribs were still sore and his knee swollen, but he could get around more easily after days of rest and Zica's care. Outside, he saw the villagers crowded around the opening in the boma. In the middle of the crowd stood the shaman, Wakakan, who was even shorter than most of the men from the village. He wore a feathered headdress with a feathered skirt over his loincloth. There was a straight bone through his nose, and he carried an ornately carved staff.

The shaman walked through the villagers, right up to Ryan, and eyed him up and down. "Your ribs seem better, and the cuts on your legs and arms healed well."

"Yes. I am healing quickly," Ryan said. "Zica is an excellent nurse."

"She is a good woman, but the quick healing is the magic within you."

"Magic? What magic. I don't have any magic." Ryan shook his head. *What kind of character is the shaman?*

"You are not from this world," Wakakan said, looking him squarely in the eyes. "Tell me how you came here."

Zica came up, interrupting them. "Wakakan, I have refreshments inside. Come into the hut where you can sit and talk. I am sure Nanhin will tell you all he knows." She led the shaman into the hut, and Ryan followed.

They sat around the fire, ate melon, and talked. Ryan told Wakakan everything he remembered about waking in the strange land and everything leading up to Wanika's people bringing him to their village.

"You do not see the magic in these things?" Wakakan said. "You are not the first stranger I have come across. Many come through the doors, but few survive. The beasts or the people from the coast kill most. But all who come through have magic. It is what attracts them to the portal."

"You have seen others like me?" Ryan said.

"Yes. Almirosia is a land with many doorways. People and animals come through occasionally. Even these people, the Oyato, originally came through many ages ago. Now, they and the dark-skinned people of the coast populate this world."

"If people come through, do they ever go back?" Ryan leaned toward the shaman. *Maybe there is hope.*

"I do not know of any, but I can check the cave walls. It might be possible to return, though I think few have stayed here for as many months as you have. Do you want to return?"

"Yes. I want to go home."

"Very well. I will check the spirit cave to see what I can learn there. I will send for you when I know anything."

"Thank you, Wakakan," Ryan said.

After the shaman left the hut to visit others in the village, Zica would not look at Ryan. She busied herself doing various chores, but she ignored him. *What's wrong with her? She should be happy. I could go home to Emily.*

Then he realized why she was upset. She wanted him to stay with her.

CHAPTER ELEVEN

TO THE MOUNTAINS

It took two nights of sleeping back-to-back for Zica's anger to subside. Before they went to bed on the third night, while they sat at the fire, she asked, "Do you like me?"

"I like you, and I have accepted you as my wife and promised to take care of you as long as I can," Ryan told her. "I don't know if I will ever be able to go back to my old life, and even if I do, I will always remember you and love you. You need to accept this." Ryan reached up and took her hand. "Sit with me. My old life was peaceful. I didn't need to hunt or gather to survive. My home had indoor running water. My wife, Emily, is a little like you. We have been together for over twenty years, and I worry she may not understand why I have been gone so long."

"You were with her that long?" She sat beside him. "No wonder you want to go back to her. I was only with my first husband six years, but I missed him so much when he died. I will accept you for as long as you stay, Nanhin. But I do not want you to go away."

They spent the night in each other's arms. After that, things returned to normal for the next three weeks until a young warrior came to the village with a message for Ryan from Wakakan.

"Nanhin, I am Topa," he said. "Wakakan would like you to come to the spirit cave. He has information about the magic that brought you here and would like to show you the marks on the cave wall."

"Thank you, Topa. I will go to the spirit cave if you guide me. When do we leave?"

"We leave in two days. It will be good if two or three warriors accompany us. The manetoo are hunting along the trail, and we believe they killed the first runner Wakakan sent for you," Topa said. "It will take a few days to get to the cave. Wakakan will meet us there."

When he returned to the hut, Zica's eyes were moist, and the trail of a recent tear marked her cheek. She put her arms around him. "You must take Toby with you. He will alert you to the manetoo and protect you."

"Don't worry. I will come back to you. Wakakan only wants to show me the caves. I do not think he has an answer yet."

When the day of his departure arrived, two warriors from the village joined Ryan, Topa, and Topa's companion for the trip to the spirit cave. They left about midmorning and walked at a rapid pace toward the north. The trail took them up through the forest to a high plateau covered in short grass, sagebrush, and alpine flowers, where they spent the night under the stars. They could hear the manetoo howling in the distance. At the first howl, Toby came and curled up next to Ryan and whined quietly.

At daybreak, they set out across the plateau, then entered a forest of scrub pine and brush that had grown over the trail. They stopped frequently because of the higher altitude and the slow progress through the brush. When the sun set, Topa located a small clearing in the bushes where they set up camp.

After he started a fire, Topa said, "We must keep the fire burning all night to discourage the manetoo, so gather as much wood as you can."

They sat around the fire and ate a cold meal of dried meat, listening to the howls of the manetoo getting closer. They spent the night taking turns tending the fire and trying to sleep but woke often to the ever nearer howls. Toby never left Ryan's side. Just before dawn, Toby growled and stood, waking Ryan. The dog's hackles stood up and his ears pointed forward. He growled and occasionally let out a sharp bark that woke everyone else. The howling had stopped.

Topa picked up his spear and said, "Get your weapons and grab a brand from the fire. We will stand in a circle with our backs to the fire. Maybe we can hold them at bay until the sun comes up."

Growls came from the shadows where the large pack of manetoo circled the camp. They started probing the defenses with one or two of the beasts running in toward the circle.

Twice the size of Toby, the manetoo had thick gray fur and long legs. They stood nearly chest high to the warriors.

The warriors held their ground, jabbing at the beasts with their spears. Then the manetoo charged, attacking just like Ryan and the hunters did with the bison, trying to separate someone from the circle. Ryan had to keep Toby under control so he wouldn't go after the wolves, especially when one came straight at them.

After an hour of holding off the snarling gnashing teeth of the beasts, they were exhausted. The warrior who had accompanied Topa fell, giving the manetoo a chance to grab him and drag him off, screaming. The fire was dying, and their strength was fading when Ryan heard and felt a low roar vibrate through his body. Topa yelled something he didn't understand. The manetoo yelped, and a dark form came out of the east, blocking the light of the rising sun.

The warriors fell to the ground, and as Ryan went down, he saw two long taloned feet pick up one manetoo and carry it away. As it lifted the wolf, its wings stirred up the sand and dust and ash around them, making it difficult to see the monster.

When the air settled, he looked at Topa, who sat in the dirt shaking his head. "What was that?" Ryan asked.

"A suzuecu, an ancient beast that lives in the mountains above the spirit cave. Few people who have seen it have lived, and many believe them to be myths. Many believe that they can carry off a mature thanka and swallow a man whole," he answered.

"Have you seen one before?"

"No, this is the first and I cannot tell you what it looks like, only that it is huge, and its wings blot out the sun." Topa shook his head. "God has smiled upon us today. We are fortunate to be alive."

The party sat on the ground watching the sky for another suzuecu and the ground for more manetoo. They huddled quietly for a little while until Topa told them to get their stuff so they could continue their journey to the spirit cave.

Topa led them uphill and by midmorning they were out of the scrub and climbing a rock-strewn path up the side of a mountain. When they stopped to rest, Ryan looked back at the panoramic view below. He could see the scrub forest with the darker pine forest below it, where the land plateaued. Farther out, he could just make out the plains through the hazy, humid air. There were varmints on the rocks nearby. One resembled a large ground hog and the other a small rabbit that would look at them and peep before running off into the grass and weeds. They reminded him of marmots and picas. Neither seemed to fear the human intruders.

They continued up the mountain, and the trail became steeper. Finally, in the late afternoon, they climbed a steep face to a ledge twenty feet above the trail. Once on the broad, flat ledge, Ryan saw a series of caves in the cliff face. Wakakan stood in the largest opening.

He motioned them inside where he had a fire burning. It lit up the walls, which were covered in crude paintings of animals and people. He had them sit on rocks arranged around the fire and dished up large bowls of stew and smaller bowls of the sweet beer. "How was your journey? I was afraid for your safety when I heard the manetoo howling this morning."

Topa told him all that had happened during the night and the morning, focusing on the manetoo attack and the suzuecu carrying the wolf away.

"A suzuecu?" Wakakan said. "That is amazing." He put his bowl down, stood, and looked at Ryan. "You still don't believe in the magic inside you. Yet, to have a suzuecu come to your rescue is indeed magic."

"Have you ever seen a suzuecu?" Ryan asked.

"Yes. Finish your food and I will show you something."

Ryan and the warriors who were from Wanika's village asked Wakakan about the caves, since neither had ever been here before.

"The caves are ancient and go back to the beginning when the first of our people came to Almirosia. They used these caves for shelter and defense against the suzuecu and other wild creatures of this land. The paintings on these walls are the history of our people. When you finish eating, I will explain some of it to you."

When everyone finished eating, Wakakan led them back deeper into the cave. "Before I start on the history, I want to show you this." They entered a side passage that led to a small, dark room. Wakakan lit torches along the walls that illuminated a massive skull. It was a good four or five feet long with teeth like daggers. The skull had a long, narrow nose sloping up to a broad flat head that flared out into two small horns.

"This is the skull of a suzuecu. They live in caves like this throughout the mountains." Wakakan showed them the paintings on the walls of the room, which showed giant beasts with two legs and gigantic wings. The creatures had moderately long necks, a short tapering tail, and enormous heads. "These are the only paintings of the suzuecu. Few people have ever seen them, though I think they are plentiful here in the mountains."

"No wonder they block the sun," Ryan said. "The wings must be huge to carry a body with a head this large."

They spent the rest of the afternoon going through the paintings on the walls of the large chamber where they ate. They portrayed mostly daily activities, hunting, dancing around the fire, and depictions of the various animals common to the land—many that Ryan recognized. When darkness came, the shaman took them to a chamber with mats arranged for sleeping and lit a fire close to the sloped wall of the cavern that reflected the heat back into the chamber.

Chapter Twelve

Spirit Caves

Exhausted from the rigors of the day and the previous night, Ryan quickly dropped off into a deep sleep as soon as he settled onto his mat. He awoke during the night, needing to go outside. He wrapped a pelt around himself and stepped out to the area designated as the latrine. The night was dark and cold; clouds covered the stars and hid the smaller of the two moons. The wind blew, muffling most of the usual night sounds. He could barely hear the howls of the manetoo in the distance. Suddenly, the loud shriek of a suzuecu drowned out the wind. He froze, watching for a hint of movement across the sky that did not come. The next shriek was farther away. Relieved, he turned and went back into the cave.

Wakakan stood there, just inside the entrance. "That was very close. Closer to the cave than I have ever heard. Did you see it, Nanhin?"

"No, with the clouds, it was too dark."

"I'm sure that woke everyone and may cause a restless few hours before sunrise. But we should try to sleep." Wakakan turned and went to the fire where he added more wood.

Ryan returned to his mat. The flickering of the firelight on the walls made the paintings appear to dance. He watched them, then fell asleep and dreamed of dragons until the movement and conversations of the others woke him. They talked about the suzuecu, both last night's flyby and the encounter from the previous morning, followed by tales the others had heard. Wakakan served fruit and smoked meat with a hot bowl of bitter tea. The clouds from the night had dissipated, allowing the sun to warm the rocks.

After breakfast, Wakakan assigned the others to gather more firewood, to search for berries and other edible plants, and to clear debris from the stream that brought water into the cave. While they busied themselves with these tasks, he took Ryan outside. They climbed a series of steps carved into the white cliff face.

At the top of the steps, another ledge extended back about eight feet into the cliff face and ran twenty feet along it, leading to a small opening. Ryan had to get on his hands and knees to go through the passage that opened into a cavern larger than the one they were in yesterday. Instead of images of animals and plants, lines, arcs, and circles in random positions covered the walls. Occasionally, images of people or animals appeared at various intersections where lines looped and crossed. At some intersections, multiple figures appeared.

"This is the magic of Almirosia," Wakakan said. "Each of the lines represents a different time or place. Where the lines cross is an opening between worlds. Unique events surrounding these openings punctuate the history of Almirosia. I believe you came here through one of these doors. The images at the intersections represent recorded occurrences when someone or something came through."

"Has anyone ever gone back through the portal into their world?" Ryan asked.

"I still don't know. I will have to continue studying history to determine if that has happened. There was an order of shamans in the old temple to the north who studied the portals and knew much more about the lines than I do. But several years ago, someone killed those shamans and their knowledge died with them."

"How can you determine which of the lines is the line I am from?"

"I will need to study the lines carefully, and you will need to tell me where and when you first came to Almirosia."

He showed Ryan through the cavern, stopping occasionally to explain some of the key events he knew, including when his people arrived. "They have lived here for hundreds of years, but like you, they also came here through the portal," he said.

"Did they try to get back to where they came from?"

"No, I don't think so. They didn't understand, and the magic frightened them. They believed their Creator put them here for a purpose. We are still a superstitious people and believe the events and circumstances around us accomplish the Creator's will."

"What about me?" Ryan said.

Wakakan looked down at the ground and remained silent for a moment before he answered. "I believe you are here for a purpose. The Creator brought you here and allowed you to survive because He has a plan. The magic I see in you is more than I have seen in anyone else."

Ryan shook his head. "I still don't understand this thing about magic. I don't know any magic."

"You think of magic as something purely supernatural. We see it as natural. It is the nature of the Creator to make things happen." The shaman pointed to the lines. "The openings are magic, and only those with magic can pass through. My people can walk through the point where the portal exists and never pass through it. For them, it does not exist."

"I still don't understand," Ryan said.

"In time, you may learn to understand, but it is not required." Wakakan pointed to the entrance. "Let's sit in the sunshine and you can tell me about how you came to Almirosia."

They went to the ledge and sat in the sun while Ryan told him everything he could remember about the day he arrived and the succeeding days until he met Weeko and her people. Wakakan listened silently. When Ryan finished, he asked him to tell him again and asked if he could tell him which direction he traveled. Ryan answered the best he could, then they went back into the cavern.

Wakakan took Ryan to another chamber with a rough map painted on it, but Ryan couldn't tell what it represented. Wakakan went to the center of the wall and pointed to some symbols. "This is the location of the spirit cave."

Ryan looked closer and figured out that the symbols around the cave stood for mountains. The map was all Almirosia. The land was much larger than he imagined. Wakakan used his finger and traced a path along the map, stopping to point out the location of Wanika's village. He continued moving east to the river. Ryan got a feel for the map, so the next time Wakakan stopped, Ryan knew it was the area where he awoke.

They went back into the other chamber and walked over to the wall. The shaman pointed to a line that was straighter than all the others. It didn't contain any loops or swirls, though it contained large peaks and valleys. "This is the path of life on Almirosia." He pointed to the place where the line ended. "This is today. Tomorrow the line will move farther. The magic extends the line on its own."

"You are telling me the lines draw themselves. I don't believe you," Ryan said.

"You don't have to believe." Wakakan moved back along the Almirosia line, one finger width at a time, counting the number of days Ryan remembered being here. When he stopped, a loop crossed the Almirosia line another finger width farther. "This would be the line for your world." Using his other hand, he traced the loop until it ended a few inches back from where it crossed.

"That makes little sense. The line goes backward," Ryan said.

"Yes, but I don't know why. It doesn't matter. What matters is that at some point, it looks like it will cross again. I must study this and other lines to know if you can return. But your world's line crosses Almirosia's line often, so I think it is possible. I will study and watch. When I know more, I will send someone for you. For now, you still have hope."

Ryan didn't feel very hopeful. It looked like a lot of mumbo jumbo to him. But Wakakan continued to reassure him before they went down to the lower level where the others waited. Hunters had returned just before them with a small deer that they were skinning.

Topa came up. "Tonight, we will sleep with our bellies full of fresh meat," he said.

"Well done, Topa," Wakakan said. "You can start back in the morning. You should be far enough away by nightfall to avoid the manetoo."

That night they feasted on the deer, drank beer, and listened to Wakakan tell stories of the people's arrival in Almirosia. Ryan slept hard and dreamed of riding on the back of a dragon, soaring over the plains as it dove to snatch a bison from the herd.

"Nanhin, it is time to get up." A warrior jostled him with his foot. "You sleep like an old man."

"I am an old man," Ryan said.

They ate and packed quickly and the three of them started down the mountain in the orange-tinted sky of the sunrise. The trip back to the village was uneventful, though they heard the suzuecu shriek both nights. When they got back, the entire village turned out to greet them.

Zica ran and jumped on Ryan. She threw her arms around his neck and wrapped her legs around his waist. "I missed you," she said and kissed him.

He held her close. "I missed you too."

"Did you find out if you can return to your world?" she asked.

"No, not yet."

Her face lit up, and she squeezed him tighter.

"You're making it hard for me to breathe. Let me go. We can talk later." She let him go and went into the hut while Ryan talked with the others.

That evening, he talked with Zica before the welcome home fire, reassuring her he would let her know when things changed. She made it hard for him. *Life here is simple. She is undemanding and generous with her affections. If I ever make it back home, I don't know if or how I will tell Emily about her. Given our past, I'm not sure she would understand.*

CHAPTER THIRTEEN

RAIDERS

During the three weeks after Ryan's return from the spirit caves, he and Zica became closer emotionally and physically. They talked more about their pasts, their feelings, the ties that bound them to each other, and their feelings for those they had loved and still love. Though Zica didn't express it, he felt she had resigned herself to his leaving. Having been through the loss of one husband and knowing the dangers of life in the village probably prepared her, at least intellectually, for that day. But now, he had to leave for another thanka hunt.

It took two days to find the herd, and now Ryan and the other hunters crouched on a rise, watching the thanka as they grazed. The wind blew in his face, assailing him with the stench of the herd. Clouds hid the sun, hinting at the coming rain and foreshadowing the winter to come. The village needed at least two kills to provide enough meat for the months ahead.

The migration of the thanka would take the animals too far away for any more hunts this year. They watched the herd move through the tall yellow grass of the plains below. Ryan saw a lone predator moving parallel to the herd between the hunting party and the thanka.

"Wanika, look." Ryan pointed to the predator's location.

"It is a hiwatoga. We must let it pass before we can make a move," Wanika said.

The hiwatoga, or saber-toothed cat, presented too great a danger to their small hunting party. It could easily kill or severely injure four of them before they could kill it. So, they waited on the hill and watched, hoping the main body of the herd didn't move too far. If it did, the hyenas and lions that followed, waiting to pick off stragglers, also presented a danger to the hunters.

After an hour, the saber-tooth was no longer in sight, and Wanika started the attack. They used the same tactics as before, rushing into the side of the herd, hoping to separate one or two animals that they could kill. Time and practice had prepared Ryan for the speed and size of the thanka. He had become more proficient with his spear hunting smaller game.

Their first rush separated three animals from the herd. Wanika and Ryan got between one of them and the main body. With just the two hunters separating it from the herd, it charged and ran between them. Ryan stood close enough to drive his spear into the beast's flank. Wanika also hit his mark, and the animal tumbled over its broad head, landing on its back, unable to get up. Wanika ran up and cut its throat to ensure its death. Ryan saw that the other hunters had another thanka down.

Together, they worked at the messy job of gutting, skinning, and boning the animals. They wanted to finish so they could move away from the smell of the kill. Blood covered their arms and chests. Ryan could already hear the chortling of the hyenas as they moved toward the scent. Their hunting party was large enough to deter an attack from a small pack, but he knew it was safer to move away and let the hyenas spend their time on what they left behind. They piled the meat on the hides and used them as sleds to drag the loads. Ryan and the others started up the hill, hoping to reach the trees before dark.

They camped once they reached the trees. Wanika had them build a small boma and gather enough wood to keep the fire going. With the smell of fresh meat, Wanika assigned guards to protect the camp through the night. Ryan had the first watch. He sat near the fire listening to the hyenas and lions quarrel over the carcasses. As long as they fought, the camp remained out of danger. He could also hear the screams of a hiwatoga. If it came after the meat, their small fence wouldn't deter it.

As he listened, his mind returned to Emily and the hope of returning home. Since his visit to the spirit cave, his thoughts often took him home. Maybe Zica sensed this, and it made her seek his reassurance in their physical relationship. He didn't know. Sometimes, he was no longer certain he wanted to return. Life here was hard but rewarding, with tangible results from hunting and everyday skills. Zica knew his past and accepted him, giving herself freely.

After he roused the warrior who would take the next watch, he went to his mat and slept. He dreamed of the saber-tooth chasing him and Emily and Zica. As the big cat jumped to grab him, he awoke to the sunrise.

He helped gather poles and build travois, stretching the hides between poles to make it easier to drag the loads of meat. This time, Ryan could keep up with the party and stayed alert to any danger from hungry predators. Later that morning, the slate gray skies opened, and the rain started, forcing them to change course. They hoped to cross the stream in the open valley, where Ryan first found water.

Trudging through the mud in the driving rain and wind proved difficult. Though the travois slid easily in the mud, so did Ryan's feet, which frequently slid out from under him, sending him to his knees. The others didn't seem to fare any better, but they slogged forward. When they finally reached the valley, the stream ran out of its banks. The narrow creek was now a river ten yards across and four feet deep. They stopped and looked for a way across.

"We will need to carry the meat across," Wanika said, as they huddled under a tree.

They got into two groups and lifted the travois. But when Ryan lifted his end, the load shifted, and the meat nearly tumbled to the ground.

"Nanhin, stay here and watch the rest of the meat and the weapons." Wanika shook his head. "You are too tall. We can't balance the load with you. Once we drop the first load on the other side, bring the weapons across while we come back for the meat."

When the first load was safely on the ground, Ryan gathered up all the weapons and waded across the cold torrent. Wanika and the other warriors passed him, going to retrieve the rest of the meat. Once across, he waited for them to return. The strength of the warriors was clear as they waded through the current in nearly shoulder-deep water with the heavy loads.

When all the meat was across, they went up the hill to the trees and fashioned a rough shelter from the wind and rain. The dead wood around them was too wet to make a fire, so they ate dried meat and huddled together for warmth. They left before sunup the next morning. The rain, now a drizzle, shrouded the landscape, keeping them chilled and forcing them to move just to stay warm. Ryan didn't look forward to another cold night, though he knew that awaited him as the hunters followed the ridgeline that paralleled the creek. Just before sunset, they made camp. The drizzle stopped, and the sky cleared as a portent of a frigid night.

They left before sunup again. There was no frost on the ground, but each cloud of breath was clearly visible once the sun rose. Exhausted, hungry, and cold, they continued along the ridge at a quicker pace, anticipating their arrival at the village. They arrived about midday and received a warm reception after the success of the hunt. All Ryan wanted was a warm fire, a hot meal, and a nap.

Zica didn't disappoint him. She had the fire burning in the hut and she cooked some of the fresh thanka he brought home. That night, she and Toby cuddled with him on the bed to warm his cold, achy body. He drifted off into a sound sleep, only to be awakened when Toby jumped up and barked. Zica held him tightly and said something he didn't understand.

He went to the door, where he saw a group of dark-skinned men fighting with the warriors and dragging away the women of the village. The attackers wore pants, and many had scarves wrapped around their heads.

Ryan grabbed his weapons and pointed out the back of the hut. "Get out of the hut and go by the lake to the forest and hide."

Zica ran out the back and he watched as she made it to the reeds along the lakeshore and headed toward the trees. Then he went out the front to join the battle. Outside, one attacker pulled a girl by the hair from the hut to his left. He threw his rabbit stick, striking him in the head, knocking him down and allowing the girl to run away. The attacker got up and came at him with a metal sword, but the blow to the head must have stunned him because the attacker was too slow to keep Ryan from plunging his spear into the man's chest. He fell, bleeding profusely from the wound. Ryan went to him and cut his throat.

More attackers streamed in through the gate of the boma. They outnumbered the villagers, and they carried metal swords, and some carried crossbows. The women and children of the village ran toward the lake while the warriors tried to slow down the invaders, who attempted to capture the women and girls. He saw Weeko struggling with an assailant near the firepit at the center of the village. He ran toward her, but Toby jumped on the assailant before he reached them. The dog clamped his jaws on the attacker's arm, forcing him to release Weeko. She ran to the lake while Toby dragged the man down, jerking his now limp arm back and forth.

Ryan ran to them and stabbed the man with his spear. Then he saw someone coming at him with his crossbow ready, but Toby charged the attacker. The man shot, and the bolt went into Toby's shoulder. He fell. Ryan threw his spear, piercing the attacker's midsection. While he ran to retrieve his spear, another man stepped out from behind a hut and shot his crossbow. The bolt went into Ryan's thigh. He fell. Struggling to his feet, he faced the warrior with only his knife, but someone hit him on the back of his head, and he crumpled to his knees, then fell face down. He looked over at Toby, who lay just a foot away. He could not determine if the dog was dead or alive. Everything went black.

When he regained consciousness, his head ached and his leg throbbed. It took several minutes for his vision to clear. He tried to move, but his hands were bound behind him, around a poplar tree on the edge of a clearing in the forest. Several of the women from the village sat tied to other trees along with one warrior, Stika, whose daughter was among the women captives. The attackers had tents with a large fire burning. Guards patrolled the edge of the clearing, checking on the prisoners. When one reached Ryan, he called out, and a boy ran over with a bucket of water. The boy scooped out some water with a wooden cup and put it to his lips. After he drank, the guard put his club under Ryan's chin and lifted his head.

"You're alive," the guard said. "I hope you live to regret it. You killed my brother. I wanted to kill you, but we captured so few of you. Addah insisted we bring you to the market. I doubt you will sell." He took the club away from Ryan's chin and pressed it into his leg. "It is a long walk to Amut." The guard left him, laughing as he walked away.

Ryan woke every hour in pain and had difficulty changing positions during the long night. He thought of Zica. Did she make it? He didn't see her or Weeko among the captives. Maybe they were alive. But then, he remembered Toby lying on the ground beside him with the crossbow bolt sticking out of his side, apparently dead. He thought about Emily. He loved Zica, but Emily was his life mate. Now, it didn't look like he would ever get back to either of them. His heart ached more than his leg or his head. *God, help me get back to Emily.*

CHAPTER FOURTEEN

ADDAH

Addah waited in front of his tent for Muhad to return from his inspection of the captives. The heat and effort from the unexpectedly tough battle had left his shirt soaked with sweat. He removed his turban and wiped the moisture from his head.

The raid resulted in only six captives with one of them wounded. Three of his men had died in the raid. *I'll be lucky to cover my cost with only three young women and one healthy man. I hope we make it back before Yago returns from Jabyl.* Muhad's approach interrupted his musings.

"How are the captives?" Addah asked.

"They are fine. The women are frightened, and the warrior is defiant. The tall, light-skinned warrior should recover from his wound and survive the trip. Fortunately, the bolt went through his thigh and didn't cause any major bleeding or damage to the bone. Though Tamuz may cause problems. The light-skinned one killed his brother during the raid."

"Tell Tamuz to leave him alone or he may not make it back alive. That would be one less man to pay from the proceeds." Addah looked out over the rest of the camp. He suspected the men were quieter than normal because of the poor result of the raid. They sat in groups of two or three around the fire, talking, the light reflecting off their faces. "Have the sentries maintain their watch through the night in case the villagers make a rescue attempt."

"It will be done." Muhad returned to the fire.

Addah watched as Muhad circulated among the men. *The light-skinned captive could be a problem. It might be better for Tamuz to get his vengeance. If Yago returns to Amut before they can sell the captive, he would force Addah to give the man to him without compensation. He always insisted that outsiders get delivered to him. But since he didn't sanction the raid, I don't intend to give anything away.*

Addah remembered when Yago first arrived in Amut from Jabyl. Addah suspected he was an outsider since he was also light skinned, though not tall like the one they captured today. His dark hair, brown eyes, and stocky build resembled the inland native people. He spoke the language of both the inlanders and that of the coastal people fluently, but he had a strange accent. People in Amut say that he has a family in Jabyl, and he spends several months each year there.

Addah recalled when Yago had stepped off a pirate ship in Amut three years ago. No one knew who he was, but he had money. He bought an old warehouse near the docks and transformed it into a forge where he made weapons: swords, crossbows, and bolts. He sold these to the pirates, and soon, he had more money to finance his growing organization, which now included financing raids for slaves. Yago became the largest supplier of slave labor in the area. He now owned several drinking and gaming establishments near the docks, and had branched out into other interests, including trading goods for the ore used to manufacture the weapons. He was one of the richest, most powerful men in Amut. Yago was ruthless, eliminating his rivals or forcing them out of business through threats and violence. Addah knew that his initiative would not make Yago happy.

The frosty night air brought a chill. He put on his cloak and pulled it tightly around his broad shoulders, then went to look at the captives and estimate what price they would bring from the market. The three young women were pretty enough to bring a good price from either the brothels or wealthy old men. The warrior would probably sell to a pirate captain or mine owner, and the older woman would sell as a household slave. But the light-skinned warrior puzzled him. He appeared too old and thin for the farms, though he had shown his strength in battle. Maybe a pirate captain could use him?

When he got to the tree where the outsider was bound, he stopped. Even though he was tied sitting with his back against the tree, Addah could tell the prisoner was taller than anyone else in the camp. Nearly as tall as some of the winged demons from the East. He was also more sinewy and thinner than the typical inland warrior, and the gray in his beard and hair hinted that he was older. The bandage on his thigh showed signs of bleeding. *How had this old man been able to kill two of his men? I will be lucky to get any buyers for him. Maybe we can shave his face and head to make him look younger.* He walked back toward the fire. Before he reached it, he heard voices.

"I have to avenge my brother." He heard Tamuz speak. "I cannot face my family knowing his killer still lives."

"Addah will not allow you to kill him. He needs the money from the sale," Muhad answered.

"Addah can go to hell. His inept leadership caused the debacle of this raid. We should have waited for Yago to return. I will tell him everything. Then we will see what Addah does."

Addah crept up to the two men in the dark. "You won't have to wait," he said.

Tamuz turned to face Addah, who plunged his sword into Tamuz's belly, driving it up into his heart. "Now we will see what you tell Yago." He pulled his sword out, letting Tamuz fall, blood from the wound pooling on the ground. "Tell the others I will not abide any insubordination," he told Muhad, and walked back to his tent wiping the blood from his sword on his cloak.

Addah knew there would be some grumbling among the men. Tamuz was popular, but they would not act rashly after tonight. In this business, fear acted as an excellent motivator for obedience. Once they returned to Amut, most would forget the incident and spend their money on drink and women. Though, he realized Yago would hear about the raid despite his efforts to do it secretly. He would handle Yago when the time came.

CHAPTER FIFTEEN

CAPTIVES

The next morning, the guard jostled Ryan awake. The restless, uncomfortable night had provided little regeneration for his body. His arms and shoulders ached, his head hurt, and the wound in his thigh throbbed. Another man joined the guard who woke Ryan. The first helped him stand while the other held his sword to Ryan's throat so they could remove his hands from around the tree. They tied his hands in front of him, providing some relief to his shoulders.

The one with the sword pushed him from behind, ordering him to walk, but when he stepped forward onto his injured leg, it gave out and he fell on his face. The dirt and dry leaves stuck to his mouth when the captors stood him up.

"We should just kill him and be done," one said.

"Addah won't allow it," the other replied. "We will get another prisoner to help. Bring the older woman."

The first guard held Ryan up while the second went down to where the woman stood. He grabbed her arm and jerked her after him, pulling her to Ryan. The guards stood her beside him and lifted his arms to put them over Kagi's shoulder. "You will help him walk," one ordered. "Keep up with the others."

The party moved through the scattered trees along the rim of the river canyon. The open ground made their journey easier, but his leg still would not fully support him. He leaned on the woman Kagi. The contact with her skin warmed that side of him. She also seemed to appreciate the warmth as the goose bumps caused by the chill air disappeared from her skin.

"Are you okay, Nanhin?" she asked after they had walked a while.

"I will be, if they let my wound heal."

"I saw you kill two of the attackers before they shot you. You fought bravely," Kagi said. "I saw Weeko escape. She ran to the lake after the manetoo grabbed her attacker."

"I think Zica escaped as well. I sent her away early. Did Chetan get away?"

"No." Kagi shook her head. "They killed him in our bed before he could get up. Then they dragged me out by my hair before they bound my hands."

"Why did they take us?" Ryan said.

"I don't know. I remember the raiders attacked our village when I was a child. They took twenty captives, including my older sister." She paused a moment. "None of them ever returned. Some say they eat the captives, but I do not believe it."

"I don't think they will eat us either, but I think they may enslave us. I will try not to be too heavy a burden for you to support. My leg should get stronger after a few days."

"You are not a burden, Nanhin," she said.

A guard came up to them. "Keep walking, don't stop!"

They continued east until midday. They stopped atop the rim of the canyon with the river to their right. It had carved out a deep gorge with sheer cliffs on both sides. The multihued strata were visible in the rock faces across the canyon. Ryan sat on a boulder overlooking the river beside Kagi. Their captors fed them dried meat and water. After they finished eating, a guard came and examined Ryan's wound, and replaced the bandage before the party moved on again.

They continued along the canyon rim. The terrain became steeper and rockier as they got closer to the river. They weaved around and through the meandering trail created by the gaps between large boulders. They stopped early, well before sunset, at the edge of an escarpment. The river below roared as it tumbled over the cliff, filling the air with a mist that blew into the camp on the breeze.

That night, their captors bound their feet and shackled them to a tree, leaving their hands tied in front. Kagi snuggled into Ryan for warmth. Though exhausted from the ordeal, he had a difficult time sleeping. His leg throbbed, and the events of the last two days replayed in his mind.

He awoke after dozing to the chuckling sound of hyenas. They were close. The guards threw more wood onto the fire.

One man screamed, which quickly woke the rest of the party. Addah ran out of his tent with his crossbow and sword barking orders. Someone came over and took Kagi and Ryan closer to the fire, where they huddled with the other captives.

The screams of men and hyenas filled the next hour as the beasts probed the perimeter of the camp defenses before leaving to find easier prey. Their captors left them together in the fire's warmth. He slept and dreamed of his home in West Creek. *Emily—will I ever see her again? How am I going to get home? Have I become so used to living here that this is normal?*

He felt Kagi's skin pressed against his back as she held him, creating an all too familiar sensation. *God help me. I am so weak and easily drawn into the desire for physical relationships. First with Zica, now with Kagi. I am afraid it will hold me here.*

Before dawn, his dreams changed. He stood in the spirit cave with Wakakan, asking him how to get back. "You must want to return even more than you want to stay. The magic that brought you here is very strong. But it brought you here for a purpose you must fulfill before you can leave. The Creator will guide you if you listen." He woke up more confused. *How am I to determine my purpose?*

After eating, their captors tied a rope between all the captives before leading them, single file, along a narrow trail down the face of the escarpment. The steep trail along the rock face often became so narrow only one person could move along it. The wet, moss-covered rocks made the footing hazardous. As they moved along a narrow shelf in single file, the girl in the center of the captives slipped off the ledge. The momentum of her fall pulled the girls in front and behind her off the ledge as well.

Ryan felt a jerk on Kagi as the girl's combined weight pulled her toward the edge. He tightened his hold on her, pulling her into his arms, but the rocks were too slick, and they slid over the edge. She screamed in pain when the rope stopped their fall. Somehow, the captors had gotten enough people holding onto the end of the rope to keep them from falling to the scree at the bottom of the cliff.

"Nanhin, hold me. Don't let me fall. The rope is cutting into my side," Kagi said.

"I will not let you go." He moved his arms down her body slowly until he could grip the rope in his hands. He pulled against it, easing some of the tension on her body. When he felt her relax, he turned his body enough that he could get his feet against the cliff face. As their captors hauled them up, he used his legs to keep them from banging into the wall. It took almost an hour for them to haul all the captives up to the ledge.

When they started back down the trail, the raiders carried the three injured girls piggyback to the bottom. Though Kagi was to be his support, Ryan now provided support for her, despite the pain in his leg.

Once at the base of the cliff, the party moved away from the waterfall to a small, sheltered clearing where they camped for the night. Addah came to look at the captives again and spoke to the one who changed Ryan's bandage. He immediately checked the condition of all their prisoners. He examined the three girls by looking at their sides, and when he pushed on their ribs, they moaned or screamed. He wrapped a cloth tightly around each of them, then he came to Kagi and examined her in the same way. She had a bruised side and a red rope burn around her waist. As he pushed against her side, she yelped. He wrapped her ribs as he had the others.

"You were lucky. This could have been worse, but your friend helped prevent more ribs from breaking. You will be sore for several days. Be happy we're only walking one more day." Then he turned his attention to Ryan. "You were unhurt in the fall, though I think your shoulder will be sore. Your leg is mending well and should hold your weight better."

That night, they kept a large fire burning, but their captors appeared more relaxed than before. They had a stash of supplies hidden in a cave at the base of the cliff and brought out a cask of ale and more food to the camp.

Ryan ate the dried, salty fish and drank the warm, bitter ale they gave him. This allowed them all to talk about the village and the attack. Many of his friends had died that day. He remembered seeing Toby lying there bleeding before he lost consciousness. But nobody knew what lay ahead of them. As Kagi had said earlier, no one had ever returned to tell what happened to them after being captured.

Chapter Sixteen

Down the River

The laughter and excited conversations of Ryan's captors as they broke camp woke him. The atmosphere in the camp seemed more relaxed. They had let the captives sleep until the sun was well above the horizon before they started down a well-worn trail through the trees. Sweat ran down Ryan's skin as the humidity wrapped him in a wet blanket. Just after midday, they stepped out of the trees onto the banks of a small clear stream where they stopped.

The captors untied the tether between the prisoners and took one young girl to the stream where they bathed her. They held her arms and legs to prevent her from escaping. They laughed and made crude comments as they ran their hands over her and dunked her in the cool water. Then they bathed the other two girls and Kagi in the same manner, before they forced Stika and Ryan into the stream. The captors allowed the two men to bathe themselves under the close watch of several guards. Ryan enjoyed the coolness of the water and submerged himself in it, taking as much time as the raiders let him.

The guards took the two male prisoners back to the women and retethered all the captives together before starting downstream. The trail ran alongside the stream through scattered trees that allowed the breeze to dry Ryan and cool his skin. He no longer needed Kagi's support. A guard had rewrapped her ribs after the bath, but Ryan could tell they were still hurting by the way she clenched her arms against herself as she walked. They walked without talking until they came to a wide, slow-flowing river.

On the riverbank, just below where the stream joined the river, were several barges. They looked to be made of reeds with woven pontoons on each side and a twenty-foot-wide bamboo-like deck between the pontoons. A shelter stood in the center of each. Their captors separated the women and herded them onto the first barge. They led Ryan and Stika to the second, where they chained them to a post near the door. Their captors then joined forces with the men who guarded the barges. Once everyone was onboard, the crews picked up poles and pushed the barges away from the bank. Here the river that had been a raging torrent in the highlands was now a broad gently moving highway.

They floated downstream until just before sunset. The crews poled the barges over to the bank and tied them to the overhanging trees. Wear along the gentle slope of the bank showed regular use. There were paths leading into the forest, which had become denser as they went downstream, and some trees had pieces of rope tied to them. Most of the captors left the barges to sleep on the shore. They left the captives tied and guarded on the barges. As the sun went down, the insects swarmed, forcing Ryan and Stika into the shelter in search of some relief. When darkness fell, the swarms dissipated until sunrise.

After breakfast, the captors used their poles to maneuver the barges away from the bank and continue down the river. Ryan watched as the forest along the banks changed to palm trees and ferns mixed with a few large deciduous trees like those of the earlier pine forest. He also saw enormous crocodiles lying on the banks in the sun. There were other creatures as well, that looked like giant frogs with short hind legs and tails. The longer front legs and colossal heads full of teeth reminded Ryan of some prehistoric beast. The crocodiles did not occupy the same shores as these new creatures. They appeared to alternate sections of shoreline as the barges floated down the river.

The crews moved the boats away from whichever side of the river had the most animals. At one point, Ryan saw a crocodile twice the length of the barge swim past. The crew on that side of the boat held their poles out of the water, apparently not wanting to antagonize the monster. Stika looked wide-eyed as it swam past.

"What are those monsters?" Stika said.

"Where I come from, we call the long ones 'crocodiles,' but I don't know what the others are called," Ryan said. "I think both are very dangerous, and both will eat us if they get the opportunity. They usually lay in the sun during the day, then hunt at night. My guess is our captors have some idea of where it is safe to haul out at night."

Stika stared wide-eyed at the riverbank. "Are we safe here on the boat?"

Ryan shook his head. "I'm not sure. One of those big 'crocs' could easily climb aboard and get us. I wish they hadn't chained us to the boat."

As the boats proceeded farther down, the forest turned into a dense jungle with few sunny banks, so Ryan saw fewer of the big reptiles along the shore. When they stopped for the night, they tied the barges to tree branches that stretched out over the river, staying away from the bank, and everyone stayed aboard the boats. There was little conversation that night as the humid air and insects pressed in on them.

Ryan woke later that night to screaming. He looked out the door of the hut. The raiders had gathered at the stern of the boat. They waved torches and brandished weapons. He moved closer to the door to get a better look and saw a gigantic snake. Its head was ten or twelve feet above the water, looking down at the men at the rear of the barge. The crew yelled and waved torches. Some fired their crossbows, but the bolts bounced off the creature's scales. Its head swayed back and forth until it shot forward and grabbed one man in its jaws, pulling him into the water.

All the men ran toward the bow of the barge. In the panic, one dropped his torch, which ignited the reeds used to make the boat. Ryan and Stika moved out of the hut, but their chains prevented them from moving much farther. The flames spread across the deck and forced them back into the hut. They tried in vain to pull their chains free.

As the fire burned the reeds closer and closer to them, Ryan thought of what the shaman had said. "The Creator brought you here and allowed you to survive because He has a plan." *God, unless your plan is to have me roasted alive, we need your help.*

Stika hit Ryan on the arm and pointed to a hole in the deck just outside the door where the fire burned. "We must jump," he said, and leaped through the flames into the void. Ryan followed, holding on to his chain with both hands, expecting it to jerk him back at any moment. Instead, the warm water broke his fall. Submerged, he kicked to the surface and saw Stika in the light from the fire reflecting off the river.

"Don't thrash around too much," Stika said. "We don't want to attract any river monsters. Maybe the flames will free our chains."

"Even if they do, I'm not sure we can make it back up the river," Ryan said. "They will look for us once the fire is out."

They worked to keep their heads above water, listening to the yells of their captors who were trying to put out the fire. The river current gradually took them downstream until their chains tightened, causing a wave to wash over their heads. They had to fight hard just to get a breath and lost track of the yells and the light of the fire. Eventually, they felt the chains pulling them upstream. Their captors hauled them out of the water onto the charred deck of the barge.

"Remove the chains and tie their hands then bring them and follow me," said one guard. "Addah will be glad to have them alive. We can put them with the women."

They took both Ryan and Stika to the other barge across a plank and chained them again to the hut with the women. Kagi came to sit beside Ryan. "What happened over there, Nanhin? All we heard was screams and then the fire."

"It was a monster. A giant snake ate one of our captors. In the panic, the fire started," Ryan said.

"Will the snake come back? Are we safe?" Kagi gripped his arm and pulled herself closer to him.

"No, I don't think it will come back." Ryan moved his arm around her shoulders. "In my world, snakes eat only every few days. I think we are safe for now."

The captives got little sleep that night because of the noise from their captors, who stayed up all night and watched and talked about the monster. Ryan heard Addah yell at several of the men, probably wanting to know who started the fire. When the sun rose, the remaining two barges continued back down the river. It took several hours for the smell of smoke to leave. Just before sunset, they left the jungle and came to a broad flat plain. The current slowed, and they poled the barges to shore on a sandy island.

The men left their captives on the boat, and they set up camp on the beach. They kept a big fire burning through the night. Ryan slept with Kagi's sweat-slicked skin pressed against his side until they woke him for breakfast.

The captors talked excitedly, so Ryan guessed they would arrive at their destination soon. They got a late start, poling down the meandering river through the reeds. Shortly after midday, the barges stopped at a pier that extended out into the river.

The guards loaded the captives into a cart pulled by an enormous ox-like animal. It had large horns extending out three to four feet on each side of its head. It was taller than a man, with a hump over its front shoulders. A man led the animal by a rope tied to a ring through its nose. The cart jostled the prisoners, throwing them from side to side and jarring them with each bump as the tropical sun burned them from a clear sky. At one point, Ryan saw and heard waves crashing against the rocks of the nearby shore. The sea birds soared and called overhead, and the salt smell of the ocean came to them on a cool and welcome breeze.

The cart stopped at a compound on the outskirts of a village not long after dark. Their captors took them into a stone building with cells where they chained the doors and left them. The cells reeked of urine and rats scurried through the straw strewn about the dirt floor. Ryan no longer had ropes tied to his hands and feet.

He spent a restless night on the straw and the next day he paced in the cell he shared with Stika, who sat in the corner with his chin on his chest.

This must be our destination. God, how will I ever make it back from here?

CHAPTER SEVENTEEN

SHERA

The sun warmed the cool morning air as Shera's cart wound through the streets of Amut. The cart jostled her in the seat as the wheels slipped in and out of the rutted dirt road. Maslic, her driver and house overseer, tried to take the smoothest track, but with so many deep ruts, the cart continued to slide from one to another. Only the ox seemed oblivious to the jerking, its large split hooves giving it stability on the rough ground. Someday, Shera thought, paving stones would eliminate the ruts here in town, just as they had on the hill where her house sat. But she had paid to have that road paved. Here, no one wanted to spend that much gold on something that would benefit others.

The smell of fish that had hung too long in the sun drifted on the breeze when the cart neared the docks. It was unfortunate she had to go by the wharf where the fishing boats unloaded their catch. Perhaps, before they returned home, she would have Maslic pick out a fresh fish for dinner.

A boardwalk built for the carts made the ride easier when they finally reached the dock area. She passed the fishing boats, their nets filled, hanging over the pier from wooden booms. Here, the fish smell was fresher, mixed with the distinctive smell of salt water.

Once they passed the fishing boats, there were commercial trading ships tied to the docks. Workers transferred the cargos to the neighboring warehouses. Her warehouse was halfway down the boardwalk. Today a ship from the eastern islands arrived with a load of spices: qarfa, zanjib, and jawzat. She wanted to see the cargo and examine the warehouse records.

Hanno, her warehouse overseer, met them when they arrived, and led them inside. Men with their sweat-shined skin carried the large bags of raw spices into the warehouse where they would be ground in the stone mill enclosed in the warehouse's courtyard. After grinding, they re-bagged the powders and sold them to merchants all along the coast.

Hanno met Shera as she entered the warehouse. He led her to the courtyard where two men led oxen to the mill. "Mistress, the mill is clean and ready to grind the new shipment. What would you like ground first?" Hanno said.

"If I remember correctly, the jawzat inventory is low. Start with that," Shera said.

"Excellent, we will begin this morning." Hanno passed the information on to the men before he continued across the courtyard.

They passed the bags of ground spices stacked on the floor, and up a flight of wooden stairs to a loft that Hanno used as his office. Shera recognized Captain Qutan, who sat at the table at the far end of the loft. He stood when he saw her and bowed. "Mistress, it is good to see you."

"It is good to see you as well, Captain." Shera returned his bow. "It looks like a successful voyage."

"Yes, Mistress," Qutan said. "We brought in a large shipment that I purchased for a good price. The winds were fair, and we arrived before most of the other vessels."

"No pirate trouble this time?" Shera said as she took a seat at the table.

"No, Mistress. I paid the fee before we left."

She hated having to pay the pirates, but they controlled the shipping lanes and attacked any vessel that had not paid. They would kill the crew and steal the cargo. She believed Yago controlled the pirates since the extortion began after he arrived in Amut, and they were all armed with weapons from his factory. "How much did that set me back?"

"Two hundred gold rani, Mistress," the captain said.

Shera estimated that would be ten percent of her profits. But it was better than one hundred percent. They sat at the table and completed their business. Shera had Maslic pay the captain from the box he had carried in from the cart.

"It is always good working with you, Mistress," Qutan said and left. Shera, Hanno, and Maslic remained in the loft. Shera looked out over the bags of ground spices in inventory. It was a profitable business, but these additional charges troubled her. She had grown the business after her father died on a trading voyage in a pirate attack five years ago. The other merchants tried to prevent her from keeping it. They didn't think a woman should run a business. Especially one that required occasional long sea voyages to visit trading partners in the East. But she quickly learned the power of money, information, and friendship, building ties with her partners, and buying out her competitors. She knew how to run a business.

Shera went through the books with Hanno. Scanning the inventories, she noticed a larger than normal loss. "Why did we lose five bags of jawzat? One or two is more typical."

"It is the rats, Mistress," Hanno said. "They are thick and ruined more bags this month. Even if they don't eat the bag, they ruin it when they burrow into them. No one will buy a bag the rats entered."

"What are you doing to prevent this?"

"What can I do, Mistress? The pests are thick and get into everything."

"Set traps, poison them, get the bags off the floor. Do something." Shera slapped her hand down on the table. "A five-bag loss is unacceptable."

"Yes, Mistress." Hanno avoided eye contact with her.

"I will be back in a few days, and I expect to see changes," she said. "Let's go, Maslic, and leave Hanno to his work."

When they returned to the cart, Maslic asked, "Where to, Mistress? Home?"

"No. Take me into town. I want to check out the slave market. You mentioned we need another house slave."

Maslic led the cart down the boardwalk to a street that would take them through town. Shera watched the activity along the dock. *Five bags? The losses were getting very high. Maybe I need to replace Hanno, but finding someone who could read and keep books was hard. I certainly wouldn't find anyone at the slave market. I might find a house slave for a good price since Yago is out of town. If he were here, he would force the prices up just to make me pay more.*

Amut was the largest port on the East Coast, but you couldn't tell by the buildings. The weather-worn mud brick structures with their flat roofs gave the impression of poverty. Only on the hill overlooking the town did the buildings show any sign of wealth. The narrow streets, crowded with pedestrians, provided barely enough room for the cart. Maslic flicked his whip occasionally to hurry a dawdling walker out of their way. As they neared the slave market, the buildings became more rundown, without doors or windows and with sagging roofs. Here, the poor lived, many stealing to survive.

Maslic stopped the cart outside the wall surrounding the slave market. "Stay here with the cart," Shera said. She took the box from beneath the seat and put it into a satchel she carried. "I will be back soon. The crowd is small. They must not have many slaves to sell."

The two guards, in their yellow vests and headbands, stood at the gate. They had short swords belted to their waists. Neither of them acknowledged her, but they let her enter freely. She meandered through the crowd of onlookers, all men, to the bidder's area, where she found an empty bench. The market master led the first of the day's offerings onto the raised platform, a frightened young girl who could not have been over fourteen. The onlookers howled and cat-called, making rude remarks about her naked body. An older man seated in front of Shera, the owner of a brothel along the wharf, opened the bidding for the girl with an unreasonably low bid, but others soon joined in, and the girl sold to the owner of a larger brothel for a good price.

The next two girls sold similarly, with one going to another brothel and one going to the owner of a large farm north of town. After the girls, the market master brought a woman out. She stood erect and defiant, not trying to cover herself. Shera made a low but reasonable bid. *She might work as a house slave. She seems strong.* But the price quickly exceeded what she would pay. In the end, an old merchant bought the woman. Shera knew the man, and she felt sorry for the woman. He would probably abuse her until she died.

The male slave that was led out next appeared to be in prime condition. Probably a warrior. He also stood tall and proud, staring defiantly at the crowd, occasionally pulling at his restraints. The same landowner that bought the girl earlier also bought him. He would probably spend his days in the fields under the whip of the overseer until either his spirit broke, or he died.

The last slave brought to the platform was an extremely tall, white-skinned male with an obvious wound to his left leg. Too skinny to interest the farmers or others looking for manual laborers, there were no immediate bids. But something about his face spoke of intelligence, even with his gray beard. Just before the market master led him off the platform, Shera bid one rani.

The market master stared at her and waited for another bid, but there was none. "Sold to Mistress Shera for one rani."

Two of the market workers led the man out to her cart while she went to pay. *What was I thinking?*

Chapter Eighteen

Slavery

The morning of the sale, Ryan paced in his cell, waiting to see what would happen to him. *How will I get out of this?* It almost seemed that any hope of returning to his real life was gone. They took the girls out first, and he heard the shouts and laughter at what he assumed were obscene comments through the walls. When they took Kagi, the volume of comments decreased and when they took Stika, the crowd noise stopped.

They came to get him and stripped off his clothes and doused him with water to clean most of the filth from his body. Two men led him onto the platform. He stood straight with his manacled hands in front of him. The auctioneer made him turn in a slow circle so the bidders could see everything. When he presented his back to the crowd, someone shouted, and the crowd murmured, but the auctioneer ignored them. After Ryan finished turning, the bidding began.

Initially, no one bid. All he heard was more yells. The auctioneer pulled on his beard after one, and he slapped Ryan's leg near the wound. He assumed to show his fitness. The auctioneer took his arm. A black woman in a red turban yelled out a bid. When the auctioneer repeated what she said, the crowd laughed. Ryan sensed she had made a ridiculously low offer, but no other bids came.

The auctioneer shook his head and motioned to the two men who brought him out. The handlers came up onto the platform, then took him out of the market through a gate to a cart. They chained him to the back of it and left him with a black man in knee length brown trousers and a blue vest. The man eyed him, displaying no emotion, and said nothing.

When the woman in the red turban came through the gate, she climbed into the cart. She said something to the man, and he led the ox away from the market, through the rutted streets of the town. Ryan had to watch his step to keep from falling. The mud bricks of the buildings looked like adobe. The morning sun's heat reflected off the buildings into the street. Sweat ran down his face and back as he trudged after the cart. If he didn't keep up, it would drag him through the dirt. Everyone he saw on the street was black. In town, they gawked as he passed, but remained silent. Once they left the main part of the village, the streets had bricks for paving and the well-dressed pedestrians showered him with what sounded like crude insults. He was grateful that he didn't understand everything.

The shouts seemed to have no effect on the turbaned woman, who sat straight and ignored those they passed. The cart stopped at the gate of a walled compound that the ox driver opened. He then led them inside. They stopped at a large mud-plastered two-story house. The woman got down, turned to the driver, and gave him instructions before going inside.

The ox herder led the cart, with Ryan still chained, around to the side of the house to a long, single-story mud brick building with multiple doors. He stopped the cart and came back to Ryan. "This is your new home," he said in the language Ryan knew. "You may call me Maslic."

He unlocked the chain holding him to the cart and led him inside the nearest door. Inside, a ring on the wall provided an anchor for the chain. "I will be back after I see to the ox."

He stood in the small room. The open door in front and a small window in the back wall provided light. A hammock strung between the two sidewalls under the window, a table with a candle, and a rough three-legged stool comprised the only furnishings. The hard-packed dirt floor appeared to have been recently swept. At least it was better than his cell in the slave market. Maybe he could figure out a way to escape.

Maslic came back a few minutes later with some clothing that he put on the table. "Do not try to escape. When they catch you, they will cut your tendons to prevent any more attempts. It will make you useless as a slave. They will leave you to starve." To emphasize what he was saying, he made a cutting motion on the back of his leg. He pointed to the clothes and removed Ryan's chains.

Ryan put on the brown pants and the coarsely woven blue tunic. He thought the pants were probably knickers like Maslic's, but his legs were longer, so the pant legs barely reached his knees. Maslic led him out of his room to the back of the main house. As they went through the kitchen, Maslic stopped and talked to a woman, who joined them when they went out the other side into a courtyard.

The woman was lighter skinned than most of the people he had seen in the town. She wore a blue shift the same color as Ryan's shirt and Maslic's vest. As they entered the courtyard, she said, "I am Jin. I will be your interpreter until you become more familiar with the language of Amut."

The rectangular courtyard had palm trees and other plants arranged between the pathways running diagonally across the opening. Roofs extended over the first six feet of the opening, providing shade. Chairs and tables sat under the roofs. Maslic took him to his new owner seated at one of these tables. She still wore her red turban.

"Mistress, here is the new slave," Maslic said.

"Thank you, Maslic. You may leave. Jin will oversee him the rest of the day." She eyed Ryan from head to foot. "We will have to do something about those pants. What do they call you?"

Jin translated, though Ryan had understood some of what she said. "My name is Ryan, but the people of my village call me Nanhin," he answered.

"You are no longer in the village. I will call you Ryan," the woman said. "I can understand why they called you Gray Beard, but here you will shave. You will address me as Mistress or Mistress Shera." She waited for Jin to translate.

"You will work as a household slave under Jin's supervision. If you attempt to escape, they will disable your legs when they catch you. And they will catch you. You cannot hide your white skin. We easily find even the darker-skinned savages. Do you understand this?"

"Yes."

"Yes, Mistress," she corrected.

"Yes, Mistress. I understand," he said.

"Good. Jin, take him to the cellar and have him put the fresh supplies away."

Jin touched his arm, and they went back across the courtyard and through the kitchen to stairs leading under the house. She lit an oil lamp to illuminate the room. In the middle of the floor lay several large bags of vegetables and a crate containing clay bottles and jars.

"You will put the vegetables in the bins over there." She pointed to the wall on the right. "Arrange the rest on the shelves with similar items. When you have finished, I will be in the kitchen."

Jin left and Ryan started on the vegetables. Under normal circumstances, he could have lifted the bags and dumped them into the bins, but his leg had not completely healed, so he had to drag them over and empty enough by hand to lighten them before he could dump the rest. His leg was still in pain after the walk behind the cart. The strain of dragging and lifting the bags had opened his wound. Blood trickled down his thigh. After he finished with the bags, he moved on to the crate. He could tell the sun was setting by the orange-tinted light streaming in the cellar door. The lamp offered little extra light, so he had to look carefully in each container to determine what it held. The shelves had labels, but he didn't know what the words meant, so he had to compare the contents of the new containers with those already on the shelves.

When he finished, he limped up the stairs and into the kitchen. The women from earlier were busy cooking. The aroma of freshly baked bread and spices made his stomach growl. How long had it been since he ate real bread, warm from the oven with butter melting into it? His mouth watered.

Jin came over to him. "What did you do?" She pointed to his leg.

"It is a wound from when they captured me. The strain of the day has reopened it."

"Sit at the table and pull up your pant leg."

He did as he was told. Jin removed the blood-soaked bandage and examined his wound. "It is healing well." She cleaned it and put a salve on it before putting on the new dressing.

"How come you speak the language of hill people so well?" he asked her.

"My mother came from the hills. They captured her before I was born. She taught me."

"She taught you well. What about your father?"

"He was an evil man who owned my mother. He raped her regularly. She died when I was ten, then he raped me. He cut my face and said I would always belong to him. Luckily, another captive slave killed him soon after that and Mistress Shera bought me. She treats me well."

Jin was beautiful with a round face, soft brown eyes, and long dark hair she wore unbound. He hadn't even noticed the scar running down her face from her left ear to her chin. "I am sorry about your mother and glad you got out of that situation."

"What about you? You don't look like the hill people."

"I am not, but they gave me shelter and helped me learn to survive in this strange world."

She finished dressing his wound and stood. "You came through the magic. That is why your skin is so white. Maslic will bring you new pants in the morning. Mistress Shera would not approve of the blood. Dinner will be ready soon. We all eat at the long table under the anoka tree by the barn. You can wait there and meet the others."

Ryan limped to the tree and saw the table Jin told him about. He sat on the ground under the tree, leaning back against the trunk. The light of the setting sun flickered through the overhanging leaves as a light wind blew. He closed his eyes.

He didn't know how long he had been asleep when Jin shook him awake. "Get up, Ryan. It is time to eat. You can sleep after dinner."

He struggled to get up, favoring his injured leg. The sun had set below the hills to the west, leaving a soft twilight. The other slaves occupied the seats around the table, their lighter skin testifying to their hill country origins. Two women from the kitchen carried out a large pot of the aromatic stew they had been cooking, and others carried trays with the bread he smelled when Jin dressed his wound.

The coarse bread had a nutty flavor, and even with no butter, it seemed to melt in his mouth. It was perfect for dipping into the fish stew that tasted of cumin and pepper. The large chunks of fish and roughly cut vegetables that filled his bowl reminded him of home. He could really go for some of Emily's fish tacos.

Jin introduced him to most of the others after they ate, but he was too tired to remember their names or to follow the surrounding conversations. As a household slave, he had to help clear the table. When that was done, Jin said, "You're finished for the night, and can talk with the others, or since you seem to be so tired, you can go to your room and sleep."

He went to his room and climbed into the hammock, quickly falling asleep. He dreamed about home and how his unfaithfulness had hurt Emily. Then he dreamed about the story of Joseph being sold into slavery by his brothers and how God used his misfortune to save the Israelites.

When he woke the next morning, it took a few minutes for his head to clear. He rolled to get up but fell out of the hammock. Someone laughed. A woman stood silhouetted in the door.

"I brought you some longer pants." He recognized Jin's voice. "You have only a few minutes before breakfast. How is your leg?"

"It seems better this morning."

"Good. Mistress Shera has a lot for you to do today."

Ryan watched her shapely figure go out the door. Joseph had resisted the advances of Potiphar's wife, but he hadn't kept his hands off Zica or his eyes off Jin or Kagi since he fell through the looking glass.

CHAPTER NINETEEN

YAGO

Yago waited at the boarding ramp of the ship for his daughter Yasmin as she ran down the pier. She jumped into his arms and squeezed his neck.

"Do you have to go, Papa?" she asked.

"You know I do. I have business in Amut."

"But why?"

"That is where my factory is located and where I conduct my trading. It is a much larger town with a better port and warehouses, so it is easier for me to sell my goods."

"Come, Yasmin. Let your father go," Tanyth, Yago's wife, said. "Your father will be back."

Yago put the child on the ground. "I will miss you too, but I must go. You stay with your mother." He went up the ramp. Tanyth was a good wife and mother, but she stayed in Jabyl and would not move the family to Amut. He had agreed with her decision, because some of his business dealings needed to be kept from innocent eight-year-old eyes and ears. He had heard disturbing rumors about Addah, one of his associates, wanting to strike off on his own.

Donis, the tall, muscular ship's captain, met him at the top of the ramp. "We are ready to depart. I will have a crewman carry your baggage to your cabin."

Yago nodded and waited. Donis's ship was one of four trading vessels he owned, and the captain had important contacts with the pirates. Yago traded crossbows for the goods they gained and sold the people they captured in the ports across the eastern sea. He would spend time during the two-day trip planning for meetings with the pirate captains after he arrived in Amut.

After the uneventful voyage, Balzer, his assistant, was waiting at the dock in Amut. "Master Yago, so good to have you back." The balding black man bowed.

"It is good to be back. We have a lot of work to do while I am here. Let's go to the factory and see if they have increased their output as I ordered."

"Yes, sir. The cart is waiting." Balzer took him to an oxcart tied up at the end of the pier.

He climbed up on the cart and Balzer led the ox down the wharf to the edge of town where smoke billowed from the chimney of a large wood-frame building that joined another pier jutting out into the bay. Two barges moored there contained piles of red earth and stone. The iron ore was used to forge the lath, or limb, and other parts of the crossbows that he had fashioned after the one he brought with him when he first arrived in this strange country.

The foundry looked like a scene from *Dante's Inferno*. Crucibles sat in open wood-fired kilns where they melted the iron ore. When ready, Mexicas slaves, their backs glistening from sweat, used tongs to carry the crucible to the mold for pouring. Other Mexicas, Yago's name for the natives from inland who resembled the indigenous people from the Indies he fought with Cortes, removed the cooled casting from the mold and carried them to the smiths for forging.

"Master." Balzer came up to him, accompanied by Sakarbal, the plant overseer.

"Master." Sakarbal bowed in greeting. "How may I serve you today?"

"Tell me you have increased production as I asked." Yago watched the overseer's eyes for indications of falsehood.

"Yes, Master. But not as much as you requested. We currently meet most of your requirements. We need more slaves. The strenuous work and long hours result in many accidents that disable or kill the workers. We have lost four men this week," Sakarbal explained.

Yago stepped closer to the big man. "I will get you your slaves. You have one month to reach the new production levels." The overseer's honesty pleased him.

"Yes, Master."

After looking over the rest of the factory, he left. Balzer led the oxcart to the slave market at the opposite end of town. He needed to know more about the rumors that Addah had made a raid without his authorization, and what kind of profit resulted from the sale of the captives. Then he would summon Addah.

That evening, Yago sat in the courtyard of his house above the city. A cool breeze that blew in from the ocean and the shade of the overhanging roof made it cooler than the rest of the house. Slaves brought him a mug of ale, cool from the barrel in the cellar and fresh fruit—a welcomed respite before Addah arrived. He watched the young woman who had brought the ale. She would make an agreeable companion later; another advantage of having two households.

Balzer interrupted his musings. "Master, Addah is waiting at the entrance."

"We will let him wait a few more minutes." Yago smiled. It was always good to make those who served him wait. They needed time to consider their actions and what repercussions they might incur. Yago finished his ale and called for a servant to bring two mugs up before he turned to Balzer. "You may bring Addah in now."

Balzer brought him into the courtyard. Yago had intentionally chosen his seat because it forced Addah to stand two steps below him. The slaver fidgeted, darting his eyes from side to side. He appeared nervous. *The wait inside seems to have had its expected effect.*

He stared at the raider. "Addah, I hear you authorized a raid while I was away."

"Yes, sir. I did."

At least he didn't lie. "So, you think you can go out on your own despite your oath to me?"

"No, sir. I—I was just trying to make a little extra. I am still your servant."

Yago picked up the papers from the table and scanned the top two sheets. "Apparently, you barely made enough to buy a mug of the bad ale from the tavern in town. You sold five captives at market prices, but you lost a boat and several men while bringing them to town. I assume that was not the outcome you wanted."

"No, sir, it was not. I am sorry. It seemed easy. I will not do it again. If you give me a chance, I will fulfill my oath," Addah said.

Yago signaled to two slaves standing in the shadows to Addah's right. "You failed me, and you failed yourself. There is a price for failure."

The two slaves grabbed Addah's arms and forced him to his knees. The one on his left extended his left arm up to the table. "Spread your fingers if you want to keep your hand," Yago ordered.

Addah spread his fingers and closed his eyes. Balzer brought his short sword down onto the table with a *thunk*, severing Addah's pinky and ring finger from his hand as the blade buried itself in the wood. Then the slaves jerked him up to a standing position and handed him a rag to wrap around the wound.

Yago continued to scan the papers. "That is the price of failure. Fail me again and you will lose your hand. You may go."

As they turned to leave, Yago noticed something unusual on the list. "Wait!"

The slaves brought Addah back to stand before him. "An unusual, white-skinned slave sold for the minimum price. You had wounded him in the raid, and he appeared to be old. Is this true?"

"Ye-yes, sir," Addah said.

Yago stood and clenched his fists at his side. "You know you must bring all unusual captives to me, yet you did not."

"I know, sir. But he was not of value, so I didn't think it would be necessary."

"You didn't think. You are a stupid man. I gave explicit orders, but you did not obey." Yago moved around the table to stand in front of Addah. "If you live, know that I require obedience." Yago punched him in the stomach, then in the face, before nodding to Balzer.

Balzer continued to beat him while the slaves held his arms. When he could no longer stand, Balzer and the slaves kicked him while Yago watched.

After several minutes, he waved them off. "Take him into town and have the healer tend to him. If he lives, he may still be of use."

The slaves carried Addah out, and he turned to Balzer. "Arrange a meeting with Shera, preferably at her home. I want to look at this white slave myself. Since she paid so little for him, perhaps I can buy him from her."

CHAPTER TWENTY

YAGO SEES RYAN

I t had been two weeks since the sale, and Ryan finally understood most of his duties as Shera's house slave. He learned quickly as Jin explained his duties. It helped him to focus when he remembered the biblical account of Joseph's faithfulness to Potiphar. Still, he watched for opportunities that might present a way for him to escape and return to the mountains. He had to find a way home.

He carried the last of the dishes from the breakfast table into the kitchen. When he entered, Jin asked to see him. "Ryan, Mistress Shera has guests arriving this morning, and we will serve them lunch. You must be careful. Yago is coming. He does not treat his slaves well. Don't speak to him and let me do the work in the courtyard. You will stay inside and out of the way as much as possible."

"I will do as you say. But why are you so concerned?" he said.

"He buys the light skinned, and others he thinks have come through the magic. We never see them again, and his slaves say he tortures and kills them."

"I will be careful."

"Good," she said. "Now we must prepare for their arrival. Mistress Shera will assign your duties today."

They spent the next hour arranging furniture in the courtyard under Maslic's direction. When they finished, Shera came out and evaluated their work. "Well done, Maslic. Yago says he wants to talk about a new trade route and the opportunity to sell my spices there. I don't believe him. He has another motive. We could discuss the trade route through our agents."

"Yes, Mistress," Maslic said. "You are wise to suspect him."

Shera turned to Jin. "Have Ryan clean the floors in the main house. I do not want him out here with our guests."

"Yes, Mistress." Jin signaled for him to follow. When they were inside, she said, "Even Mistress Shera understands the danger. You must stay out of sight." She led him to the large room reserved for gatherings. "Sweep and scrub the floors. That should see you through the visit."

Jin left him to complete his work. While he swept the floor, he heard Maslic lead the guests out to the courtyard. "Your mistress has a delightful house," he overheard one guest say.

"Yes, Master Yago," Maslic said. "She takes pride in it. She has prepared for your arrival and will meet you in the courtyard." Their footsteps faded as they went down the hall.

Yago has a strange accent. It seems familiar. Ryan finished sweeping and went out through the kitchen to get water to use on the floor. As he went through, he heard Jin talking to the other women.

"Yago is such an awful man. He paws at me each time I serve him something. He is trying to get Mistress Shera angry, and I think it is working. I can see it in her eyes. To think, she once considered marrying him until she learned he already had a wife in Jabyl." The other women consoled her.

Ryan went out to the well, and when he returned through the kitchen, Jin was not there. He had nearly completed cleaning the floor when he heard voices in the hall.

"Thank you, Shera, that was a wonderful meal, and I think we may have an opportunity once the new market opens." Ryan recognized the accent and assumed it was Yago. "By the way, I heard you purchased a new household slave while I was away. Could I see him?"

"Maslic, where is Nanhin?" Ryan heard Shera use his native name.

"He is cleaning floors and has much to do," Maslic answered.

"Perhaps we can just go by the door," Yago said. "I would like to see him."

"Very well. We will go by the door, but he needs to finish his work," Shera said.

Ryan saw them standing in the doorway. There were two strangers. One was a tall, muscular black man with a purple sash and turban. The other was nearly as light skinned as he was and wore an embroidered shirt with the purple sash, but no turban covering his light brown hair.

The light-skinned one must be Yago. He acted as if he was ignoring them, but he listened carefully as they spoke.

"He is very white," Yago said. "I would like to buy him. I can give you a good price, especially since you paid practically nothing for him."

"He is not for sale," Shera said. "I also find him interesting and want to know more about him. It is fortunate for me you were away."

"Yes, very fortunate. But if you change your mind, you know how to contact me."

They left the doorway and Ryan heard nothing else. *I don't like Yago. Though, his accent reminds me of Emily's family.*

A little later, Shera and Jin came into the room.

"Ryan," Shera said.

"Yes, Mistress Shera." Ryan stood and faced her.

"What do you know about Yago?"

"Only the rumors I have heard from the other slaves." Ryan cocked his head and looked at Jin.

"Well, he seems very interested in you, and offered to pay me well for you." She put her fists on her hips. "But I don't trust him, and I don't like him. You may bring trouble to me if I don't sell you." She turned to leave, then stopped. "Jin tells me you can read. Can you work with numbers as well?"

"Yes, Mistress. I can read a little but haven't had enough exposure to your written language to read everything. I can work with numbers."

"Good." She turned to Jin. "Have him ready to go to the warehouse with me in one hour." Shera left.

"Why is she taking me to the warehouse?" Ryan asked.

"She wants to know if you will be worth the trouble Yago is going to start," Jin said.

"Is what you said true? He kills those who have come through the portals, the magic."

"It is. I'm worried for you, Ryan," she said. "Now go wash and straighten your clothing. You will want to look good when you go through town."

"At least this time, I won't be naked."

After Ryan had cleaned up, he waited in the shade near the slave's table. Maslic found him there and led him out front to the oxcart. "I assume you cannot drive an ox," he said, holding a rod in his hand.

"No, sir. I have never learned how to do that," Ryan said. "But I can learn if you teach me."

"Maybe another day." Maslic pointed to the back of the cart. "Sit there on the bags. Mistress Shera will be down soon."

Ryan climbed up and sat on a pile of empty cloth bags with his back against the side of the cart bed. He remembered being tied to the back of this same cart naked when they brought him here from the slave market. He still thought it odd that the people in town ignored him. *They must not think of me as a person. Just a piece of property like the ox.*

When Shera joined them, Maslic helped her up to the front seat. He said something to her then tapped the ox's rear with the rod, and the cart moved. Maslic walked beside the huge ox. Whenever they needed to change directions, he would voice a command and tap the ox with his rod.

After the bumpy ride, they pulled up in front of a large, busy warehouse that smelled of spices. Muscular men, some black and others from the mountains, carried large sacks into the open door of the warehouse. Inside, he saw where they stacked the bags in piles separated into different types. Ryan thought it looked like a typical warehouse, not much different from one back in his world, except for fewer shelves and no forklifts. They went through the warehouse to the grinding mill, where the plant overseer, Hanno, greeted Shera, ignoring Maslic and him.

While Hanno and Shera talked, Maslic took him to the far side of the grinding area, to a pile of broken bags.

"What are these?" Ryan asked.

"These are scrap bags." He pointed to a tear on the side of one bag. "The rats have burrowed into them."

Ryan bent down to look closer. The smell of cinnamon drifted up from the hole. Ryan licked his finger and put it into the torn bag. He pulled it out and tasted the rust colored powder that adhered to it. It was cinnamon, but he thought rats avoided strong spices like cinnamon and pepper. The hole also appeared to have straight edges, more like a cut than a hole gnawed by rats.

"What do they do with these bags?" Ryan said.

"I believe they throw them away. No one will buy a bag fouled by rats," Maslic said.

Ryan sat on a low stack at the right edge of the pile. The dust covering the floor had no tracks or other signs of rodents. He looked at several other bags near where he sat. One looked bright red like paprika and another looked yellowish brown, like cumin. Each bag had a straight cut through the side. He thought it odd, but kept it to himself.

Shera signaled Maslic from the bottom of a set of stairs leading up to a loft. They followed her up. When they got to the top, they sat by the rail that overlooked the warehouse floor. Shera and Hanno sat at a table. Hanno had his back to Ryan, who watched Shera going through some papers.

She looked up. "I thought we talked about the inventory losses last time. Yet we have even bigger losses now. Did you do anything to prevent them?" She glared across the table at Hanno.

"Yes, Mistress," Hanno said. "I had the bags put up on pallets and set traps, but they were ineffective. As you can see, the losses were greater this time. The rats multiply quickly."

"You must do better, or I will have you replaced. I don't want to hear any excuses next time." Shera stood, still holding the papers, and looked at Maslic. "Let's go. We will be back." She strode to the stairs, ignoring Hanno's response.

Ryan followed them down the stairs to the cart. Maslic took them back to the house. Ryan wondered why they had brought him. It seemed like a waste. Shera sat in silence and gripped the papers the entire trip back to the villa.

Chapter Twenty-One

Yago Plots

After Yago and Balzer left Shera's, they met with several associates before returning to his estate. Except for the stubbornness of that idiot woman, things had gone well. His assets and influence were growing. Maybe he could force Shera to sell if he could undermine her business dealings.

When the slave returned with another cool beer, he said, "Have Balzer join me out here."

"Yes, Master."

A few minutes later, Balzer came to the table. "You wanted to see me?"

"Yes, sit. What were your thoughts on the white slave?"

"He is not from Almirosia, though he spoke like it. He is too tall, and his skin is even lighter than yours," Balzer said, then took a swig of his beer. "I do not understand why Shera would not sell. Either she is holding out for a better price, or she is being spiteful. You have crossed her in the past. I don't believe she would do anything to help you."

Yago sat silently for a few moments, staring into his beer. "I think you are right about her. She needs to be convinced. What can we do to change her mind? Don't we have one or two of her employees on our payroll?"

"Yes. Hanno, her warehouse overseer, siphons off spices for us to sell. Though it is not much, it gives us information about her operations. We also have one of her slaves that talks for favors."

"Good, we can start with Hanno. He must increase the amount he siphons." Yago drained his cup. "Then take the auction manifest. We will buy the other male and the older woman from the new masters. I want to know more about this slave."

"As you wish." Balzer rose and left.

The next day, Yago was in his courtyard when Balzer returned. From the look on his face, Yago knew he had brought bad news. "What did you learn from Hanno?"

"He will do what he can," Balzer said. "But he says Shera is suspicious of the losses and he fears she may not keep him on."

Yago stood and paced. "Do we have an alternative?"

"Possibly." Balzer walked with him. "Hanno says that Shera will sail next week on the trading voyage to the islands."

"Interesting. That may solve our problem. Thank Hanno for the information and tell him we will reward him if he loses his position." He turned to Balzer. "With Shera gone, we can snatch the white slave from her compound and spread the rumor that he fled. Do we have anyone inside her staff we can rely on?"

"I think we can find someone," Balzer said. "All slaves look to better their position."

"Good, get to work on that. Meanwhile, what of the other slaves from the sale?"

"The male slave was badly beaten for trying to escape and cannot talk. But I have purchased the female you requested. Her owner had tired of her and sold her for what he paid. They will deliver her tomorrow."

"Good. Maybe she will tell us where he came from." Yago smiled and sat at a table. "Now, go to the wharf and arrange for me to meet with Ahram and Hailama. Shera's voyage will be very eventful."

Balzer left the courtyard.

The next morning, Yago sat eating his breakfast in the court-yard of his villa. The cool breeze from the ocean and the shade of the trees made it very comfortable to sit outside. Balzer came up to him.

"Master, the woman slave you requested has arrived. Would you like her brought out here?"

"No. Take her to the study. I will be in shortly."

"As you wish." Balzer went back into the house, leaving Yago to finish his breakfast.

Now that he had the woman, he would find out if Shera's white slave came through the portal. When he entered his study, the woman was on her knees in front of the table that served as his desk. She was completely naked, with her arms drawn in and leaning over her knees. He saw the dark bruises on her back and sides as he walked by her.

"Lift your head," he ordered the woman. Her right eye was also bruised and her lip split. "Stand up." He looked her over and saw the fear in her eyes as she stood totally exposed. He turned to Balzer. "Get her a robe and have someone bring in food and water."

He sat and watched her while Balzer fetched the robe. When he returned with it, he cut the ropes from her hands. She put on the robe and drew it around her. Once dressed, she stood taller, looking less afraid. She appeared to relax more when they brought in the food and water. Yago had her sit at the table across from him while she gulped down the water and stuffed fruit into her mouth.

When she finished, Yago asked, "What is your name?"

"Kagi."

"Well, Kagi, it appears your previous owner mistreated you. Things will be different while you are here." He leaned toward her. "But I would like you to tell me about another captive that was taken from your village. He is tall and light skinned. Do you know him?"

Kagi drank more water. "Yes, he is a brave man and a mighty warrior. We call him Nanhin because of the hair on his face."

"That is the one. How long has he lived in your village?"

"Since the spring. He and the manetoo that obeys him rescued one of the village girls from two tanwakuas."

"He has a manetoo?" Yago guessed it was a dog and not a wolf.

"Yes, but a raider shot it. I don't know if it is dead or alive."

"Did he talk about where he came from before he arrived at your village?"

"No. He only talked about finding a way back. He wanted to go to his wife even after Wakakan gave Zica to him."

"Who is Wakakan?"

"The shaman. He had Nanhin go to the spirit caves to see if they could find a way for him to return."

"This Nanhin sounds like an interesting man. If possible, I am going to purchase him from his present owner. Perhaps he may join you here." He stood. "Eat and drink as much as you like. When you finish, Balzer will take you out and show you where you will stay."

"Thank you, Master."

Yago looked at Balzer. "You know what to do." Then he left the room, knowing Balzer would take her out back and kill her. She could wait for Nanhin in hell.

Later that afternoon, Balzer brought Addah to Yago. "Addah, I see you are healing from your injuries," Yago said.

"Yes. I am nearly recovered." Addah stood with his head down.

"Recovered enough to do a simple job?"

Addah looked up. "I believe I am. What sort of job?"

"I want you to get me the white slave you sold after your recent misadventure." Yago put his hand on Addah's shoulder. "Do you know where he is?"

"Yes. He is at Mistress Shera's compound," Addah said.

"You are familiar with the compound? How many men would you need to raid it and bring me the slave?"

"I could do it with two men, but what about the mistress and the other merchants? Won't they respond?"

Yago smiled. "They will respond if they know who is responsible. You are responsible and must keep it a secret." He took a couple of steps away from Addah. "Bring the white slave to me. You may keep the women slaves for yourself, but you must take them away from Amut. Kill everyone else and burn the compound. Don't leave any witnesses."

Now, Addah smiled. "I will not fail you."

"See that you don't. Now get your men. Balzer will see you out."

Yago walked to the window. He knew he would have to kill Addah and his men before any of them talked. Perhaps he could arrange their escape on a ship. They could disappear at sea.

CHAPTER TWENTY-TWO

SHERA CONFRONTS HANNO

Shera went through the accounts from the warehouse. There was something wrong, but she couldn't pinpoint it. She straightened and stretched her back as Maslic came into the room.

"Mistress, you sent for me."

"Yes, Maslic. Have you made all the arrangements for my trip next week?" She walked away from the table, leaned from side to side at the waist, and continued to stretch.

"Yes, Mistress. Qutan will have accommodations for both of us on his ship." He paused. "Do you require anything else?"

"Not unless you can enlighten me on the warehouse accounts. They make little sense to me. Something's off."

"I don't know accounts, as you know," Maslic said. "But I have been talking with the white-skinned slave. He said things did not look right at the warehouse, especially with the contaminated bags."

"What did he say?"

"He said that rodents didn't tear the holes in the bags he saw. Someone cut the holes with a sharp-edged blade. He also thought that the rodents didn't eat the spices. Where he was from, rats avoided spicy things."

"He told you that?" When Maslic nodded assent, she said, "Bring him in. I want to talk to him."

"Yes, Mistress." Maslic left while Shera thought about what she had heard. *Was Hanno siphoning off profits by stealing spices?*

When Maslic returned with Ryan, she asked them to sit. "Ryan, Maslic relayed a conversation you had with him concerning things you saw at the warehouse. What did you see?"

"Mistress, while we waited for you and Hanno, I sat on the bags designated as bad. I looked at the bag I was on, and I noticed the hole had very straight, uniform edges. If rodents had gotten into the bag, they would have left ragged edges with bits of cloth scattered. Curious, I looked at the others and saw the same type of hole. Also, there were no tracks in the dust. I do not believe rodents caused the holes."

"That is interesting, but how can you be sure?" Shera said.

"I cannot. I would suggest you talk to a ship captain to see if he has had any losses because of rodents aboard ship, since they surely have rodents," he said.

Shera turned to Maslic. "Is Qutan's ship at the dock?"

"Yes, Mistress."

"Go get the cart. We will go down there now." Maslic and Ryan got up to leave, but Shera said, "Ryan, you stay here with me. You said you could work with numbers. Can you go through the accounts with me while Maslic gets the cart?"

"Yes, Mistress."

Shera took Ryan to the table and handed him the latest account sheet. He studied it for a few minutes. "The numbers add up correctly, but there may be an issue with the scrap quantities. It shows twelve bags as scrap, but during our visit, there were only six bags and a couple of them appeared to be older."

"Thank you. Let's go to the wharf." *My suspicions of Hanno seem well founded. I need to make a change quickly, especially if Captain Qutan confirms what Ryan said about the rats.*

On the trip into town, Ryan told her more about the rodents he knew. She asked many questions that Ryan answered. When they got to the docks, Maslic took the cart down the pier to Qutan's ship.

The captain was up on deck when they got there and waved to them. "Come aboard. This is a surprise. I wasn't expecting to see you until next week."

"This is an unplanned visit," Shera said as they went up the gangplank to the ship. "Can we talk in private?"

"Of course. Let's go to my cabin. Would you like something cool to drink? Your trip down here was probably hot."

"Yes, thank you."

Inside the small compartment that served as the captain's quarters, Shera sat across the table from Qutan, and Ryan and Maslic sat on a bench near the door.

After the young sailor, who brought in glasses of cool beer, left, Shera asked, "How long have you been sailing for me?"

"I have worked only for you the last four years, but I also did a couple of voyages as a free agent the year before," Qutan said.

"During that time, have you had any issues with rodents getting into the cargo?"

Qutan tilted his head slightly. "As a sailing vessel, we always have issues with rodents. But they are only a problem with the provision we carry for the voyage. They do not get into the cargo, not even to nest. Why do you ask?"

"I am looking into an issue at the warehouse. What can you tell me about Hanno?"

"Not much, Mistress. I have only known him while he has been at the warehouse, though there are rumors he has some relationship with Yago," Qutan said. "But, to my knowledge, they are just rumors."

Shera finished her beer and stood. "Thank you, Captain. You have been very helpful. Please keep our conversation just between us."

Qutan stood and bowed. "It was my pleasure, Mistress. Your concerns will not leave this room. I look forward to traveling with you next week."

When they got back to the cart, Maslic asked, "Shall we go to the warehouse?"

"No, not today. Take me back home and we will talk," Shera said. "I have a job for you."

When they returned to her compound, she took Maslic and Ryan out to the courtyard where she had one of her female slaves bring drinks. She sat at a table in the shade and signaled the two men to sit as well. She looked at Maslic. "You have contacts in town who can help you monitor Hanno's activities, don't you?"

"Yes, Mistress."

"Good. I want you to spend a few days in town watching the warehouse and Hanno. You must be discreet. Can you do that?"

"Yes, Mistress," he said. "But what about my duties here?"

"For now, I will let Ryan run things in the household." She turned to Ryan. "Can you handle that?"

"I think so, Mistress," Ryan said. "But unlike Maslic, I am a slave and have limited authority."

"Is there anything he and I cannot do while you complete your assignment?" she asked Maslic.

"You are more than capable of doing everything, Mistress," he said. "If you give Ryan the authority to assign tasks to others, they will do as you say. I will let Jin and a few others know of the change to ease the transition."

"Good. Ryan will also help me with the accounts from the warehouse. Perhaps he can see what I cannot."

For the next three days, she met with Maslic every evening after his return from town. He told of witnesses to Hanno allowing men to remove two or three bags from the warehouse on two different occasions. They followed the men to a ship on the wharf where they loaded the bags. He provided Shera with details of the times and quantity of bags, as well as the names of the ships.

Hanno was a thief, and she decided she must remove him immediately.

The next day, she returned to the warehouse with Maslic and Ryan. Hanno seemed surprised at the unexpected visit, but he took them up to the office. Again, Shera sat at the table with Hanno, while Ryan and Maslic sat along the railing.

"I think you are a thief," Shera said. "You have been stealing bags of spices from me and hiding the shortages as inventory losses."

Hanno stood and glared over the table. "You are mistaken, Mistress."

Shera sat calmly and glared back. "I have witnesses I trust who saw you help men take bags from the warehouse to ships on the wharf under the cover of darkness. I can no longer have you work for me. Gather your belongings and leave immediately."

Hanno moved around the table, but Ryan and Maslic both jumped up and moved toward him. He turned to face them and put his hand on the knife in his belt.

Maslic already had his sword drawn. "You will be dead before it clears the scabbard."

"You will regret this," Hanno said. "I have friends, and you won't find anyone else to run this place."

Shera pushed her chair back and stood. "I have friends as well and will see that you do not find an honest job in Amut." She looked at Maslic. "Get him out of my sight."

Maslic put the point of his sword into Hanno's back and Ryan took the knife from his belt. Then Maslic took the thief down the stairs and out of the building.

Shera and Ryan gathered the workers together. "You will not allow Hanno back into the building. He is a thief. For now, you will receive your instructions from Maslic. Is that understood?"

"Yes, Mistress," they all replied.

"Good. Back to work," Shera said, then turned to Maslic, who had returned. "Have men you can trust watch the doors. Then join us upstairs."

When Maslic joined them, they all sat at the table. Shera handed the books over to Ryan. "You will go through these and help Maslic understand how to use them. You have two days."

"Yes, Mistress," they answered.

"Maslic, how many of the workers are not slaves but paid workers?" she asked.

"Four, Mistress. And I do not trust three of them," he said.

"Fire them. I will buy more slaves if needed. I do not want any of Hanno's men still working here. You will need to have firm control while I am gone."

Maslic shook his head. "I do not think it is a good idea for you to go on the voyage alone, Mistress."

"I will not be going alone," she said. "Ryan will go with me. He is adept at numbers and strong enough to act as my protector."

"But he is a slave."

"Yes. I trust him, even though he is a slave." She turned to Ryan. "Will you accompany me and act as my protector without trying to escape?"

"Yes, Mistress. I swear it," Ryan said.

"Good. It's settled. Ryan will take me back home while you get things going here. I will send him back with men from the house to help you. Then he can start on the books."

She turned to Ryan. "Can you handle the ox?"

"I think so, Mistress."

CHAPTER TWENTY-THREE

SET SAIL

The morning of their departure, Ryan and Shera returned to the docks. This time, he rode in the cart with Shera and another slave, Towah, acted as ox driver. Shera had provided him with new clothing for the voyage. He wore tan pants, a blue vest over a white smock, a blue turban, and leather sandals. All to disguise the fact that he was a slave when they met her business partners.

Captain Qutan greeted them when they arrived at the dock. "Mistress Shera, welcome aboard. I will have someone bring your luggage to your quarters." He led them up the gangway and into a small compartment at the ship's stern. "Unfortunately, this is a small ship, so you will need to share quarters. I had a curtain installed for your privacy, Mistress."

"Thank you, Captain. I am used to the arrangements having sailed on your ship on other occasions, and the arrangements on other ships are similar. How soon do we depart?"

"We leave on the tide in another hour."

"Captain." A sailor stood at the door with the luggage. "Where shall I put these?"

"On the floor at the foot of the bed." The captain turned to Shera. "You can stow them from there. Now I must tend to my duties. Will you join me in my cabin for dinner tonight?"

"It will be my pleasure," she said as the captain and the sailor left. "Ryan, you will sleep over there." She pointed to a hammock hung near the wall on the left. "You can pull the curtain across to separate the hammock from the bed on the other side of the room. The latrine is through the small door at the back. It is not much, just a bench with a hole above the water where the deck extends beyond the ship's hull."

Ryan nodded and picked up his bundle of clothing and moved it to a shelf below his hammock. He put Shera's bag in the wardrobe that stood beside the lavatory door before they went out onto the deck. The sailors scurried about, moving supplies from the pier to the hold of the ship and securing items on the deck to prepare for their departure.

Captain Qutan stood on the raised deck, the poop deck, above their quarters and waved them up to join him there. They watched until the crew had stored all the provisions. Then Captain Qutan ordered the moorings released. A large rowboat, attached to the ship by a heavy rope, pulled the prow away from the pier. It continued to pull until the ship was well clear of the dock and the captain ordered the release of the connecting line and the lowering of the sails.

Ryan watched the coast as the ship sailed through the clear waters of the bay. Once they went through the narrow inlet, the waves of the open ocean rolled under the ship. He remembered being slightly seasick when he and Emily went whale watching while on vacation in Monterey. But this was different. He felt like his head was spinning. He could barely stand. Soon nausea overtook him, and he bent over the rail of the ship and purged his stomach.

Captain Qutan came and stood beside him. "You will get used to the sea soon enough." He put his hand on Ryan's shoulder. "Everyone has some difficulty when we start. Try to breathe slowly and watch the horizon. Then, when you are able, sleep."

Ryan remained bent over the rail for several minutes before standing. He followed the captain's advice and took several deep breaths while watching the horizon. The coast was a thin green line in the hazy distance. He closed his eyes, held onto the rail, and relaxed before going down to the main deck. Along the rail of the ship, he saw that even a few of the crew were sick. He went into the cabin and climbed into his hammock and slept. He could not join Shera and the captain for dinner that evening or the next. After the first two days of the two-week voyage, the seasickness gradually subsided. On the third day, he could stay on deck, walk around, interact with the crew, and eat regular meals.

Shipboard life was boring. He had nothing to do to keep himself occupied. He often sat at the stern of the ship with his legs hanging over the edge, staring into the uninterrupted expanse. His mind often went back to that final evening at home. Emily stood at the sink, her long ponytail swinging as she sang and did the dishes. He was more homesick now than at any time since his arrival in Almirosia. *Will I ever go back there? God, you rescued Joseph from his slavery, and I believe you will rescue me, but please don't take that long.*

One week into the voyage, he and Shera sat in the captain's quarters eating dinner. Shera leaned over to Ryan. "You have been silent, Ryan. What is bothering you?"

"I've seen that look before," Qutan said. "He is homesick. The sea does that to people. It gives them too much time to think."

"Is that true, Ryan?"

"Yes, Mistress. I miss my wife and my home."

She stared at him with a puzzled expression. "You miss your village? I have given you a home with shelter and food and things to occupy your time."

He didn't know how to answer her. She had been kind, but he told the truth. "Yes, I miss my home, my wife, and Toby. I miss the village and the freedom it provided, and my friends. But mostly I miss the home I had before I came to Almirosia and before the villagers took me in."

Just then, a knock on the door interrupted them, and a sailor entered. "Captain, there is a ship off our port. It is closing fast and looks like a pirate vessel."

The captain stood. "Nonsense. Let me see this vessel. We paid for protection from the pirates."

Ryan and Shera stayed at the table and waited. Soon, the captain returned. "Go to your cabin and stay there. Don't come out until I tell you it is clear." He turned and went back out.

They got up and hurried to their cabin next door. On their way, Ryan spotted a boat hook. He thought it looked like a pike. He could use it as a weapon. Inside, he bolted the door and waited. It wasn't long until he heard fighting outside, men yelling, the dull *thunks* as men or other things fell to the deck. When it finally got quiet outside, he heard someone say, "Search the cabins. Find the woman and the white slave."

Ryan waited with the hook ready while they used an axe on the door. When they broke through, Shera screamed, and he drove the hook into the chest of the first one that came through the door. But there were too many. While he pulled the hook from the first, three more entered with crossbows ready.

"Don't kill them," he heard someone say. "Yago wants the man alive, and we will sell the woman."

He dropped the hook and two of them grabbed him and took him outside. More followed, bringing Shera out. Captain Qutan was on his knees in front of six remaining crewmen, all surrounded by twice that many pirates on the torchlit deck.

"Is that everyone?" said the pirate who stood in front of Captain Qutan.

"Aye, Captain. We searched the whole ship. All the others are dead."

"Good. Start loading the cargo into our ship." The pirate captain turned to Qutan. "Your crew did not fight well, Captain Qutan. We only lost the man your passenger killed."

Qutan stared up at the pirate. "I did not expect a fight. We paid the protection fee. Why did you attack us?"

"I'll just say an interested party offered more for your capture than the value of your entire cargo. Though we will take it as well." He pointed his crossbow at Qutan's chest.

"You are a mud-sucking sea worm. What will you do with us?" Qutan said.

"We will sell your crew to the mine owners in Donaica. But you, Captain, are of no value." The pirate captain fired his crossbow, and the bolt went into Captain Qutan's chest. He fell forward, the weight of his body driving the bolt deeper. The flames of the torches reflected in the blood that pooled around him.

The pirate captain turned to his crew. "Now, take the rest of them to the cells on our ship and lock them up. Then, after you have transferred all the cargo, burn the ship."

They took Ryan, Shera, and the surviving crew members across a plank tied between the two ships, then down into the bowels of the other vessel and locked them in a cage that reeked of human waste.

Shera clung to Ryan's arm. "What will we do?"

"What can we do?" Ryan looked around the cell at the other prisoners. "I have been through this once already. We do as we are told and try to stay alive. That is our only hope."

CHAPTER TWENTY-FOUR

LOOSE ENDS

As the sun rose over the blue lagoon at the bottom of the hill, Addah watched for the ship that Yago promised would be there. It had been a long night trekking through the hills after the raid on Shera's compound. They had executed the attack at sunset after Hanno's associates had set fire to the vacant building next to Shera's warehouse. The fire guaranteed that Maslic, reputedly a formidable fighter, would not be at the compound during the attack. Addah knew Maslic's presence at the compound would increase the probability of failure.

Though Addah didn't like Hanno, his help had been essential before the raid. Now he was a thorn in his side. Hanno insisted on carrying too much loot from Shera's compound. That slowed their progress. They should already be on the beach below. Once the ship rounded the point and entered the lagoon, he would eliminate Hanno.

He called Muhad when he saw the ship appear in the distance. "Get the women up. We are going down to the beach."

Muhad grabbed the rope that bound the four captive women and jerked it. They all stood and followed as he led them down the hill.

Hanno scrambled to pick up the two sacks of loot so he could follow. "Give me a hand, Addah."

"You took it. You carry it." Addah started down the hill. He and Muhad would share the loot once they reached the beach. Yago had been clear about Hanno's fate.

They followed a game trail through the scattered trees. The morning sun quickly heated the still air. Addah's body was wet with sweat when they finally stepped out of the trees into the long grass that covered the dunes guarding the lagoon. They made slow progress as they climbed and descended each dune. Their feet slipped on the loose sand and long grass. Hanno fell farther behind and whined for help. He would get none.

The grass ended at the peak of the last dune, which descended to smaller dunes leading to the beach. These provided little hindrance as they reached the smooth, white sand beach.

"Have the women sit," he said to Muhad. "Let's get the signal fire started." He could see the ship already in the lagoon.

"Why wouldn't you help me carry this?" Hanno said when he finally got to the beach and dropped the sacks.

"I told you. You took it. You carry it. Now, go help Muhad get more wood for the fire."

"I am not your servant. I need to rest. Muhad can get enough wood himself." Hanno plopped down on the sand.

"Yes, he can." Addah pointed his crossbow at Hanno.

"What is this?"

"This was always the plan. Yago has no further need for you." He pulled the release, sending the bolt into Hanno's chest. "Thank you for bringing the loot. Muhad and I would have been happy with the price of the women, but this is a bonus." He kicked sand over Hanno's body.

When Muhad returned, they lit the fire and threw green grass on it to increase the smoke. The ship drew closer and stopped a hundred yards from the beach. Its crew lowered a boat over the side, and two men rowed it to shore.

Addah tossed Hanno's sacks into the boat and helped Muhad load the women. Once everyone was in the boat, they pushed out into the light surf. The sailors didn't talk, which suited Addah. He was ready to be away somewhere he could start anew. The loot and sale of the women would make a good start.

They pulled up alongside the ship to a rope ladder that hung down the side. Addah was the first to climb aboard. The captain met him. "I am Captain Hailama. Welcome aboard."

"Thank you, Captain. Yago said you would meet us. How long will we be aboard?"

"Not long. We will only be at sea for a few days."

Muhad and the sailors finished boarding along with the captive women. "We will put the women below. Botrys will show you to your cabin." The captain pointed to a sailor nearby.

The sailor led them to a cabin at the stern of the ship. "We sail immediately. Mess is at sunset amidship. Until then, you may spend time on deck or rest here," Botrys said and left, closing the door behind him.

"I'm going to rest." Muhad climbed into one hammock that hung along the wall. "It was a long night. What about you?"

"I think I will go out on deck," Addah said. "I didn't like the way the crew eyed the women. The captain and I need to talk."

The captain stood at the rail on the small upper deck, where the steering wheel was located. He yelled orders to the crew. They pulled up the anchor and unfurled the sails in the light breeze that blew in from the open ocean. Addah went to the side rail and watched as the ship left the lagoon. Once they passed through the reef that guarded the lagoon entrance, activity on deck decreased. He looked back up toward the captain, who waved him up to the upper deck.

"Are your quarters acceptable?" the captain said.

"Yes, the cabin is fine," Addah said. "Do you mind if I ask a couple of questions?"

"No. Ask what you will."

"Where are we headed?"

"We are going north to Jabyl, and who knows where from there?"

"What about our captives?" Addah pointed to a group of sailors on the deck below. "The crew was eyeing them. I worry about their value if they abuse the women."

"The crew is used to having slaves aboard." The captain put his hand on Addah's shoulder. "They know the rules and will not touch the women without my permission. I run a tight ship."

By sunset, he and Muhad were seasick, so they stayed in their cabin. They didn't eat the next morning either. Around midday, Addah went out on deck. The open sea was calm, with gently rolling swells. His stomach seemed better, and he felt hungry, but he would have to wait to eat until the evening mess.

He heard a commotion behind him. He turned and saw two sailors bringing one woman up on deck. It was the one with the scarred face. They tore her tunic off and tied her over a barrel.

He looked up to where the captain stood at the rail. "Captain, I thought you said they would leave the women alone."

The captain waved, and two sailors came over to him. "I said they wouldn't touch them without my permission." They grabbed Addah's arms and held him while two more entered the cabin. They brought out Muhad, then tied the hands of both men. The captain descended the stairs and stood in front of Addah. "Yago does not like failure."

The pirates laughed as they ran a long plank out over the port side of the ship. "What are you going to do?" he yelled. *This can't be happening. I did as Yago ordered.* He struggled against his bonds.

The captain watched as the sailors lifted him up onto the plank. "I'm going to do what Yago paid me to do. Now off you go."

Addah felt the point of a sword on his back. "No!"

The pirate behind him prodded him forward, out to the edge of the plank.

"It is a long way to shore. Don't waste your strength fighting," the captain said, and the sailor pushed Addah off the end.

He hit the water and kicked his feet to get to the surface. Before he went back under, he heard Muhad screaming and the pirates laughing. He kicked to the surface again, but it was impossible to stay afloat with his hands tied. Sinking again, he swallowed the salty water. He fought to stay at the surface, but he could not.

Chapter Twenty-Five

Prisoners

Ryan and Shera sat inside a cage, in a corner away from the other captive sailors from Qutan's ship. It didn't take long for the smell and motion of the ship to make him nauseous. He spent the first night curled up on the floor or bent over the bucket in the cell's rear that was used as a toilet. It soon overflowed because he wasn't the only one sick.

Late the next day, though he couldn't really know the time, his stomach settled down, but he was still lightheaded. He heard a scream. He looked and three of the captive sailors had Shera pinned in the corner. One held her while a second pulled at her clothing.

Ryan stood and moved toward them. "Stop!"

"We'll stop when we finish with her." The biggest of the three puffed his chest and stepped between Ryan and Shera. "So shut up and go back to the hole you crawled out of, or we'll stuff you back in it."

Ryan looked him in the eyes. *He's mean, but only a brawler, a bully. He is not a killer.* "I can't do that. Now, leave her alone."

The big man ran at him, but he sidestepped and used the assailant's momentum to throw him into the wall. He bounced off, landing on his rear. He yelled to the others, "Get him!"

One grabbed Ryan from behind, pinning his arms back. The big man got up and faced him. "I'm going to beat the life out of you."

Ryan kicked him in the groin, and then he kicked him in the face when he bent over, knocking him back onto his butt. Blood poured from the man's nose. The smallest of the three stood behind him, and said, "Be careful, Zido. Remember, he killed a pirate."

"I'm going to kill him. He can't do this to me." Zido came back to Ryan. This time, Ryan used both feet to kick the man in the chest. The force sent both Zido and the one holding him backward. Ryan fell on top of the man and rolled off. He jumped up and backed against the bars of the cage, ready for the next assault, when something hit his head, knocking him to his knees.

As he tried to clear his head, he felt Shera throw her arms around him. "Don't touch him!" she yelled.

When his vision cleared, the pirates had entered the cage with weapons. They had separated Shera and him from the other prisoners, still pointing some of their swords at Ryan.

The captain walked in. "What's all the noise?" He looked at the big assailant. "You—you must be the troublemaker." Then turning to Ryan and Shera. "Why are they in here with the others? They are worth more than all the others combined. Yago wants the man returned to Amut, and the woman goes with us to the slave market at Donaica. Take them to the other cell."

They grabbed Ryan's arms and pulled him to his feet, then took them out of the cell to another farther back into the stern of the ship. They threw them to the floor, and he heard the cage lock when they shut the door.

"Get some clothes for the woman," the captain said as he walked away. "I don't want to have her strutting around, enticing the crew."

Shera came over to Ryan and kneeled beside him, looking at his head. She tore a small rag from her ripped shirt and wiped the blood from his forehead. "Tilt your head forward. I want to look where they hit you."

She lightly dabbed the spot with her rag. The lump throbbed, and he winced each time she touched it. "I'll be okay. I just want to sit and rest for a few minutes." He looked around the cell and pointed to a bucket near the door. "Did they leave us any water?"

Shera went to the bucket and returned with a cup of tepid water. After he drank some, she dipped her rag in the cup and used it to clean more blood from his face. "You don't appear to be cut. Where did all this blood come from?"

"I think it is splatter from the big guy Zido. His nose was bleeding profusely."

She continued to clean his face, gently wiping and looking at his face and head. When she stopped, she said, "Thank you. You risked your life for me."

"I promised to protect you before we left." He looked into her eyes.

She kissed him and held his face in her hands. He didn't know what to say.

They heard someone coming. Shera turned away and pulled her ripped shirt together to cover her breasts. A crewman stood at the door. He reached through the bars and dropped some clothes on the floor. "The captain sent these for you." He stood at the door and watched as she went over to pick them up. "It is a shame, but he's the captain." He turned and left, shaking his head.

She grabbed the clothes and went to the far bulkhead, where she removed her torn clothing. Ryan watched her, the beam of light coming through the hatch above, glistening off the sweat on her body. *God help me. I don't know if I can resist being this close to her for long.* She put on the tunic and pants provided. Both were slightly small, fitting tightly around her breasts and butt.

He spent the rest of the day resting. His head hurt. That night he slept fitfully. Though he could not see the other cell because of the cargo stacked between them, he heard someone moaning loudly. He guessed it was Zido.

The next morning, they brought food and fresh water to the cell. Again, the crewman stayed at the bars and watched as Shera took the food back to where Ryan sat. She tore a chunk of the bread off and handed it to him. "What did you do to Yago? Why would he spend so much to have you taken back to Amut?"

"I don't know," he said. "I had never heard of him until he came to visit you. Who is he?"

"He is a stranger from Jabyl. He runs the foundry that makes the crossbows, and he handles most of the slave trade around Amut. I know nothing, other than he would like to take over my spice trade. He has offered to buy it and once he even asked me to marry him, but rumors say he has a wife in Jabyl." She ate her bread and sipped some water. "Many believe he came through the magic."

"If he came through the magic, maybe he wants me because I also came through it." He sat for a moment thinking about the day Yago came to Shera's. There had been something familiar about his accent.

They spent the next two days talking to pass the time. Ryan told her of his world, and she listened in disbelief when he tried to explain the technology. Though she was more interested in his adventures once he arrived in Almirosia.

"Did you really kill two 'tanwakuas'?"

"What is Toby?"

"You saw a 'suzuecu'?"

He answered her questions the best he could, then asked about her life. She told him about her father, who started the business and tried to marry her off. But she wasn't interested in having a man tell her what to do. After he died and she took the business over, all the men who approached were more interested in the business than in her.

"What about Maslic?" he asked.

"Maslic has worked for me since just after my father died."

"Why do you think he stayed with you for so long?"

"He is loyal, and I pay him well." She looked at him like she had another question, but she didn't ask it.

"Maybe," he said, "he is more interested in you than in your business."

They talked very little the rest of the day. Ryan felt like he had upset her, but that evening when they were brought more food, she came and sat close to him.

"What happens if you can't return to your world? Where will you stay?"

"I don't know. I haven't considered not being able to return. The shaman seemed to think I could go back if I fulfilled my purpose."

She took his hand. "If we get out of this, you could stay with me. Not as a slave, but as a husband."

He looked into her eyes. "I am honored, but I already have a wife here in Almirosia. I think if I must stay, I will return to the village to be with her."

"It is not unheard of for a man to have more than one wife here. I think I could share you with her." She leaned over and kissed him again. "Think about it. I could make you happy, and

I would serve you." She stayed next to him, holding his hand and leaning against him.

CHAPTER TWENTY-SIX

NICHE

The darkness of the moonless night enveloped Niche. Feathers rustled as they flew through the quartering wind. The familiar patterns of the stars and his innate sense of direction guided them. The serenity of the night allowed him to center his thoughts on the battle ahead. Scouts had spotted the ship early in the day and reported its location. Now he and a dozen warriors flew to attack it.

Just one year ago, he never would have considered fighting. But, since the day the land dwellers murdered his wife and daughter, he would do whatever it took to prevent the deaths of more women and children. That day, he didn't understand how anyone could kill and mutilate innocents. Now he knew the enemy only wanted their feathers. They considered his race demons, but they are the demons, and must die. His memories hardened his heart, allowing him to kill them like the animals they were.

A whistle to his right brought him back to the moment. The calls continued with chirps and shrill sounds, telling him they had spotted the ship. He focused on the surface in the direction indicated and spotted the faint glow of lamps. He called back a reply, telling the others to descend in slow circles and watch for anyone on deck. Surprise was their best weapon. The weapons of the land dwellers were deadly and accurate at a distance. If the sentries saw them, they would be easy targets, but in the dark, they could silently glide in before those on the ship saw them.

When he got closer, there were only two sentries on deck. He whistled to the warriors on his right. They swooped in behind the two pirates. Niche drove his spear through one's heart and Natan smashed the skull of the other with his war club. The rest of the ship's crew slept in the hammocks on deck at the bow of the ship or in the hold below. His warriors landed and started killing the crew while they slept, but the noise woke the sleepers, who ran to their weapons. The shouts of the men on deck woke those below who came up through the hatch, armed and ready to fight. But by then it was too late. The winged demons had killed everyone on deck. When no more pirates came out of the hatch, his warriors went below to search for survivors, and to look for wings.

One of his warriors called from below and he went down to investigate. Two of his band had several land dwellers trapped in a cage. They must have been prisoners since they were unarmed, and one appeared injured from a beating. The winged men poked at the prisoners, taunting them.

Niche left them and went aft, checking the cargo for feathers. He had to bend down to move through the ship to prevent his folded wings from hitting the ceiling. "Niche," he heard someone call him further aft. When he got there, Remi stood in front of another cage. Inside were two more prisoners. One was a dark-skinned female, and the other, a male, had skin even lighter than his.

"What do you want me to do with these two?" Remi asked.

"Leave them for now. I don't like the idea of killing women. If we do that, we are no better than the dark-skinned land dwellers who attack our villages."

Natan came up to him with three other warriors. "The front of the ship is clear. We found nothing."

"Good," Niche said. "Continue searching the rest. I will decide what to do with these two."

He stood outside the cage. The light-skinned male kept himself between the warriors outside and the dark-skinned female. He whistled signals to the warriors, having them change positions while he watched. The light-skinned one repositioned himself with the warriors, attempting to shield the female. *She must be his mate. I would do the same thing.*

After several minutes, he ordered the warriors to take them up on deck. When his men went into the cage, the light-skinned man didn't attack. *He is not foolish.* The warriors tied his hands behind him before binding the female's hands. Niche went up on deck with them, glad to stand tall. Once there, he had their feet tied with a rope connected to those that bound their hands. They had them kneel on a sail that was spread out on deck.

Natan came up from below. "We have found no one else. We did not find any wings or feathers. What do you want us to do?"

"How are the rest of the warriors?" he asked.

"They wounded two of them. Cyri has a minor wound to his leg, but Gaita took a bolt to his shoulder and cannot use his right wing. He will need help to get back home." He pointed to the prisoners. "What will you do with these two?"

"We will take them with us. I sense they may be useful. I need to know more about the male. He seems very attached to the female. If nothing else, we can use her as leverage to get information from him."

The warrior circling above alerted them. "There is another ship approaching. We need to leave."

Niche whistled the order to the others and turned back to Natan. "We leave now. Our warriors will carry these two prisoners. They can use the sail as a sack. Tie it securely. We don't want to drop them. Leave the other prisoners in the cell below. Burn the ship."

The warriors took flight. The captives screamed when they lifted them off the deck, while Natan set the vessel ablaze using the oil from its lamps. Niche left just before Natan and circled high above as the other ship approached. They would be miles away before it reached the burning ship below.

As they flew, they took turns carrying the prisoners and Gaita. When they approached the trees, they called to the village in loud whistles. The village sentries replied and lit lamps on the treetop platforms. They dropped the sack with the prisoners on a high platform before they glided onto the landing area. Niche landed last and folded his wings.

Gaita's mate rushed to him when she saw him covered in blood from the wound to his shoulder. She wept as she followed the warriors who took him to their nest. Other women gathered around her to console her. Niche knew the healer would be at the nest to tend to his wound. The other warriors' mates greeted them with chirps and hugs before going off to their own nests. He missed Gizzi's warm embrace and gentle coos.

"Natan," he said. "Take the prisoners to the highest vacant nest and have them guarded. I am going to find Dimo."

"I will see to it."

Niche went across the suspended walkways between the trees. Dimo lived on the far edge of the village. He spoke the language of the dark skins better than anyone else. The oldest of the Erotae, he remembered the times before the land dwellers began attacking and killing the people. His understanding of their language would help him when he talked to the light-skinned male.

Dimo stood outside the entrance to his nest and waved to him as he approached. "Niche, good to see you. What brings you to me at this late hour?"

"Good to see you also, my friend." He clasped the elder's arm. "I came to ask for your help. We brought prisoners back with us tonight, and I would like you to be with me when I try to talk to them."

"I would be glad to help, but you speak their language almost as well as I do." Dimo cocked his head. "But I am surprised to hear you brought prisoners back. What makes them so special?"

"One is a female, and the other is a male who has skin lighter than ours. There is something intriguing about him. I sensed he might be important."

"Lighter skinned than us? You are right. He might be important. But it is late, and I am old. Before I join you, I need my rest."

"I understand. I will hold off until midday. Thank you." He turned to leave, and Dimo whistled adieu.

Niche's sadness returned as he walked back to his own nest. It would be cold there without Gizzi. He missed her and Sella, his daughter, so much. He didn't know how well he would sleep; the sight of their mutilated bodies haunted his dreams.

CHAPTER TWENTY-SEVEN

WINGED DEMONS

The night of the attack on the pirate ship, Ryan was sleeping curled around Shera on the floor of their cell. The screams from the deck woke them. He got up and peered through the cell bars, trying to see anything in the darkness. The only thing he understood was when someone shouted, "Demon!"

They moved to the back of the cell. Shera stood directly behind him against the wall. The noise on deck increased when the hatch opened, and the crewmen went up on deck. In the dim light of the lamps, he saw three of the pirates, who had climbed out to the deck, fall back into the hold.

When the noise stopped, large, dark shapes descended through the hatch. Two of the shapes came to the cell with a lantern. The creatures were bent over with large, feathered humps on their backs. They spoke to each other in whistles and chirps. One carried a long lance and the other a large club.

"Demons!" Shera screamed when she saw them—just like the pirates on deck had earlier.

The demon with the club left and brought a third demon to the cell. He came right up to the bars and stared at the two of them with icy-blue eyes. He whistled and the first two creatures moved to the sides of the cell. His eyes never left Ryan. After several minutes of the two moving along the sides, he whistled again, and the demons entered the cell and took them up onto the deck. They forced them to their knees on what looked like a sail.

Bodies of the pirate crew lay scattered around the deck, with many in or near the hammocks at the bow. The light from the lamps on deck gave Ryan his first clear view of the demons. They were nearly seven feet tall. The folded wings on their backs stuck up another two feet. Feathers covered areas on their long bodies: their groins, the back of their legs, and the top of their shoulders. They looked more like the angels depicted in art than demons. But demons were just fallen angels.

While they were on their knees, the creatures tied their hands and feet, hog-tying them together. They kneeled there until the demon with the icy stare came and seemed to order the others to leave. When they unfolded their huge wings, Ryan's jaw dropped. They were magnificent creatures. They easily flew off the deck and as they got higher, ropes attached to the edges of the sail lifted it around them. This forced Shera and him together into an uncomfortable ball at the bottom of the sack.

He sensed the motion as they flew, but couldn't see anything, and could only hear the occasional whistles of their new captors. After what seemed hours, their captors let the sail down onto a hard, flat surface. Once down, they removed the ropes from their feet and led them across a narrow bridge to another platform. This one had a shelter with rough walls extending up to Ryan's waist, and a roof supported by poles. The demons pushed them inside the enclosure and remained outside, probably as guards. Inside the enclosure was a thick bed of leaves.

Ryan bent close to Shera's ear. "What are those creatures?"

"I only know them as demons from childhood stories. My father said they would steal children away in the night and eat them."

"I don't think they will eat us. But I don't know why they didn't kill us like they did the others." He pointed to the bed. "We should rest. I'm exhausted."

They sat on the bed of leaves with their backs against the wall. She leaned on him, and they slept.

The next morning, he woke to the icy stare of the leader from the night's attack. He stood at the entrance to the enclosure. When Ryan stood, the demon whistled, and two others came into the room. They grabbed his arms and removed the ropes from his hands. He shook them and flexed his fingers to ease the pins and needles. They woke Shera, pulling her up by her arms and removing her bonds. The blue-eyed leader and the two guards left them in the enclosure.

Shera came to his side and clung to his arm. "People say they eat their captives, but I think you were right. If they were going to do that, they wouldn't have untied us."

He walked out to the edge of the platform, which was built on the top of a tall tree at least eighty feet above the ocean's surface. The blue-green water below appeared shallow compared to the dark blue water farther out. Large fish swam below the surface. When he looked around the platform, he saw the only way onto or off it was the narrow bridge they crossed in the night. A guard stood on the platform across the bridge.

They walked around the platform. Shera held his hand so tight, he had to move her hand up onto his arm. "You can relax for now. I think if they wanted us dead, they would have killed us last night. For now, we are prisoners. I don't see any way we can get down from here."

"But they killed the pirate crew."

"Yes. But they rescued us from the pirates. I don't know why. Maybe we will find out soon."

"I am so scared. How do we survive?"

"We continue to live. This is not the first time someone has taken me since I arrived in Almirosia. Remember, you bought me as a slave."

Shera looked into his eyes, tearing up. "I am sorry. I don't think I ever understood how hard it must be to be taken from everything you know."

"It is hard, but you can survive and there is always hope that you can return. We are alive. That is our hope."

The flapping of wings interrupted their conversation. One of the winged creatures flew to the platform. She appeared to be female, shorter than the males that captured them. In her arms, she carried a bundle wrapped in green leaves. She took it into the shelter, laid it on the floor, then unwrapped the leaves and took out a small piece of fruit and put it in her mouth. As she left, she pointed to the open bundle.

The leaves held fruit, fish, and a jar of clear liquid. Shera grabbed a small fruit and took a bite. Juice ran down her chin. Ryan took the jar. The clear liquid was water. They sat and ate in silence. It was their best meal since being captured by the pirates.

When Shera finished, she plopped onto the bed and said, "I am alive. I have hope."

The sun continued to rise, and it got hotter, but the cool ocean breeze through the trees helped to make it bearable. About midday, the demon with the icy-blue eyes returned with two companions. One Ryan recognized as a warrior from the previous night. The other appeared older and used a staff when he walked across the bridge.

The icy-eyed one stood at the entrance of the enclosure and spoke in a language Ryan didn't understand. *So, they can talk and not just whistle.*

The older one then spoke in the language of Amut. "I am Dimo and will translate for our leader Niche." He pointed to his icy-eyed companion. "As the leader of this Erotae village, he wants to know who you are and why you were captives of the pirates."

"I am Ryan, and this is Shera." He put his hand on her shoulder. "I believe an enemy in Amut paid the pirates to capture us."

Dimo translated for Niche.

"Why were you separated from the other prisoners?"

"They separated us to protect Shera from the others who tried to assault her."

"You do not look like the others."

"No, I came from a place far away and lived in the mountains until slavers captured me and sold me as a slave."

"She is not your mate? Still, you protected her as if she were. Why?"

"When she brought me on the ship, I promised to protect her. Why did you not kill us like the others?"

"I dislike killing women. But your fate is yet to be determined. Some believe you may be important to us, while others, like Natan, believe we should toss you into the sea." Dimo pointed at the other warrior to show who Natan was. "I am still thinking."

The birdmen left, leaving only the guard at the far end of the bridge.

"Do you think they will kill us?" Shera asked.

"Maybe, but I think their leader may look for ways to keep us alive. Somehow, we need to convince him of our value."

"How do we do that?"

He shrugged his shoulders. "I don't know."

They barely talked the rest of the day. He looked closely at the guard across the bridge. His brown plumage and dark eyes differed greatly from the blue and gray feathers and icy-blue eyes of Niche. Shera came to him later before sunset and cuddled next to him as he sat on the edge of the platform, looking at the ocean. "I don't want to die here. But if I do, I am thankful that you protected me."

"Wakakan, the shaman, told me I had a purpose here, and that I needed to fulfill it before I could go home. I believe God will provide a way for us to get out of this situation. Dying in the ocean is not my purpose."

He had just finished speaking when Niche and Natan returned. Natan was carrying a crossbow like those used by the pirates.

This doesn't look good. They did not bring the translator. But he didn't wait to find out. "Greetings, Niche. Have you made your decision?" He watched Natan while he spoke.

"I have not," Niche said in the language of Amut. "I have more questions."

He is looking to keep us alive. "You speak the language of Amut well. You didn't need Dimo to translate earlier."

"Dimo speaks it better than me, and I wanted to watch your response." He took the crossbow from Natan. "Do you know how this works?"

"Yes. I can show you if you would like. Why?"

"Ever since the pirates gained this weapon, they no longer fear us. They raid our villages, killing our people for their wings. We cannot fight them during the day because of these." He held the crossbow out and shook it.

"I can show you how to use it, but I am not proficient at it. And you would require more than one to fight. It takes practice if you want to use it well."

Niche handed him the crossbow. "Show me."

Ryan took the weapon and looked it over. "Do you have the cocking lever?"

"What is a cocking lever?"

"It is a metal piece used to pull the bowstring back to the firing position."

Niche turned to Natan and spoke in their language. "We do not have it," he said.

"I will try to show you without it, but it may be too difficult." He held the butt of the crossbow with the bow arms on the platform and with his foot on one arm, pulled up on the bowstring with both hands. It took him three tries before he got it all the way back to the firing position. "Do you have a bolt? The thing it shoots."

Niche handed him a blood-stained bolt. He put it in the bow and showed them how to fire it. Natan took it and aimed it at the floor. When he pulled the lever, the bolt shot out, burying itself two inches into the floor. Natan then sat with both feet in the bow arms and re-cocked the bow, pulling against his feet.

He got it on the first try. He dug out the bolt and shot again. Excited, Natan flapped his wings and whistled.

Niche turned to Ryan. "Can you make more of these?"

"You can make more bolts, but you do not have the facilities or materials to make more crossbows. It takes a furnace to melt and mold the metal. You can make the arms out of wood, but it would not be as strong or as durable. It probably would not penetrate any armor the pirates might wear."

"Let me think about this. You are safe for now. Natan is happy and says you may be useful, though we have no need for the woman. You may keep her." They flew off to another part of the village.

Shera poked him in the back. "You may keep me. Hah! Who does he think he is? I will stay with you because I cannot leave."

CHAPTER TWENTY-EIGHT

THE EROTAE

Ryan expected a visit from Niche the next morning, but he didn't come. Instead, two other warriors flew up and grabbed him and Shera and flew through the trees, down to the surface of the sea. They deposited them on a large platform with an open pool in the center. Several females and small young sat around the pool or swam in it.

Dimo came up to them. "We would like you to bathe. You stink, and the women who bring you food are complaining."

Ryan was ready to jump in, but Dimo grabbed his arm. He motioned to the female standing next to him. "You should remove your clothes and give them to Chilla. She will clean them."

Ryan looked at Shera and shrugged before removing his clothing. Then he jumped into the warm water. It wasn't as salty as he expected. The pool was shallow enough that he stood in shoulder-deep water. Shera joined him but had to stand on tiptoes to keep her mouth above the water.

Ryan ducked his head under and rinsed his hair. Coming up, he shook his head and heard the laughter of the Erotae on the platform. They whispered and pointed at them.

Shera bobbed over to him. "Are they laughing at us?"

"I think so. They have probably never seen anyone like us, especially naked, before."

"That's not very polite." She gripped his arm to help hold herself up. "Can you help me? It is too deep, and I can't swim."

"Sure. Why don't you hold my hands and go under to rinse your hair? I will help you pull yourself up. Then we can wash each other's backs."

While Shera washed his back, she got a little too fresh. He was afraid his arousal would be visible, so he took her hands away. "Let's not go there. Here, let me teach you to float."

He put his hands under her arms. "Now, relax and let your feet come to the surface. Breathe slowly. Remember, I have you."

It took her a couple of minutes, but she eventually relaxed and allowed her feet to come up. He held her there and talked her through it while gradually releasing his hold. Soon, she was floating on her own. "See, you can do this," Ryan said. "Once you can float, you have less chance of drowning. Now use your hands to propel yourself."

She moved her arms too fast and panicked. He put his arms back under her. "Not so fast and not such big motions. Just use your hands and move slowly." After about thirty minutes, she could float and move across the pool on her own. When Ryan floated beside her, the onlookers laughed again, but he ignored them and concentrated on her.

They returned to the edge of the platform, where Dimo helped them up. "Do you feel better now?"

Shera was wringing out her hair. "Yes, that was great, but why were they laughing at us?"

"You look strange to us. Most have never seen land dwellers before, and even those who have, have never seen one un-clothed."

"Well, you look just as strange to us, and you don't wear clothes."

"True, but we have feathers."

Chilla came up to Dimo and said something. He turned to Ryan. "The warriors will be here soon to return you to your nest. Your clothing is clean and hung up to dry over there. I'm afraid you will have to remain naked for a little longer."

While they sat drying on the platform rail, Ryan asked, "How did you learn the language of Amut?"

"I am old enough to remember the time before the pirates when the Erotae and the land dwellers could trade." He stared at the trees for a moment. "Back then, we could fly to the coast in daylight. I have been to the settlement you call Amut. I was young, but I remember. We were never really friends with the land dwellers; they have always feared us."

"What changed?"

"The pirates came and started killing us. They even killed children and cut off their wings. Over the last few years, we deemed all land dwellers pirates." He looked at them. "You are helping to change that perception."

Two warriors descended onto the platform, interrupting their conversation. "They are here to return you to your nest. I will talk more with you later."

"Thank you, Dimo. I will look forward to it."

The warriors grabbed them and flew to their platform. When they alighted, Ryan went to the bundle of clothes and checked to see if they were dry. "Well, everything is still soaking wet. We will have to wait for them."

Shera came over and took his hand. "We can find something to do while they dry." Her deep brown eyes looked into his. "I can see your attraction to me. Why don't we take advantage of our circumstances?"

He pushed her away, holding onto her arms. "I have told you. I have a wife and family at home that I will return to if I can. If I can't, I will return to the village and Zica. You are beautiful, and I am physically attracted to you. It would be easy, but it would not be right." He let her go and stepped back. "We will not always be here. Our circumstances will change."

She extended her lower lip. "I do not understand you. Why can't you be like other men?"

"You would not like me if I were like other men." He walked into the shelter and sat on the sleeping mat.

She came and sat next to him. "I suppose you are right. I like you because you are different."

They didn't talk the rest of the morning. Shera dozed on the mat and Ryan sat on the shady side of the shelter until the clothes dried. He took Shera's to her just before the women flew up with a midday meal.

While they ate, Niche landed on the platform. "Welcome, Niche," Ryan said. "Would you like to join us?"

"No. I have already eaten. But I would like to talk to you while you eat."

"Sit, and we can talk."

Niche sat cross-legged across from Ryan. "Natan is happy that you showed him how to operate the pirate weapon. He no longer calls for your death. But he does not want to release you, because he feels you are still too dangerous to us. He wants to capture more enemy weapons and have you train others in how to use them."

"I told you; I am not proficient with the crossbow. Natan can probably show others as well as I can." He looked at Niche for a moment. "And prisoners do not make reliable helpers. What do I get if I help you?"

"You get to live, and maybe in time you can be free."

Ryan ate and thought a few minutes before answering. "I will help train more warriors for now. But at some point, you will need to have your own warriors do the training. I don't think you will capture enough crossbows to make a difference. And if they break, you can't repair them."

Niche stood. "I will speak to the others. For now, you will need to train everyone who has a weapon." He flew away, leaving them to finish their meal.

"Why can't they just kill us and get it over with?" Shera threw the piece of fruit she was eating onto the platform. "These constant threats drive me crazy." She stomped into the shelter.

Ryan heard her crying softly, but he left her alone, not wanting to reopen their previous discussion. He had to think of a way to get them on land, but from here, it seemed impossible. The ocean was too big, and they didn't have a boat or supplies. They had to rely on their captors.

Chapter Twenty-Nine

Niche's Dilemma

After meeting with the captives, Niche flew to Dimo's nest. The old warrior looked to be asleep on the edge of the platform, but when Niche alit, he opened his eyes. "Hello, my friend, you look troubled."

"I am troubled. I've just come from the land dweller's nest." He sat down next to the Dimo. "He seems to be cooperative but continues to tell me we cannot hope to gather enough of the pirate weapons to defeat them."

"Why does that trouble you? I think he is only telling you the truth."

Niche shook his head. "I know he is truthful. But the others may decide it is too much trouble if we allow them to live and he cannot be more helpful."

The old warrior looked him in the eyes. "They have their reasons for feeling that way, just as you have. Yet that troubles you. Why?"

"I know I should hate them, and I did, but seeing him protect the female made me realize he is not so different from us." He stood and paced behind Dimo. "Now that I have spent time with him and talked to him, I like him. He could be my friend. I don't believe he is like those that attack us."

"I feel the same way you do. He is not like the pirates; I know that from talking to him, though I am not sure he trusts us."

Niche continued to pace. "I am taking a party out tonight. A vessel was spotted sailing south. We hope to capture more weapons. It will be another chance for him to help us."

"If he doesn't help, what will you do? Will you kill them?"

He stopped and thought for a minute. "I don't need to kill him. I only need to threaten the female. He will not let harm come to her. Now, I must prepare for the raid." Niche flew to meet with his warriors.

That night, he led the raiding party. They circled the ship in the dark, looking at their defenses. The pirates had more lanterns lit and at least five sentries. This would not be easy. He didn't think they could take out the sentries without at least one sounding the alarm. They needed to hurry if they expected to take the ship. He whistled the instructions to the others. They dove with five warriors leading and each targeting one sentry.

Three of them dispatched their targets immediately, but two were a few seconds late, allowing the sentries to sound the alarm.

Niche led the rest of the warriors to the deck and charged into the sailors, who were jumping out of their hammocks. He killed two with his lance before the sailors grouped together with their weapons in a defensive circle.

He signaled for them to take to the air so they could attack from above. But he saw Natan stand with his crossbow and fire into the circle. His bolt hit one sailor, but before he could reload, a sailor's bolt hit him in the middle of his chest. Niche and the remaining warriors circled high, out of the light, then dove from above, picking off the pirates one or two at a time. Each time, the defensive circle reformed. Eventually, the pirates fired randomly into the air.

Niche had his warriors drop and circle outside the halo of the lanterns. Now they attacked at deck level, swooping in on the pirates. After a two-hour battle, they finally killed the last of the defenders and landed on the ship's deck. Their search of the vessel revealed no survivors. The hold of the ship was full of the wings from mutilated Erotae. It looked like the monsters had killed at least a hundred of his kind.

When they completed the search, he looked at his warriors. Three had died and three more wounded. The remaining six of them would need to work hard to carry the bodies and help the wounded on the return flight. They poured oil from the lamps out onto the deck and into the hold before they torched the ship. He picked up Natan's body.

On the flight home, he understood what the stranger was saying. Each warrior could only carry one or two crossbows, especially with their other burdens. *How can we defeat them?*

When they got back to the village, the reception was not joyous. Two of the wounded and one of the dead warriors had mates waiting. Their anguished cries filled the emptiness of the still, dark night. Niche cried for Natan, whose mate pirates had killed months before. Her death had fueled his hatred of the land dwellers.

The next afternoon, after a troubled rest, Niche flew to the captive's nest. The male, Ryan, paced along the edge of the platform. "I suppose you have killed more land dwellers and have brought more weapons."

"I have, and I need you to show us how to use them."

"You know I could kill you as a demonstration."

"I know, but it would mean we would hurt your female while you watched." He walked up to the captive and looked down at him. "I do not want to do that."

Ryan glared up into Niche's face. "And I do not want to make it easier for you to kill the land dwellers. Not all of us are pirates. What is to prevent you from attacking the innocent people on shore if, by some slight chance, you get enough weapons?"

Niche took a step back. "You have my promise that we will not attack the innocent. Besides, I believe you are telling me the truth. We will never capture enough weapons to defeat them. But we must be able to defend ourselves." He sat on the edge of the platform and motioned for Ryan to sit as well. When he did, Niche said, "I did not always fight your kind. I lived in peace with my wife and daughter in a village much like this one."

The captive turned slightly. "I have not seen your mate."

"You will not. She and my daughter are dead—killed by the pirates. I was on my way home from fishing carrying a good catch when I saw smoke rising from the grove where we lived. I hurried to the grove. The entire village was in flames. When I got to my nest, I saw the bodies of my wife and daughter laying there mutilated. The murderers had chopped off their wings. I bent down to my wife. She looked at me and whispered my daughter's name as she died." He stopped and tried to quench the sadness welling within his chest.

"I'm sorry. I did not know." The captive bowed his head. "No wonder you hate us."

"I do—I hate them. But somehow, I don't hate you. Dimo tells me there are more land dwellers like you than there are pirates. I don't know if I believe him. I know I want no more of my people killed and mutilated by them. But we are almost defenseless against their weapons. I need your help." He stood. "I will send a warrior for you after the morning meal tomorrow. You will do the demonstration."

He flew away, wanting to be alone. His tears fell to the ocean below as he soared above the village. He had told the stranger more than he wanted to and opened himself to the grief of losing his family, Natan, and so many others. The killing had to stop.

Chapter Thirty

Ryan's Decision

Ryan watched Niche fly away. But unlike his other visits, he didn't fly back to the village. Instead, he flew in circles so high Ryan could just see a speck against the clear blue sky.

Shera came up behind him. "You don't want to help him do you?" She put her arms around his waist and leaned her head against his back.

He put his hands over her arms. "I don't know what to do. No matter what I do, more of our people and more of his will die. I cannot end the war or eliminate the hatred between the two groups."

She held him tightly for a few minutes. "You can keep us alive. You told me that if we are alive, we have hope." She released her hold and stepped around to face him. "I didn't believe it then, but now I know it is true. You have given me the hope that I might live through this. You will do what you think is necessary to get us back to dry land."

He looked into her eyes. They were moist with tears. He held her face in his hands and wiped a tear from her cheek. "We are alive, and I will do my best to ensure we stay that way." They spent the rest of the day together in the shelter. Her closeness comforted him. He had to admit, his hope had waned. She had helped to restore it.

The next morning, when Niche arrived, Ryan still didn't know what to do. He thought he would continue showing them how to use the crossbow. When he got to the assembled warriors, he looked over their haul. They had just over a dozen crossbows, two spanning levers, but only a handful of bolts.

Niche handed him a crossbow and pointed to the shelter wall on the platform across the bridge where four rectangular mats hung. Ryan picked up a spanning lever and a bolt. He showed Niche how to operate the lever and waited until he had translated the instructions for the others. He repeated the instructions and showed each step. When the crossbow was ready, he raised it and pointed it at Niche. The birdman didn't flinch. Ryan turned and fired into a target, then handed the crossbow to Niche.

After he picked up another bow, Ryan went through the same procedure without using the spanning lever. When he finished, he handed the bow to another warrior. Niche organized the warriors into groups of four and they rotated through, arming the crossbows and firing at the targets. After two rounds, they had run out of bolts. Niche sent several warriors over to the targets to retrieve what they could. However, about half of the shots had gone wide and dropped into the ocean.

While his warriors retrieved the bolts, Niche looked at Ryan. "We will never capture enough of these to defeat the pirates. It is as you said. What can we do?"

When everyone was back on the platform, Ryan took a bolt and held it up in front of Niche. "You cannot make crossbows, but you can make bolts. You have plenty of wood and feathers."

Niche nodded to him, then said something to the others who flew off. He pointed to a section of log used as a seat. "Sit. Thank you for helping us. I worry we will just lose more men now that they think they can fight the pirates. But they must do something. Like me, many have lost their families to the raiders."

They sat without talking until the warriors returned with armloads of wood that they piled on the platform. Ryan picked up a bolt and sorted through the wood to find the best pieces to use. Then he had Niche explain how to cut and shape the bolts using their knives and axes.

While the warriors were busy, he explained to Niche about putting points on the bolts and fletching them. He helped when needed, but mostly he watched.

Ryan picked up a stick that was obviously too large to cut into bolts. It was six feet long and two plus inches in diameter. Holding his foot on one end, he tried to bend it. The stick bent with difficulty and sprang back. He asked Niche for a knife and began scraping the stick. After removing the bark, he tapered it from the center out to each end. Then he thinned it and tested the flex.

Under Niche's instructions, the warriors had finished making the bolt shafts. Then he sent them back to their homes.

"Are you ready to go back to your nest?"

Ryan looked up. "Yes—may I take these with me?" He held up the knife and stick.

"Yes, what are you making?"

"Just something to keep me busy. There is not much for me to do but sit around and stare at the ocean."

"Very well. I will return you to your nest."

"Let me get a few more sticks first." He picked up several thin straight sticks to take back.

Niche set him down when they got to the nest. "I will remove the guard. You are free to walk around the village."

"Thank you."

Niche flew to the guard and they both left. Shera came out of the shelter and stood next to him. "How did it go?"

"It went okay. Niche realizes they will never capture enough weapons to defeat the pirates, and he allowed me to bring back a knife." He held it up for her to see. "He also removed the guard, so we may roam the village freely. Would you like to take a walk?"

"Yes. Where do you want to go?"

"Let me put these inside." He left her and put the sticks and the knife in the shelter. When he returned, he took her arm. "I thought we could just walk around this level. Maybe later we can go to the bathing area if you think you can manage the ladders."

"No ladders today. I am afraid of heights. I don't even like being close to the edge of our platform."

"Well, the bridges aren't very wide, but you can hold on to me."

She took his arm, and they crossed the bridge with her clinging to him. He held the rope rail with his other hand. The top level of the village extended about a quarter of a mile east and west from their shelter. They stayed on the main walkways, which were wider than the bridges. A short distance from their platform, they came to the larger common platform. The tops of the trees shaded it on three sides. A few of the Erotae had gathered under the shade, but they ignored the land dwellers. Wide walkways went from all four sides of the common platform connecting it to others. They stayed on these wide walkways which seemed to be anchored in the trees. From these, the narrower bridges, suspended by ropes, led to individual nests. Some occupants stared at them as they walked past. Rope ladders also ran down to the lower levels from the common platforms.

They walked out to the far east end of the village. From the last common area, they saw Dimo sitting outside his shelter. When he saw them, he stood and waved them over.

"I see Niche gave you some freedom," he said when they reached him. "It is about time. Where were you going to go?"

"We certainly can't swim far enough or fly to leave. So, we are just walking around the village," Ryan said.

Dimo pointed to a bench built along the wall of his shelter. "Sit. I will get some cool water." He went inside and returned with cups of water, then he sat next to Ryan. "How did the training go?"

"It was fine. The warriors made bolts."

"It is a vain hope to think they can defeat the pirates." He turned to Ryan. "I know you have told him that, but still the people hope."

"I think Niche realizes it is futile." He took a drink, then stared into his cup. "I fear he will never let us leave."

"You underestimate Niche." The old Erotae stood and walked to the edge of the platform. "If it were only his decision, he would take you back now. The minds of the other warriors will take more time to change. They are seeing you as real people for the first time."

Dimo returned to the bench and sat back down. "Be patient. I believe as they get to know you, they will see the truth."

After a few silent minutes, Shera said, "You knew my people before the pirates became a problem?"

He leaned forward to see her better, since Ryan was between them. "Yes, and not that long ago. Many people along the coast traded with us. Though we have always been called demons by those that didn't take the time to know us. That is probably what you were told when you were young."

"It was. When the warriors first brought us here, I thought you would eat us."

Dimo laughed. "I am glad we surprised you. I hope we continue to surprise you."

Ryan finished his water and stood, handing his cup to Dimo. "We should probably head back before dark. Thank you for your hospitality."

Shera handed her cup back as well. "Thank you, Dimo. You helped me to not be so afraid."

She took Ryan's arm, and they headed across the bridge. On their way back, whenever they passed a nest and the resident stared at them, she waved and smiled. Most of them smiled back, and a few returned the wave.

Over the next eight days, they walked around the top level and the level below their shelter. The villagers seemed to accept them, no longer calling their young in when they approached and many smiled and waved at them. They also went to see Dimo regularly and asked him to teach them some simple phrases in the Erotae language. Their new freedom seemed to ease Shera's fears. She no longer clung to him so tightly. Soon, they could greet the villagers appropriately. Ryan spent time every day working on his sticks.

When Niche finally came to take him to do more training, Ryan said, "Before we go, what must I do for you to take us back to dry land?"

"I cannot say. It is more of a feeling. You need to provide hope that we can defeat the pirates."

"I cannot do that." Ryan stepped back. "Even with enough crossbows and bolts, you do not have enough to defeat all the pirates. There are too many and their defenses will improve rapidly. They could also turn the rest of the coastal people against you."

"What can we do?" The birdman hung his head. "I know you are telling me the truth. But I must give my people hope."

"If I can give you a weapon that you can make yourself, and that you can use more quickly than the pirates' crossbows, will you take us back to land?"

"Will we be able to defeat them?"

Ryan knew he had piqued his interest. "You will win some battles, but not the war. You should be able to defend your villages and reduce the number of your people the pirates kill. And if you repair relations with the coastal people, you could reduce their support for the pirates."

"If you can prove this to me, I will have you returned to the land."

"Good." Ryan turned and went into the shelter and brought out a bundle of sticks wrapped in a piece of cloth. "I am ready to go to the other warriors."

CHAPTER THIRTY-ONE

NEW WEAPON

Niche let Ryan down before landing on the platform where the other warriors had gathered. Niche went over to them and had them form four lines, then he walked back to Ryan. "They have been practicing and are much better at hitting the targets."

Ryan watched for a few minutes as the warriors shot at the targets, then handed the crossbows to the next man in line. It seemed to Ryan that there were fewer warriors than there had been last time he joined them. "How many warriors did you lose last night?"

"Three more." Niche shook his head. "At this rate, we will have lost so many men that we will soon have enough weapons to arm all the warriors."

"I am sorry about the men, but I believe you need to rethink your strategy." He bent down and unwrapped the bundle he brought. He pulled out a long bow and strung it.

Niche moved closer. "What is that?"

"It is called a longbow." Ryan handed it to him. "It works on the same principle as the crossbow, without all the mechanical parts. You just use your arms. Would you like me to show you?"

"Yes, show us." Niche had the warriors stop their practice. They formed a semicircle around Ryan at the edge of the platform. He held the bow and the handful of arrows.

He nocked an arrow, drew back, and shot it at the target. The arrow hit the upper right portion and vibrated. He picked up another arrow and carefully explained to Niche how to use the bow. After going through the process a couple more times, he handed the bow to Niche. It looked small in his hands. Ryan talked the birdman through the process, making sure he didn't pull the bow back too far. Niche's shot hit the bottom of the target. The other warriors cheered.

"Just like the crossbow," Ryan said, "you must practice in order to become good at hitting your target." He took the bow back. "You can see how I made the bow's proportions to fit my body. It will work better for you if you make it longer. The arrows must also be longer. I did all this using the materials you have available. You won't need to raid pirate ships to get weapons."

When Niche translated not having to raid to get weapons, they chittered among themselves for a few minutes, then one asked Niche how the new weapon would help.

Ryan turned to his feathered friend. "Who is the best warrior with the crossbow?"

"Aymera, bring your weapon." The warrior came to the front with them.

Ryan took a handful of arrows and stuck the points in a seam of the platform in front of him. "Aymera will shoot his crossbow at the target, and I will shoot the longbow until one of us hits the target four times."

Aymera put his bolts in a pouch strapped to his leg. Ryan had Niche tell them to aim, then fire. Aymera's bolt hit the dead center of his target. Ryan's arrow hit high on his target. But before Aymera could reload, Ryan had shot and hit the target three more times, though none were as accurate as Aymera's first shot.

Sounds of approval came from the warriors behind them, along with a few japes Ryan could understand, directed at Aymera. "It will take practice, but your warriors should be able to make their own weapons and shoot them faster than the pirates can shoot their crossbows." He paused while Niche translated. "You still won't defeat the pirates, but you should be able to defend your village."

The warriors gathered around their leader, chattering. Ryan went to the other side of the platform and sat to watch and listen to the discussion. *I hope I haven't opened Pandora's box.*

After an hour, the discussion died down and Ryan heard a general agreement coming from the group. Niche came over to him. "They agree that the new weapon is good and want you to teach us how to make it."

"Will you return us to the land if I do?"

"You must stay until we are certain the weapons will work."

Ryan stood and faced Niche. "I trust you are being truthful with me. Have the warriors gather the materials. The wood for the bow will need to be about this much longer." He held the bow vertically with a hand over the top.

Niche took the bow and an arrow and examined the wood, running his finger along the grain and flexing it. Then he returned to the warriors. Soon they scattered, and he returned to Ryan. "They will gather the materials. I will return you to your nest and we can start the instruction tomorrow." They flew back to the nest. Before he left, he looked at Ryan. "You also said we need to change our strategy. What did you mean?"

"I think you need to stop going out and attacking the ships. Instead, set a watch to warn the village if a ship approaches. Then put your people in defensive positions to prevent the pirates from getting from their vessel to your village. I am sure you can develop some ideas that might work to make it hard for the pirates to enter the grove. It would also be wise to teach your women and children how to use the bow."

Niche looked at him and shook his head. "Our women have never been warriors. I will think about that." He flew away.

Shera stood at the shelter door to greet him. She was smiling. "How did it go? Will he let us leave?"

"I don't know if he will, not yet anyway. He liked the bow, and I will teach them how to make more of them tomorrow. But he wants proof they will work against the pirates. I am still uncertain that we can trust them." They turned to go inside. "How about you? You seem happy."

"Tatian came to see me today. She is Dimo's daughter, and she speaks our language. It was so nice to talk with another woman. It made me feel less lonely." She took his arm, and they went inside. "Tomorrow, she is coming back to help me with my hair and show me where they cook our meals. She said I speak enough of their language to meet some of the other women. I am excited."

They spent the rest of the afternoon out of the heat. Shera told him about Tatian. The change in her amazed him. She smiled and laughed. She even puttered about moving things until she finally sat back down beside him just before they brought up their evening meal.

After dinner, they sat on the platform and looked into the night sky. She told him the names of some stars and talked about her father. When they went to bed for the night, she curled her body around him.

When he woke the next morning to the sun shining into the shelter, she still held him. He could feel her breathing. She mumbled something when he rolled away and got up.

Out on the platform, he stretched and looked at the sunlight reflecting off the calm waters of the ocean beyond the trees. Three Erotae silhouettes appeared in the sun, carrying some sort of basket. He assumed they had been fishing. *It can be so peaceful here. There are things I will miss, but I still need to get home, if home still exists. It is getting harder and harder not to become intimate with Shera. Needing the warmth of her body.*

Shera interrupted his thoughts. "Thinking about your other life? You have that distant look on your face."

"Yes. Right now, I don't even know if I still have a home. It's been almost half a year, and I am further away than ever."

She scooted closer and held his arm. "I know you want to go home, and you miss your wife. But if you can't, you can stay with me."

The flapping of wings interrupted them as their breakfast arrived. They went to the front of the platform and Shera said, "Good morning," in Erotae to the young woman who set the food down.

She smiled and replied with her own, "Good morning," before flying away.

While they were still eating, Niche arrived and took Ryan away as soon as he finished his meal. The warriors had piled the middle of the platform high with sticks for arrows and larger branches for bows. Using his bow, he showed how to shape the limbs with a knife.

The warriors worked on their bows while he oversaw their progress, making suggestions when needed. After an hour, they continued without help. He sat and Niche joined him, working on his own bow. "You said you would help us with our defenses. What do you need to do that?"

"Is there anyone here who has survived a pirate raid?"

"I survived," the birdman said.

"But you didn't witness the attack. I would like someone to tell me how the pirates attacked. Are there any surviving witnesses?"

"There are two, but they were young and are now adolescents." He stopped working on his bow and looked at Ryan. "I don't know how reliable they will be. It was a very traumatic experience."

"If they are the only witnesses, I need to talk to them."

"I will do what I can." Niche went back to work on his bow. "I will bring you to them if they are willing."

Ryan watched for several hours as the warriors worked, and he made more arrows for himself before Niche took him back to his platform. When he got there, Shera was gone. *She must be off somewhere with Tatian. I never realized how much joy I got from her greeting me after I spent the day with the Erotae warriors.*

Chapter Thirty-Two

Survivors

It surprised Ryan when Shera returned, accompanied by Dimo and a female. *What do they have planned?*

Dimo broke the silence. "You did not expect us."

"Yes. I wasn't expecting to see the two of you."

Shera came up and hugged him. "This is Tatian, Dimo's daughter. I told you about her. She took me down to the lower level to the community kitchen. The other women are friendly, and I had fun."

Ryan smiled and squeezed her hand. "It's been a long time since either of us has had fun."

"Well, unfortunately, you probably won't have any more fun tonight," Dimo said. "Niche has asked you to join us for the evening meal tonight. He has a couple of young people for you to meet."

They must be the survivors he told me about. "When will you come get us?"

"We will take you both to my nest now. The women are preparing to bring the meal as we speak."

"Both?" Ryan looked over to Shera.

"Niche, though it would be less threatening if I'm with you. Besides, I helped cook." Shera smiled at him. "Are you ready to go?" She released his hand and went over to Tatian.

"Sure."

Dimo lifted him, and they flew to his nest. When they alighted, Niche and a pair of adolescent Erotae sat around a low table. The women were already bringing the food up. It looked like a feast. Ryan furrowed his brow and glanced at Dimo.

"We are just in time to eat." The old Erotae pointed to empty seats at the table. "This will give our young guests time to get accustomed to you. Please, don't ask about their past until after the meal."

He and Shera sat across from the two young survivors. The male had bright blue and gray plumage. He appeared to be twelve or thirteen years old, if he had been human. The female appeared younger, with teal and white feathers. They avoided eye contact with him.

Niche introduced them. "Ryan and Shera, this is Breece and Danyl. They will join us for dinner tonight, so let's eat."

Shera took some of the orange fish and put it on a large leaf along with the red berry sauce the Erotae ate regularly. She handed the leaf to Ryan and dished herself some. "The other women taught me how to make the sauce today. I hope it is as good as they make it." She smiled and looked at Tatian, who nodded, smiling back.

The fish was oily and tasted a lot like salmon. The flakey orange meat melted in Ryan's mouth, and the tart berry sauce was perfect. "This is delicious. Thank you. It reminds me of a fish I had in my previous home."

While they ate, Dimo told Ryan and Shera about how the men caught the fish in nets and the women gathered the berries from a grove of trees to the west. He told them how they had traded the fish with the land dwellers when he was young. Then he asked Ryan about the fish from his home. Ryan told them about the salmon and trout from his home and about the trout he caught to survive when he first arrived in Almirosia.

When they finished eating, Niche looked at Ryan. "Why don't you tell Breece and Danyl about your time in the mountains, and how you came to be aboard the pirate ship?"

The young Erotae listened as Ryan told them of his arrival in the strange land, of his time in the village, but when he told of his capture by the slavers, Breece interrupted. "They shot you with a crossbow bolt? They also shot me." He moved the feathers on his chest to reveal the scar near his shoulder.

Ryan stood. "I think I can get the pant leg up far enough." He pulled it up as far as he could to show the scar where the slaver's bolt had gone through his thigh. Then he sat and continued the rest of his story. When he finished, he said, "The pirates, like the slavers, are violent, evil people, and I want to help your people protect themselves from their raids. Would you help me by telling me your story?" He looked at the two young Erotae.

They looked at Niche who nodded his approval. "I will," Breece said. "It was four years ago. I was in a group of other young men from my village. We were meeting at the top level of the village, learning about wind currents and how to use hot air currents to gain elevation."

He stood and spread his wings, weaving from side to side to simulate soaring. "That's when we heard the alarm warning of danger. We all ran to the edge of the platform and saw the ship just at the edge of the trees. Several smaller boats moved through the trees to the bottom level of the village. The boats had small fires burning in the center. Before they got to the low platforms, they shot burning arrows into some nests on the first three levels. Soon everything was ablaze and there was chaos." He paused. Ryan saw tears forming in his eyes as the boy took a moment.

"The screams—I can still hear the screams. Most of the warriors were out fishing. The pirate weapons killed the ones that remained. They used ropes and hooks to climb into the upper levels. They avoided the flames and took advantage of the confusion in the village. I flew from the platform to my nest to get my own weapons. The pirates were already there. My mother lay face down, motionless on the platform—" He could no longer keep back the tears now streaming down his cheeks as he sobbed quietly. "The attacker stood over her, pulling on her wing with one hand and holding his sword in the other. Blood ran from a wound on her head and pooled under her face. I was so angry I dove at the pirate standing over my mom. But before I reached him, another one shot me with a crossbow bolt. I fell, tumbling into the sea. The impact as my back hit the water stunned me. I lost focus, but stayed afloat. When my head cleared, I swam to a clump of tree roots and hid. I was so afraid. I thought I would die."

Tatian put her arm around him and held him while he cried quietly. "You are very brave. I know it was hard to tell us."

"Tatian is right," Niche said. "You were very brave. Not only to tell the story, but also to defend your mother. There is no shame in surviving." Then he turned to Danyl. "Can you tell us your story?"

The girl sat with her head down. "When the pirates came to my village, it was as Breece described. The alarm sounded, and the ship was outside of the trees, but the small boats came." Her voice dropped to a whisper. "I was on the cooking platform with my mother when the fire rained down on us. One of the flaming bolts hit her." She paused and took several deep breaths. "I went to help her, but the flames caught my wing on fire!" She stood and spread her wings. The left wing only had a third of its feathers. Her side and left leg had large patches of red scarring. "When the pirates got to the platform, they hit me and threw me into the sea. I clung to roots to stay afloat because I was too badly injured to swim, since I could barely move my arm and leg. I remember little more than holding onto the root until a boat approached. A pirate grabbed me by my head and lifted me up. When he saw my wing, he laughed and dropped me, then said something I did not understand. They left me there until evening when a warrior came and pulled me up." She plopped down in her seat.

Both Breece and Tatian moved over to hold her.

"You are a brave young woman." Shera's tears ran down her face as she looked at Ryan. "We have to help them."

Niche turned to Ryan. "Did you get the information you needed?"

"Yes. I think we can come up with a plan to help you defend your village," Ryan said.

"Good. I will have Dimo and Tatian take you back."

They all stood, and Shera went over and hugged Danyl. She whispered something to her. Then she hugged Breece before Tatian picked her up.

Early the next morning, Ryan walked the perimeter of the village on the top level. The higher levels extended farther away from the center of the grove than the lower levels, creating an inverted pyramid shape. The bottom level consisted mainly of large heavily built public platforms anchored to the roots that spread from the trees into the sea: the cooking platform, the bathing platform, and others the villagers used for training and workshop space. Much of the next level also had these public spaces. This was where Ryan had shown the warriors how to make and use the bows. On the next three levels, dwellings on smaller platforms spread throughout the grove's canopy.

From the top west end of the village, he could see the ocean's endless expanse. The light of the rising sun shone off the waves and the light and dark lines that defined the crests and troughs moved from right to left, creating an op art image. Only two trees stood between the last platform and the ocean eighty feet below. The farthest platforms on the top level went to within two or three trees at the end of the grove. From there, the ocean extended to the horizon in all directions. His best guess was that an Erotae soaring above the village could give them almost a day's warning before a ship reached the village.

After he walked the perimeter, he climbed down to the third level, and walked its perimeter and concentrated on the surface of the water and tree roots below. The roots of each tree grew out, extending out almost as far as the upper branches. Few clear lanes existed between the trees. Anyone wanting to get to the bottom level of the village from the sea would need to go through the maze of roots. *How did the Erotae allow the raiders to get all the way to the bottom levels? They had to have had plenty of warning and opportunities to fight.*

He climbed the rope ladders back up to the top level and returned to the nest he shared with Shera.

"You were up early," she said when he walked into the shelter.

"I'm trying to figure out how to help these people defend themselves." He sat on the mat they used for a bed and took a long drink from the water jar. "Honestly, I don't understand how they allowed the pirates to attack so easily. The tree roots are like a maze on the surface. They could ambush and drive off the raiders in the tangle of roots."

"It's difficult for them to fly through the small spaces and get close enough to kill the raiders with their spears and clubs," Shera said.

Of course. He had forgotten the technological advantage the pirates possessed. The crossbows prevented the Erotae from getting close enough to repel them. He stood and took Shera in his arms, hugging her. "Thank you. You're brilliant."

He went out on the platform and sat thinking. Around midday, the warriors began returning with that morning's catch. *The men also fly away each morning, leaving only a few warriors behind.* He formed the outline of a plan to prevent the pirates from getting to the village. But would Niche and the warriors accept it?

He got up and walked across the village to Dimo's.

"Hello." The old man sat outside his shelter. "What brings you here?"

"I think I have a plan to defend your village. Can you set up a meeting with the warriors?"

"Yes, I can. When?"

"As soon as possible." They talked for a few minutes, then Ryan went back to wait for the meeting. *The hardest thing will be to convince them to spend the time arming and training their women. Empowering them could change their lives.*

CHAPTER THIRTY-THREE

SHERA AND TATIAN

Three days after the dinner with the young survivors, Tatian took Shera down to the training platform. As they watched the warriors and young men practice, Dimo came over to them.

"What do you think about what Ryan has done?" He looked at Shera.

"I have mixed feelings," she said. "I think it is good he has shown you how to defend yourselves, but I worry it will endanger my people."

"Your people already possess arms, and they know how to use their weapons." He handed the bow he carried to Tatian. "Would you like to learn?"

She paused for a moment without looking at her father. "Why would I want to learn?"

"Ryan believes that the raiders intentionally attack while the warriors are away fishing and have left only the women and children in the village." He pointed to Breece and the other adolescents practicing. "He suggested we teach the youth and the women how to defend themselves. I would like you to be the first and help convince the other women to learn."

"I guess so." Tatian turned to Shera. "Do you know how to do it?"

"No. But maybe I could learn too."

"Good." Dimo led them over to where Ryan and Niche were working with the young men. Ryan was busy instructing a boy, helping him stand correctly. He had the boy lower his draw arm slightly to get his shoulders level, then told him to relax and aim the tip of the arrow at the target. It shot forward, hitting the mark.

"Well done," Ryan said. "Keep practicing that technique. It is all about repetition."

"Did you see that?" The boy yelled to the other youths standing nearby. "I'm a natural."

The boy nocked another arrow, but his second shot went wide. He hung his head and his shoulders slumped as another youth lined up behind him giggled.

Ryan put his hand on the boy's shoulder. "Remember, relax and concentrate on your form. You will get better. They will have their chances and probably won't do any better." He turned to the two women. "Tatian, did you agree to learn?"

"Yes, and Shera wants to learn as well."

"Okay. Dimo, will you grab a bow for Shera?" He took them both to the edge of the platform and pointed to the targets set up on the adjacent platform.

After Dimo returned, he talked them through shooting the bow, and emphasized the need for consistent form. He asked Tatian to come up and guided her through the technique. Her first shot was wide to the right. After she nocked another arrow, he had her loosen her grip on the bow, cradling it between her thumb and hand. This time, the arrow hit the bottom of the target.

"Well done," he said. "Now, this time, take a few seconds to ensure the tip of the arrow is in the center of the target." Her next shot was close to the center. "Good, now you must keep practicing."

Ryan nodded to Shera, who had been paying close attention to the instructions he gave Tatian. She stood correctly and drew the bow back. He had her hold it there while he adjusted her back shoulder, then made her adjust her feet slightly. She concentrated on his instructions and after a few shots, she finally hit the center of the target. *I can do this. If I learn to use the bow, I won't have to rely on some man.*

She and Tatian continued to shoot after Ryan left to go help some of the young men. After about an hour, Shera nudged Tatian. "This is harder than it looks. I'm tired."

"Me too," Tatian said. "Let's go to the kitchen and tell the other girls what we did."

Shera flexed her hands and twisted at the waist to loosen her muscles. "And maybe get something to eat and drink."

That evening while they ate, she told Ryan how excited most of the other women were about learning to shoot. "It was fun to shoot, but, ugh, my back and fingers hurt."

"Maybe I can find something to help your fingers, but your back muscles will have to get stronger. After dinner, I will rub your back to see if that helps."

When they finished, Ryan took her into the shelter and had her remove her shirt and lie face down on the mat. He kneeled at her head and pushed his hands down her back.

"Mmmmm." She felt herself relax. Her muscles loosened as he continued to rub her back. After several minutes, he started using his thumbs and fingers on her neck. *This is wonderful.*

"Is this helping?" he asked.

"Yes, don't stop yet. You are going to put me to sleep."

After her neck, he changed positions and straddled her body, kneading her trapezius muscles, then working down to her shoulders and upper arms. She moaned in pleasure as some of the soreness left and the muscles relaxed. He finished the massage by rubbing her back again, still straddling her body. *I could get used to this. I want him to touch me more.*

When he stopped, he said, "Just relax and lie here as long as you want."

She stayed there, listening to the breeze moving through the trees. It didn't take long before she dropped off to sleep. She dreamed about shooting the bow and Ryan touching her. She woke in the middle of the night and got up to relieve herself. Ryan was asleep on the mat, lying against the wall. She sat and watched him sleep. *He's not handsome by the standards of my culture. His skin is so light, and that scraggly gray beard makes him look old. But he is the kindest man I have ever known.*

She lay back down on the mat and realized she was happier here as a captive than she had been since she was a child at home with her father. Here she had a man who cared for her and protected her. She had her first real female friend in Tatian. She had lived her life trying to compete in a man's world. Now she understood she could be happy being a woman. She could still compete. She and Tatian had competed on the archery range without having to be men. *I don't think I want to go back to the way I was.*

She drifted off to sleep and woke with the sunrise the next morning curled up against Ryan's back with her arm around him. She lay there, feeling his chest rise with each breath, smelling the familiar scent of his body, knowing it wouldn't last as long as she wanted.

When he stirred a few minutes later and rolled onto his back, she snuggled into his chest. "Thank you for the rub. It really helped."

They got up and prepared for the day. "Are you and Tatian going to practice more this morning?"

"Yes. After we do some chores. I promised I would help her," she said. "We should have some of the other women with us today."

Tatian flew up to the platform with their morning meal. She set the food down. "Ow. Are you hurting as badly as I am?" she said to Shera.

"No, Ryan rubbed my back and shoulders, and I feel better. Maybe he can rub you." *It was also very sensual.* She turned to Ryan.

He shrugged his shoulders and said, "After we eat, I will spend a few minutes massaging you, Tatian."

She and Tatian laughed as they ate and talked about the previous day. After the meal, Ryan kneeled behind the young woman who was kneeling and leaning forward. He rubbed her back, neck, and shoulders while Shera cleaned the mess from the meal.

Ryan looked at Shera when she came near to pick up. "This is harder than rubbing you. Her wings are in the way, and she has larger muscles." She felt jealous watching him rub the young Erotae. He leaned into her, pushing his hands up her back.

"Aaaah." Tatian let out a sigh of relief, just as Dimo came to take Ryan down to the training platform.

Dimo whistled. A hint of anger flashed in his eyes.

"Father," Tatian said. "It is all right. He is helping my sore muscles."

"She can tell you how to do it until she gets a man of her own." Shera shook her head and laughed.

Ryan continued to massage Tatian's back until the muscles loosened, then he left with Dimo. Tatian stood and stretched. "That helped. You are a lucky woman."

"We'll see how lucky I am when we get to the training platform later. Do you want my help this morning?"

"Yes."

They went to the kitchen and did Tatian's chores before flying up to the training platform. When they got there, Ryan came over to them carrying something.

"Here. I had these made for you." He handed each of them two pieces of leather-like material. "This should help your fingers, and this will protect your chest."

"This is regun skin," Tatian said as she fingered the tough material.

"Yes." Ryan took the smaller piece from Shera and put it on his hand over the tips of his fingers. "This will keep the string from cutting into your fingers. It should allow you to shoot more easily."

"And this?" Shera held out the larger piece, which had straps.

He showed them how to put the piece on, so that it covered their breasts. "This will keep the string from snapping into your breasts if your form changes when you get tired or if you're in a hurry."

Ryan left them, and she helped Tatian with her chest guard and they started practicing.

"Where did he learn so many things?" the young Erotae said.

"I don't know. When I bought him, he looked like an old savage from the hills. But he continues to surprise me. He can read and use numbers. He fights like a devil, and he talks of his home in another land." Shera shook her head. "I know little about him. But I trust him."

CHAPTER THIRTY-FOUR

THE ATTACK

Niche watched his people take their turns practicing with the bows and arrows. Many shot well, more accurately than the land dweller, and even the women and the adolescents appeared competent. Ryan, standing to Niche's left, helped a young woman adjust her chest guard. *Soon he will ask me to release him. He has fulfilled his bargain, yet the new weapons remain untested. My warriors need more proof that they can defend the village.*

A warning whistle came from the east. He whistled a quick reply that he was on his way. When he got to the eastern edge of the trees, a lookout pointed to a speck high in the sky. A scout was circling above, signaling the warning of an approaching ship. He and the lookout flew to meet the scout.

When they joined him, he motioned for them to follow. "Come with me. A ship approaches our grove." The scout led them east until the ship appeared on the horizon.

"Watch it carefully," Niche said. "I will send out warriors after dark to get a closer look."

The warrior pointed to a bank of low, orange clouds behind the ship. "They need to go early. The fog is moving in behind the ship and will overtake it sometime tonight."

Niche nodded to the warrior and flew back to the village center, where he called for his warriors. "Our scouts spotted a ship approaching. At sunset tonight, Aubrin, you and Balon will go with me to determine what kind of vessel it is."

They talked for several minutes before he dismissed them to prepare for an attack. He flew up to the nest where the land dwellers stayed.

Ryan came out of the shelter when he landed. "What can I do for you?"

"We need to talk." He pointed to the seats where they ate. "We spotted a vessel approaching today. I think it is pirates. The ship appears larger than most and is moving quickly toward the grove. They have the wind at their back."

"You should be ready," Ryan said. "Your warriors finished erecting the defenses you designed to block the channels, and they know the plan."

Niche stood, then paced. "Yes. We finished the defenses, but they are untested, as are the new weapons. I fear for my people."

"It is good to be afraid. We never know what battle will bring." He stood and joined the winged leader. "Your people have trained, and I think they will fight well. When do you expect the vessel to arrive?"

"Sometime tomorrow. I'll go after dark to scout the ship."

"Be careful. Don't let them see you."

"We won't." He spread his wings to leave. "I have trusted you and believe you to be a friend. If we survive this, I will release you."

He flew around the village, inspecting the defenses. Everything looked to be in place. But it didn't calm his nerves. Even with the defenses, all he could see was his wife's mutilated body.

After dark, Balon and Aubrin joined him. They flew toward the last sighting of the ship, staying high above the surface of the ocean. The brisk wind in their face slowed them, and the clouds obscured the stars ahead of them. When they finally spotted the lights on the ship, they circled down for a closer look at the deck.

The vessel was twice the size of any previous ship they had attacked. Lanterns illuminated the entire deck. At least eight humans stood watch with their crossbows ready. After two passes over the deck, Niche led his party higher and back to the village. The trailing wind shortened their return trip. Once back, they met with the other warriors. "The raiders will be here by midmorning," Niche said. "Get everyone prepared. They have eight smaller boats on deck that they can use to navigate through the trees." He peered into the faces of the warriors, trying to determine how they would react, but most stared back stone faced. "Get some rest while you can. In the morning, we will double the lookouts."

They flew away without speaking. He flew to his own nest and tried to sleep. His mind flooded with images of the village burning, women screaming, and raiders swarming up the ladders, killing everyone in sight.

The lightning and thunder interrupted his thoughts and cleared his mind temporarily, but he dozed, and the visions returned. When the dreary gray day finally dawned, his head ached, and his limbs were stiff. *How can I defend my people when I am already defeated in my mind? Creator, help me be the leader the people expect. Give me courage to face the enemy. Help us defeat the enemy that seeks to destroy your people.*

He rose and flew to rouse his warriors, then he went to the eastern edge of the grove to look for the vessel. The winds had brought the ship within a mile of the trees. He could see them lowering the smaller boats into the water. They would soon be within the grove. He flew back and alerted the warriors, setting up ambushes along the channels between the trees.

He settled into his position and summoned Balon. "Go to Dimo's and tell him the raiders are here. He must get the women ready. Then return to your position."

"As you wish." The young warrior flew off.

Niche looked again at the faces of the warriors. Some clenched their jaws in stoic determination. Other's eyes darted quickly, looking for danger, fidgeting with their weapons. A few sat with their eyes closed and their lips moving, apparently praying. Despite their different reactions to the moment, some had seen battle with him, and he knew they would fight valiantly.

The low clouds and drizzle muffled the sounds of the morning. Only a few birds sang, and the wind had stopped. The gray dawn and humid air hung like a wet cloak draped over the grove. Then he heard the faint sounds of the boats as their oars worked through the water. Low voices of the men carried through the stillness. Then the first boat appeared out of the mist to his left. It moved steadily toward the ambush. He whistled the signal to attack.

His warriors sent a volley of arrows at the boat, hitting three of the eight men working the oars. The man at the back shouted and the remaining men increased their pace. Other men in the boat shot crossbows at the warriors, but the boat hit the sunken log Niche's people had put across the channel. The men yelled as the Erotae sent another volley into their midst.

A bolt whizzed by Niche, clipping the feathers on his shoulder. The second boat had entered the channel below them. They shot at anything that moved. The cover of the trees hid most of his men, but when the third and fourth boats came, they shot flaming bolts into the trees, igniting the platforms.

He whistled for the warriors to fall back, while he and a few of the best archers sent their own flaming arrows into the boats. Niche's fist hit the steersman, who fell, hitting the side of the brazier and spilling burning coals across the bottom of the boat, igniting it in flames. The sailors jumped out and swam for the other two boats and the trees, but the blood in the water had brought the reguns into the channel. The fast ocean predators feasted on the bodies of those in the water, living and dead. Niche and the remaining warriors withdrew to the screams of raiders.

When he got to the second ambush position, Aubrin came to him. "That was a glorious victory. Surely they will flee."

"You are wrong. We have only slowed them down. Now, they will come with greater caution and more determination." He put his hand on the warrior's shoulder. "Now, take up your position and prepare for a long day."

As the day wore on, the drizzle became a steady downpour, soaking everyone and everything. The drumming of the rain on the leaves and trunks of the trees drowned out the noise from the boats. Niche had spread archers around the grove. They acted as snipers, picking off one or two sailors at a time. The boats struggled through the logs and snags placed below the surface of the channels.

When the boats finally came to the second ambush, only half of their crews still survived. The deluge of rain prevented the raiders from igniting their bolts and the Erotae overwhelmed them. A victory yell echoed through the trees. Niche and a few warriors flew down to inspect the boats and killed the few wounded sailors that remained. They tossed all the bodies into the channel for the waiting reguns.

He sent scouts to look for the ship and the other four boats he had seen on the ship's deck. When they returned, the scouts reported the ship was gone. "We have chased them away," they said. But Niche needed to know where the ship went. He sent warriors to scout the entire area. *Something is wrong. The ship could not have known about the outcome of the battle. It was too far away.*

He assembled his warriors and sent out groups of two or three to take up positions around the village. The visions from his dream troubled him. The battle wasn't over. He needed to find that ship. He flew as high as the clouds would allow, then spiraled out looking for the ship. Below, he saw his warriors scattered among the trees. Then on the western edge of the grove he saw the ship and the other four boats nearing the village.

Chapter Thirty-Five

The Battle Continues

Ryan paced inside the shelter. The rain and fog left him isolated. He needed to know what was going on. Had the raiders attacked? Were the defenses they put into the channels working? When the drizzle turned into a downpour, he kicked the basket on the floor across the room.

"Did that help?" Shera stood with her hands on her hips.

"No. I am just frustrated." He continued to pace.

"It's not something you can control." She grabbed his arm and stopped him. "You will know what is happening when it is time. Sit with me. I'm cold." She pulled him onto the bed and snuggled into him.

He put his arm around her. "Waiting is hard. I feel I should be helping."

"You already helped. You have taught them what you know. Now it is up to Niche and his warriors."

"At least the rain should help him. The raiders won't be able to burn the trees as easily." He felt her warmth and relaxed. During their time with the Erotae, she had changed. She wasn't the woman who bought him. She was becoming hard to resist. He put his other arm around her and drew her closer.

They held each other and listened to the rain until Breece came to their door. "Ryan," he said. "We need your help. The pirates have attacked from the west." The young man's voice was shaky. "Most of the warriors are fighting on the other side of the village."

"Was anyone else there? We need to gather people to fight before they get too close." Ryan picked up his weapons.

"Danyl is there alone. She cannot fly, so I had to come."

"Can you take me there?"

"I don't know. You may be too heavy for me," the young Erotae said.

"You must try."

Breece stood behind him and wrapped his arms around his chest and lifted off. They flew west and down. He could feel the young warrior struggling to hold him. "How much farther?"

"Just to the edge of the trees and down two levels. I—I don't think I can... make it." Breece was panting.

"Set me down on the platform below us. Do you know who is manning it?" He braced for a hard landing as he felt Breece falter.

They thumped onto the platform, startling the two adolescents that occupied the post. He could hear the screams from below. "Send them to find Dimo or Niche. We need help here as soon as we can. You man this post while you recover your strength. I'm going down to help Danyl."

Ryan started down the ladder. "Be brave. You must hold this position until help arrives."

He continued down to the next level and ran across the bridges as far west as he could. When he got to the far end of the village, he saw Danyl trying to beat a raider with her bow. The pirate was climbing a rope attached to a grappling hook lodged onto the platform. The raider grabbed the bow as she tried to hit him again and pulled it away from her. She screamed.

He was halfway down the ladder and jumped to the platform as the pirate stood. He didn't have time to get his bow off his shoulder, so he charged the pirate, slamming his shoulder into the man's stomach, knocking him off the platform. Danyl stood behind him, crying.

"Get up the ladder and go find help." Ryan pointed to it and waved his hand toward the center of the grove. "Breece is up another level toward the village center."

Another raider's hand reached the top of the rope, but Ryan had his bow ready and shot him as he tried to climb up. He heard another grappling hook hit the platform. Looking over the edge, he saw more raiders coming up both ropes, preparing to throw additional hooks. He shot the top raider on each rope before crossbow bolts whizzed by, forcing him away from the edge.

Looking back at the ladder, he saw Danyl had reached the platform above him and was climbing to the next level. He ran to the ladder and went up. As he got to the top, a bolt hit his right hip. He struggled but pulled himself over the edge onto the landing.

Danyl was on the platform above him. "Cut the ladder!" He pulled out his own knife. He cut through the rope that formed one side of the ladder below him. As he cut the second rope, it broke, taking a raider down with it. Still lying on the platform, he shot into the raiders gathered below him. When he stood, pain shot through his leg. He couldn't support himself and he fell. He stayed down after that and tried to shoot over the edge, but it had little effect.

"Let me get you higher." Dimo stood next to him. He picked Ryan up and lifted him to the next platform. Breece, Shera, Tatian, and two adolescents were there with Danyl. They took turns firing into the raiders, who now tried to use grappling hooks to get to the next level. The raiders had finally secured one hook, but the arrows from above prevented them from getting to the top.

Ryan tried to stand again, but fell to his knees. Shera came over to him. "Lie down," she said. "Let us get that bolt out."

She sat on Ryan's back to hold him down, and Dimo pulled the bolt out. He fought to stay conscious, screaming through his teeth. Once they removed the bolt, Tatian and Shera rolled him onto his side and bandaged it, wrapping a dressing around his thigh and up across the wound.

"Be still," Tatian said. "The bleeding should slow down."

Shera sat with him while the others continued to hold off the pirates. He could hear shouts from both sides now but couldn't see what was happening. Then Danyl yelled, "They're here!" The others on the platform shouted as well. He glimpsed several Erotae flying past the platform. *Someone must have reached the warriors.*

Danyl kneeled beside him, next to Shera. "Thank you for coming to help me." She bent closer and hugged him.

"Let's get you back to your nest." He heard Dimo's voice and felt the Erotae's firm hands lift him. They flew to the platform he shared with Shera. Dimo put him on the bed. "Tatian will be back shortly to change the bandage and apply some salve. I will have other girls bring food and water. You should rest."

Ryan drifted off to sleep, but sharp pains from the wound woke him every time he moved. Shera sat beside him and stroked his forehead with a cool rag. Then he woke with Tatian cutting his bandage. "Hold still. This part is easy."

Once she had the bandage loose, she and Shera pulled his pants off while he gritted his teeth to keep from yelling. They rolled him onto his side again. He could feel the warm blood running down his butt. Tatian applied a salve to the wound. "This will ease the pain and help stop the bleeding."

Shera held his leg up, and the Erotae wrapped a bandage back around the wound. When she finished, Shera set his leg down gently and put a covering over him. Tatian had been right. The salve eased the pain, and he slept again.

When he woke, lamps burned outside the shelter, and he could hear Shera talking to someone. He tried to sit, but it hurt too much. Shera must have heard him because she came in. "Lie still. They can come in and talk to you if you feel up to it."

"I'm fine. Who's here?"

"Everyone." She went out and returned with Niche and a cup of cool water.

Niche stood towering over the bed. "Thank you, my friend. We defeated the pirates today, killing them all. Though we offered to let them surrender, they fought on. Your plan, and the defenses we put in the channels, worked. Even the women and adolescents fought well today. If you and they had not held the western side, we might not have won."

"How many casualties?" Ryan asked.

"Six died, three warriors along with two adolescents and a woman. They wounded another dozen, including you. Tatian says it will take several weeks for your wound to heal. It's deep and may have nicked the bone." He kneeled, so he was at eye level with Ryan. "When you have healed, we will take you back to the land. You have fulfilled your promise to us. We will fulfill our promise to you, though many of us will be sad to see you leave."

Chapter Thirty-Six

Niche's Promise

It took three weeks for Ryan's leg to heal enough that he could move around on his own without a crutch. During that time, either Shera, Tatian, or Danyl stayed with him and saw to his needs. Now, though he still limped, he could walk. Shera and Tatian had gone to do Tatian's chores, leaving Danyl in the shelter with him.

"I need to move." Ryan stood, wincing.

"Let me help you." The girl grabbed his arm. "You still seem unsteady."

He pulled his arm away and glared. "I am steady enough to walk around the platform without your help." She stepped back in surprise, as if he had slapped her. "I know you just want to help me—I need to do this myself."

He walked out to the edge of the platform and gazed out at the horizon. The light blue of the cloudless sky met the dark blue of the ocean in a straight line. The tropical sun beat down on the village. Below him, he heard giggles and screams from the bathing pool. The young could bathe now that enough time had passed to allow the reguns to return to the deeper water of the open ocean.

When he turned to go back inside, Danyl stood behind him. She moved aside and let him pass, but he stopped and held his arm up so she could help support him. "Why are you here helping me?"

They entered the shelter, and she helped Ryan sit down on the bed. "You saved my life."

"It was just a battle. I did what needed to be done."

She sat beside him, looking down to avoid eye contact. "When I first met you that night at Dimo's, I hated you. You are a land dweller, just like those that killed my family and disfigured me. I knew Dimo, Tatian, and Niche said you were different. But I didn't believe them. Then you came to my rescue. You risked your life for me and nearly lost yours. You could have stayed on the upper platform and kept the raiders away from the village, but you jumped down to save me." Tears streamed down her face. "I can't fly, and I'm not pretty. I'm useless."

He put his arms around her and held her close. "You may not fly, but you are beautiful, and you did as much as anyone else to save this village. The raiders may have taken your wing, but your heart is stronger than most." He let go of her and turned to face her. He held her chin up so he could look into her eyes. "I think there are young Erotae who would gladly have you as a mate. I see the way Breece looks at you. How often has he been here since you started tending to me?"

She furrowed her brow for a moment. "At least once every day, he comes to ask if we need anything."

"Does he ask Shera or Tatian?"

"No. Usually he asks me."

Ryan laughed. "See? He comes because you are here. You need to spend more time with him. You two have a lot in common."

Shera came into the shelter and frowned when Danyl wiped the tears from her cheeks. "Did he say something to upset you? He's been a little testy lately."

"No. No. He thinks Breece likes me." A grin spread across her face.

"Of course he likes you. Everyone can see that." Shera came over and sat on the other side of Ryan. "Tatian is ready to take you home."

Danyl stood to leave, then turned and gave Ryan a hug. "Thank you."

"Niche wants to see us tonight." Shera took his hand. "I think he wants to talk about letting us go now that you have recovered."

"I'm ready. Are you?"

"Yes, and no. These people are my friends. I don't want to leave them, but I want to go home." She stood and took his hand. "Have you been up today?"

"Yes. We came inside a few minutes before you arrived."

"Let's take a walk." She led him outside to the bridge. "The people have almost completely repaired the damage from the raid."

They walked to the east end of the village. Along the way, everyone greeted them. "Remember how when we first walked through, the people ignored us?" he said.

"They were as afraid of us as I was of them." She waved to a female standing outside her door. "Now they accept us. Tatian has taught me so much."

He started limping before they reached the end of the village, so they turned around. He still had to recover his strength. When they got back, he crashed onto the bed. Listening to Shera puttering around the shelter, he drifted off to sleep.

"Wake up, sleepy head." Shera tapped his arm. "Dimo and Tatian are here to take us to the meeting."

"All right. Give me a minute." He sat up, stretched, and rubbed his eyes. He sat for a few more minutes, stretching. "How long was I asleep?"

"Just over an hour."

They went outside, where Dimo and Tatian waited.

"Are you ready? The feast is about to start," Dimo said.

"Feast? What feast?" he asked, looking at Shera who shrugged her shoulders.

"We are celebrating our victory and remembering those we lost in the battle." The old Erotae lowered his voice. "We had to wait for you to recover. You are the guest of honor. Now, come." He opened his arms so he could carry Ryan.

They flew to the large training platform. It looked like the entire village had gathered. The kaleidoscope of colors created by the plumage of the Erotae combined with their whistling songs created a very festive atmosphere. Dimo and Tatian set them down in the middle of the platform, surrounded by the colorful Erotae.

Niche came up to them. "I am glad to see you have nearly recovered. Come sit." He took them to a spot in the innermost circle. They sat and young women brought them food and a fermented drink made from the fruit of the trees surrounding the village. Once they were served, several of the women brought food up for the rest of the village.

The festivities lasted for a couple of hours. Niche talked about how the people learned to trust Ryan and Shera. Villagers would periodically come up and greet them or thank them. Ryan just wanted to fade into the background. Finally, the party broke up into small groups with the villagers flying off to their nests. Then Niche had Ryan and Shera taken to Dimo's, accompanied by several warriors.

Inside Dimo's shelter, they all gathered around a table. Niche took out a large rolled-up document and unfurled it on the table. "We found this on the raiders' ship after the battle. We thought you could help us read it."

Ryan bent over the table. The document was a map of some sort, but he couldn't determine what anything was. "It's a map." He looked over at Shera. "Can you read any of it?"

She came to the table and looked at it, turning it ninety degrees. "This is the coast of Almirosia." She pointed to a long, dark, irregular line. Then she followed it with her finger and stopped. "This is Amut. And up here is Jabyl." She straightened, spending several minutes on the chart, then pointed to a marked spot in the middle of nowhere. "I think the mark here is this village."

Ryan bent over the map, looking closely at the mark. "What is this line of islands?"

She looked and said, "I don't know. I'm not sure they are islands."

Niche looked at them. "I think they are the groves where the other clans of Erotae live." He followed the indistinct line of dots north of the mark. "This would have been my home."

Ryan continued to study the chart. He pointed to the river below Amut. "This must be the river the slavers used when they brought me down from the mountains." Then he stretched his hand to the groves. "These groves seem to come close to the mainland here."

Dimo stepped up and looked at the chart. "You are right. These groves are in a very shallow and rocky place. The villages may still be there. The water is so shallow, I don't think the raider ships can get close enough to them." He moved his hand to the mark representing one grove. "It will be difficult to carry you two from here to the land over the ocean. It is hard enough to fly that far with no load. But if we can use the groves to rest, we could take you to the river."

Niche put his hand on Ryan's shoulder. "Would that fulfill my bargain?"

He looked at Shera, who nodded. "It would fulfill your promise."

"Good. We will make plans to return you to the land. I will have Dimo keep you updated on when we will leave."

They talked a little longer, going over the map in more detail. Then Dimo took them back to their nest.

Chapter Thirty-Seven

Return to Amut

One week later, Ryan, Shera, Tatian, Dimo, Niche, and six other Erotae stood in the beach's sand as the last orange glow of the sun faded in the west. It had taken three days flying to get here, with rest stops each day at different groves along the way. The Erotae had built a crate for him and Shera. The flat floor enabled them to stand if they wanted, and a bench on one wall allowed them to sit. Three Erotae carried the crate as they flew. Though confining, it was much more comfortable than the sail the Erotae had used to haul them away from the ship.

Niche had his hand on Ryan's shoulder. "Goodbye, Ryan. We must leave before other land dwellers see us. You have been a friend to me and my people. I will miss you."

He looked up at Niche. "You have also been a friend to us. Thank you for saving us from the pirates and bringing us back here. I hope you and your people find peace." He offered his hand, which the winged man grasped.

"I hope you find your way home." He left Ryan and called to the others. All of them lifted off except Tatian, who embraced Shera and cried before she finally followed the others.

Ryan went to Shera and put his arm around her shoulder, and they watched the shadowy forms of the party fly into the darkening sky.

"What do we do now?" she asked.

"I'll take us to Amut. It's two or three hours north of here along the coast. The moon will provide some light, so we will follow the road." He led her up the beach to the rutted cart path. "We'll decide what to do next once we get to Amut."

They walked up the deserted path in silence. The musty smell from the jungle, and the steady hum of the waves breaking along the beach brought back memories of his first trip up this road. *At least now I have a chance to get back to the mountains and maybe home. But Amut could present problems. I am still Shera's slave, and who knows what Yago will do if he finds out I am here. I'll need to leave Amut quickly.*

After an hour on the road, he heard voices. He pulled Shera to the side, where they hid behind a dune. The voices grew louder. He lay on his belly and peered over the top of the dune as a group of armed men went by with two oxcarts.

"Why do we have to march so late? Couldn't we wait for morning?" he heard one say.

"Stop your whining," another said. "You can sleep on the barge. It's a long journey, and they can only travel upriver during daylight."

Ryan and Shera waited until he could no longer hear the party before moving back to the road and continuing their journey.

"Who were those men?" Shera said.

"Slavers. They are going to the docks on the river for the trip up to the mountains."

"Was the group that captured you like them?"

"Yes." He kept walking, remembering that day—watching Zica running to the lake, seeing his friends killed, lying on the ground next to Toby. The slaver's bolt sticking up from the dog's chest. He swallowed hard and clenched his fists, staring straight ahead. *Will I ever see any of them again?*

When they neared Amut, he went left, away from the road. They stopped behind a large, grass-covered dune. "When we get to Amut, where do you want me to take you?"

"Either to my home or to the warehouse," Shera said.

Even in the moonlight, he could see her biting her lip with her forehead wrinkled. She shook her head. "It's too dangerous for you to walk through town. The warehouse is closer and there will be fewer people early in the morning before the businesses open."

"The warehouse sounds like a better choice." Ryan stood and offered his hand to help Shera up.

"Let's do that. Maslic will be there early to unlock the doors. We can hide in the alley until he arrives. I don't know if I trust anyone else." She let out a long sigh. "Take me to the warehouse. How long before sunup?"

"It will be several hours. Do you want to wait out here?"

"Yes, let's wait here until just before dawn."

He led her farther off the road and found a dune with overhanging grass to provide some shelter. They huddled there and tried to sleep. He held her and wrapped the blanket used to bundle his weapons around them both. He felt her relax in his arms, her steady breathing letting him know she was asleep. He fell asleep listening to the waves.

The sound of birds singing woke Ryan just as the eastern sky grew lighter. He woke Shera, and they started into Amut. They went around the slave market, moving toward the beach. Then when it became impossible to avoid the streets, Shera led, and he carried the bundle containing their possessions. He stayed two paces behind her with his head down, trying to look the part of her slave. She kept to the side streets, avoiding the taverns.

The sun hadn't fully risen when they reached her warehouse. She went to the alley on the south side of the building. A storage shed provided some cover from the street, but still provided a view of the dock in front of the building. They didn't have to wait long before Maslic led the oxcart up and unlocked the door. While he worked the lock, Shera called out to him. "Maslic."

He jerked his head around to face them. "Mistress Shera? I heard you were dead. Lost at sea."

"As you can see, I am not dead. Can we go inside?"

"Yes. Of course." He fumbled with the lock and opened the door.

Inside the nearly empty building, Maslic hurried them to the stairs. Their footsteps echoed in the cavernous building. He led them up to the loft.

"What has happened here?" Shera pointed to the empty warehouse floor.

"Yago," he said. "The day after you left, someone attacked your estate. They killed most of your servants and carried off some women, then they burned it down. No one can prove it, but I know it was Yago."

"My house?"

"Burned down. The only building left is the barn, which sustained some damage. I was here when they told me about the fire, so I hurried up there as quickly as I could, but I was too late. I found Aradu lying in the yard with a crossbow bolt in his chest. He was still alive, and he told me Addah had shot him." Maslic shook his head and leaned over the railing. "I gathered some friends, and we followed their trail the next morning. It ended at a cove north of town. There we found Hanno's body, but no sign of Addah. Yago was tying up loose ends."

Shera joined him at the rail. "What about the warehouse? There was a shipment scheduled after I left."

"It never arrived. I haven't been able to arrange any ships. It is too expensive to buy safe passage. The only ships that come in belong to Yago. He has total control of the docks and most of the town."

"How have you survived?" Ryan said.

Maslic turned toward him. "I have friends. Besides, I am no threat. I have no money and I can't prove anything, even though everyone knows what I say is true. Eventually, though, he will tie up this loose end as well."

Shera put her hand on his shoulder. "Is there any safe place we can go?"

"My family's farm. It is about a day's walk north of town. But we can't let Yago know either of you is there." He looked at Ryan. "How did you survive?"

"It's a long story, and she can tell it to you on the way to the farm. How do we get there without being seen?"

"We wait until evening. Until then, the two of you can lie in the back of the oxcart. I will cover you with a tarp and we can go to the barn where I have been staying. No one will notice. We can leave from there after dark." He turned to Shera. "Let me go get some food and beer. You look hungry."

"I am hungry and tired."

"After we eat, you can rest here." Maslic left to get them some food.

Shera plopped down on the cot. "Yago has taken everything. What am I supposed to do now?"

Ryan sat next to her. "You keep going. Yago thinks we are dead. You can get a fresh start away from Amut, maybe with Maslic."

She punched his arm. "Do you ever lose hope?"

"Not really. Sometimes I have a hard time seeing it, but I believe in a power greater than me that has control over my life. And even when I don't do the things I should, He is still looking out for me."

"That's why you can say: as long as you live, you have hope."

"Yes." He got up and walked to the rail. "Even if it is impossible for me to return to my home, I can have hope for a future here in Almirosia."

When Maslic returned with the food, he and Shera sat at the table, while Ryan went and sat on the top step to let them talk. He finished eating before them and went downstairs. There he found one pallet of ground spices. He rearranged the bags, laid down, and slept. He dreamed of dragons.

Maslic woke him. "It is time to leave."

Ryan shook his head to clear it and sat up. "How long was I asleep?"

"Two or three hours. I'm uncertain because I was upstairs with Shera. We talked a lot after you left."

They went to the oxcart that Maslic had brought inside while Ryan slept. "Help me put a couple of those bags on her. I must make one stop on the way up the hill."

They loaded the bags, leaving a space between them and the front of the cart for Ryan and Shera. Once they were lying in the cart, Maslic covered them with a tarp. "Be still and quiet, especially when I stop. Yago has eyes and ears all over town."

CHAPTER THIRTY-EIGHT

RYAN LEAVES SHERA AND MASLIC

Once they arrived at the farm, and Maslic closed the barn door, Shera and Ryan climbed out from under the tarp. Maslic helped Shera down. "I'm sorry for the rough ride. I know it is not what you are accustomed to."

Shera smiled at him. "You don't know what I've become accustomed to lately."

"Still, you are my employer, and I should treat you with the proper respect."

"Ha!" She laughed. "You are free. I have no money and no business. You are not obligated to me. Yago has taken everything. I need to accept that, and so do you." She looked into his eyes. *It has been months since he has seen me. Yet, he remains loyal. Maybe Ryan is right about his feelings for me.*

"I still need to protect you. At least until we are clear of Amut. Please don't go outside. Someone could see you. I'm going to get a bird for dinner before we leave." He turned to go, but Shera grabbed his hand.

"Thank you. I will do as you say." She let his hand drop, but he stood and looked into her eyes a moment before leaving. *There are feelings in those deep brown eyes.*

While he was out, she went to the window. Little remained of her beautiful house. One charred black wall on the east side still stood. Burned posts, beams, and furniture lay strewn about what would have been her courtyard. Tears ran down her cheeks. She turned away, wiping her eyes. More than anything, she wanted to make Yago pay for what he had done. She wanted to see him suffer, but she knew that was not possible. At least, not yet.

After dark, Maslic had them get back in the cart covered by the tarp. She watched through a gap between the tarp and the cart as he led the ox out to the road. This far away from the town, only a few lights shone along the side of the road. Still, they traveled for a while before he stopped the cart so they could get out.

"We should be far enough away," he said. "There aren't many travelers out here, so we should be safe." He helped her up onto the seat of the cart.

"Do we continue on this road?" Ryan asked.

"Yes. The road will take us to within two hours of my family's farm."

"Then let me tend the ox while you ride with Shera." He winked at Shera. "After all, I am the slave."

"Perhaps you are right." Maslic climbed up next to Shera.

"She can tell you more about our adventures." Ryan took the goad from Maslic and went to the head of the ox.

Shera told Maslic about the voyage, the pirates, the winged demons, and the raiders. Talking to him made the time pass quickly. He seemed attentive, though she couldn't make out his expression in the dark. His body was warm and solid. She grew tired and leaned on him. He put his arm around her, and she slept.

She woke to Maslic talking to Ryan. "This is where we leave the main road."

It was still dark, and she didn't want to move from the warmth of his embrace, but he released her and climbed down. She pulled the blanket tighter to keep the warmth in. She didn't remember it being so cool around Amut.

Ryan came and sat beside her on the cart, while Maslic led the ox up a rutted path.

She leaned over Ryan. "You have been silent since we got to Amut."

"I'm thinking about the mountains and finding a way home." He turned to look into her eyes. "You know I will not be staying with you, even though your law says I am your slave."

"I know. You are no longer my slave. You have earned your freedom. I will not stop you from leaving." They sat quietly until Maslic stopped the cart.

"We will rest here until daylight," Maslic said. "The trail is rough and will be too difficult in the dark. We should be safe this far away from the main road."

Maslic prepared a bed in the back of the cart for her. He and Ryan would sleep on the ground under the cart. She lay there looking up at the stars. *It is funny how, when I was trying to be successful, I never noticed how beautiful the night sky is.*

Just after sunrise, they continued up the rutted track. Maslic talked about his father's farm where they grew pineapples, limes, and other fruit along with fields of oats and a vegetable garden. His father had twenty slaves who worked the fields and another three in the house. He said his parents would welcome her.

At midmorning, they crested a hill and Ryan said, "Stop the cart."

"The farm is just down the hill. You can see it down there. Why stop here?" Maslic pointed to a cluster of buildings in the valley below them.

Ryan walked to the back of the cart. "I see the farm, but I'm not going down there with you. I'm going to the mountains to find my village if it is still there."

"Wait. Don't go yet." Shera climbed down with Maslic's help. "I don't want you to leave."

"I must." He turned to Maslic. "Your father is a slave owner and will probably only accept me as a slave. It is better if I leave before he knows I am here. Besides, if Yago learns where you are it will be safer if your parents know nothing about me."

"But what about me?" Shera held his arm.

"Maslic will keep you as safe as possible. Yago wants me."

"He is right." Maslic took her hand away from Ryan's arm. "How will you find your village?"

"I'm not sure. I'll start heading west to the mountains."

"There is a deep, nearly impassable jungle valley to the west. If you go north, you will come to a road at the foot of the mountains leading west toward the old temple complex. It will take you about two days to reach the complex, but it will save you at least three days over the jungle route." Maslic dug into the cart and took out the last of their food and water and gave it to Ryan. "Good luck."

"Thank you." He faced Shera. "Goodbye. If things work out, this is the last time you will see me."

She looked at him, feeling the moist tears on her cheeks. "I will miss you. You have been faithful to me and taught me so much about life. You have been my friend even after all I did to you. I hope you find your way home." She embraced him, not wanting to let go. But after a few minutes, she stepped back. "May your Higher Power guide you on your journey."

He shouldered the bundle containing the supplies and his weapons and started walking away from the path.

"Ryan, the priests at the temple may give you help if they are still there," Maslic said.

He nodded and walked away into the bush. Maslic stood by Shera. She leaned her head on his shoulder and cried as she watched Ryan disappear into the bush.

Chapter Thirty-Nine

The Temple

Ryan left Shera and Maslic at the cart, hurrying into the cover of the brush before he moved west along the crest of the hill. Once he was past the farm, he turned north and climbed to the top of another ridge. This one ran north to south, and from the top, he could just make out the farm below, and the higher peaks ahead. To the west, the slope descended into the dense, green jungle.

He trusted Maslic, but he remained on alert, not wanting to be captured as an escaped slave.

The scorching sun beat down as he walked along the open ridge, which seemed to be the boundary between the jungle on the western side and the farms that dotted the eastern side. When he came upon a farm, he went down the western slope until he passed it. The steeper and more rugged slope on the western side slowed his progress. When the sun dipped below the mountains, he still hadn't reached the temple road.

He spent the night under an overhanging rock face on the western slope. It provided a good windbreak, and the rock wall reflected the heat from his small fire. He dreamed. In his dream, he woke to the suzuecu's wings beating in front of him, its black eyes staring at him. "Pilgrim," the beast said. "Your trials will continue, but you must not give up hope. The Creator is with you."

He woke up cold just as the sunlight kissed the tops of the mountains to the north. When he climbed back to the ridge crest, the sun had already reached it. *It's going to be another hot day. I hope I find the road soon.*

There were fewer farms this far north, so he made better progress. By midmorning, he reached the foothills of the northern mountain range, and then found the road an hour later.

He rested and ate before starting up the path that snaked along the side of the mountains before disappearing in the distance. The road looked unused. It was full of holes, with sections blocked by rockslides and washouts. There were no settlements or farms along the road. He spooked a massively antlered deer while climbing around one rockslide. *I'm glad that was only a deer, but I'd hate to run into a predator. I wish I had Toby with me.*

The farther he went up the road, the more abundant the wildlife became. He could hear rushing water in the canyon below. Smelling the pine forest on the slopes of the mountain brought back memories of his time in the village—and home. As the sun dipped below the mountain peaks, the road ran down along the side of a gorge, ending at the base of a large stone structure cut into the cliff that formed one gorge wall. *This must be the temple.*

Inside, he found it deserted, with symbols carved into the walls of the cavernous main room. It was too dark to determine what they said or represented. *Well, I guess I'll just have to wait until morning to see anything.* He found a small chamber on the side of the main room and settled in there to sleep.

He dreamed about the Erotae. A pirate ship anchored near the edge of a grove hurled fireballs into the trees from a catapult on its deck, engulfing the grove in flames. Screams from the inhabitants and the smell of burning feathers filled the air.

Danyl appeared in the flames. She peeled the skin from her body. "We will die if you don't help."

He jerked awake, feeling like he was going to vomit. His skin felt cold and clammy. He shook his head and rubbed his eyes. His stomach still churned. He stared into the darkness. *What was that?*

He got up and went outside, not knowing if he would throw up or not. The cool, clear morning air helped settle his stomach. Light on the eastern horizon signaled the approaching dawn.

Something is happening I can't explain. God, are you trying to talk to me? If you are, I don't understand. Help me.

He sat on the stone steps, and let the rising sun warm him as its rays moved down the face of the temple. He sat there for several minutes before he went back inside and examined the symbols on the walls. Many of them resembled those in the spirit cave. He recognized the map of Almirosia on the back wall. It revealed the location of the temple. From there, he could determine how to get back to the area of his village. After scanning the rest of the temple, he gathered his stuff and left.

"Hello, pilgrim." A voice startled him. An old man with empty eye sockets sat against the wall outside the temple door. "Did you find what you sought?"

"Yes and no," he answered. "Where did you come from?"

"I live here. I am always nearby." He stood with the help of the staff in his right hand and came to stand in front of Ryan. "You are not from around here. What is it you seek?"

"A way back home."

The old man stared at him through empty sockets. He leaned closer, his sour breath filling the air. "You are the one Wakakan spoke about. I can feel the magic in you."

"I'm not a wizard or a magician, and I don't know any magic."

"The magic is not yours. It comes from the Creator. It brought you here."

"That's what Wakakan said." He stepped back. "Why do you speak in riddles? Why can't anyone give me a straight answer?"

"I do not know the answer. Only the Creator knows what you must do to get back to your home. He will guide your path, but you may not like where He leads you. That is all I know, and the others are all gone."

"Gone. Where can I find them?"

The shaman turned toward the temple door. "You cannot. They are all dead. Killed by a stranger like you."

Ryan asked the old man more questions, but he didn't say another word. Finally, he had to give up and leave. He went down the mountain slope to the gentler terrain of the foothills. The temperate forest covered the hills and provided ample game, and the clear creeks running off the mountains provided fresh water and fish. Unlike his initial trek into the forest, he now had the skills to survive, though he still needed to stay alert to the threat of predators.

A suzuecu flew over his campsite on the second evening after leaving the temple, and a pack of manetoo howled in the distance. He slept under an overhanging rock face that night and kept the fire going as best he could. He dreamed of the suzuecu that carried the wolf away on his trip to the spirit cave. Somehow, he sensed the suzuecu presented less of a threat than the manetoo as he listened to their cries through the night. He would be near the village in the next day or two—if the village was still there.

CHAPTER FORTY

MASLIC'S FARM

Shera and Maslic stood on the hill silently for several minutes after Ryan left them. She didn't need to talk, but she needed Maslic's support. Finally, she pushed herself away from his muscular chest and looked into his eyes. "I'm ready. We can go down now."

"Let me help you up." He helped her onto the cart, then led the ox down the path.

She smelled the cut grass from the hayfield they passed, the wood smoke from the house, and manure from the barn as they neared the farm. It was all very different from the smell of the ocean and the fish she had become accustomed to over the last few months. *My whole life will be different. Will I have to live in fear that Yago will find me? Can I adapt? I have always lived in town, never on a farm. But I adapted to the life of the Erotae. I can adapt. I will adapt.*

When they got to the farm, a young man ran up to the cart. "Maslic!" he yelled and hugged the bigger man.

"Ho ho, little brother." Maslic released the young man and turned to the cart. "Arada, this is my friend Shera. Shera, this is my youngest brother Arada."

"Hello," the young man said.

She smiled. "Hello, Arada. It is nice to meet you."

Maslic helped her down from the cart. "Arada, go tell mom and dad we have a guest."

Shera walked beside Maslic as he led the ox to the barn. Someone, she assumed a slave, took over, and they turned back toward the house where a woman stood in the doorway. She appeared taller than Shera and wore a bright orange and yellow skirt with a blue smock. Her braided hair was piled on top of her head and covered with a triangular scarf. To her, the woman appeared to be of mixed race with lighter skin like Jin's. She saw a broad smile on the woman's face, even from a distance.

When they reached the door, the woman hugged Maslic. He turned to Shera. "This is my mother, Dem. Mother, this is Shera. I've asked her to stay with us."

The woman hugged her, then held her at arm's length to look at her. "You are even prettier than Maslic told us. You may stay here with us for as long as you wish." She released her hold and turned to go inside. "Come in, please. I have cool water from the spring and a freshly baked loaf of bread. Are you hungry?"

Shera followed her into the house. "Yes." The smell of freshly baked bread filled the room.

Dem went straight to a cask next to the door, and dipped out three cups of clear water, which she placed on the table in the center of the room.

Shera sat with Maslic, while his mother went to the counter and began cutting thick slices of the coarse-looking bread. Dem placed the plate with the slices on the table along with a tub of butter and a jar of honey.

Maslic didn't wait. As soon as the bread arrived, he grabbed a thick slice and began spreading butter and honey on it. "Don't be shy, Shera. Mom makes the best bread."

Shera took a slice and followed his example, spreading butter and honey on it. The warm bread melted the butter, which soaked deep into the slice. The taste of the wild, sweet honey had a slight bite to it. Combined with the nutty-tasting bread, it was as good as any pastry she had ever eaten in Amut or any foreign port. She finished the slice and took another. "Dem, this is wonderful. Will you teach me how to make it?"

Dem's smile widened. "Of course. It will be nice to have another woman to talk to. The slaves are nice, but most know little of our language."

They sat, ate, and talked for several minutes before Dem got up. "Why don't you take her out to the new cottage? She can stay there while she is here. It will give her some privacy."

Maslic stood and offered Shera his hand. As they left, she saw Dem wink at Maslic. Once outside, she asked, "Why did she wink at you?"

"She hopes you and I will become a couple. She is not very subtle." He pointed to a smaller building north of the main house. Like the other buildings, it was mud brick with a thatched roof. Slaves were working on coating the outside with a white plaster. "This is my house. They built it for when I return to the farm, whether for visits or to stay."

"What about you? Do you hope we will become a couple?" She stopped him at the door and looked into his dark eyes. She could see he cared for her, but would he say it?

"I have loved you for a long time." He looked away. "But you were always my employer. You had big ambitions and little time for relationships. So, I served you. I serve you now."

He led her inside the house, which appeared ready for occupants with wood plank floors smoothed and swept. Only the kitchen, where workers set the bricks that would make the oven, remained unfinished. A counter with benches separated the kitchen from the main room. On the east end, a fireplace burned with chairs arranged in front of it.

Though not as nice as her estate in Amut, it was nicer than the hut she and Ryan shared with the Erotae. She could live here. She might even grow to love Maslic.

They shared the small house for several weeks but slept in separate rooms. She found herself drawn to his quiet and kind personality, watching his interactions with not only his family but also their slaves.

Neither his father nor mother pressured them or interfered with their relationship. She became close to his mother, learning to make bread and preparing food grown on the farm. On special occasions, when Maslic's father, Melqarat, brought fish home from the market on the coast, she would show Dem how to prepare the fish like the Erotae did. She was happy.

One day a commotion outside brought Maslic running into the house. "Stay inside. People from Amut are coming. They might recognize you, and I don't trust them." He turned and left her standing there with his mother.

Dem took her to a bedroom where they sat. "Why is he so concerned about the people from Amut? Are you in trouble?"

"I have enemies there who would seek to harm me." Then Shera explained the trouble Yago had brought upon her. "He may also seek to harm Maslic. Especially if he knows I am alive."

"Stay here. I'm going to go outside and see what is going on." Dem left her in the bedroom.

"Maslic knows one man, Hyrum," Dem said when she returned. "There are six of them, and they will eat with us and stay the night before continuing to Amut. We hope our kindness will prevent them from becoming suspicious of Maslic's presence. He has told them he didn't see the point in hanging around Amut, waiting for a corpse."

Dem went back out to the kitchen and started the preparations for the larger meal. She left the door ajar so Shera could hear what they said inside the house. Only once did one man enter the main house. He came in to ask for more water. Dem had a slave take a jar out to them.

At full dark, Maslic came in. "Our visitors have eaten and gone to the barn to sleep. Put this over your head, and I will take you up to the cottage." He handed her a shawl that she wrapped around her head and shoulders.

The next morning, she watched from a window as the party ate and started back down the path toward Amut. Maslic returned to the cottage. "They are gone. I don't think they know you are here, but I will have someone watch them for a day."

She took his hand. "What about you? Aren't you afraid Yago might come after you?"

"No. I think he could have taken care of me while you were away." He faced her. "I think we are safe, but I will have lookouts posted in case I am wrong." He held her. She looked up at his face and kissed him.

CHAPTER FORTY-ONE

BACK TO THE VILLAGE

Ryan walked up the hill to the village, hoping to find his friends. As he approached, he saw the boma broken down and the gate open. No smoke rose from either the communal fire pit or the huts. Once he went through the gate, he knew they had deserted the village some time ago. Most of the huts had walls collapsed and a layer of fine dust covered the hard-packed floors. *Had slavers killed or taken all of them? No, they wouldn't have taken the personal possessions of the villagers.*

He found a hut that still had all its walls. Then he went to the lake to catch a fish for dinner before he gathered wood from the fallen huts. He thought about Zica while he sat by the fire, remembering her moving about the hut, tending to the fire, and sitting beside him. *Will I ever find them? Are they even alive?*

That night, he had troubled dreams. Images of the raid flashed in his mind, waking him several times during the night.

At dawn, he got up and went to the lake, where he removed his clothing and dove in. The cold water cleared his head. He got out and ran to the hut and the fire to warm up. Remembering the map from the temple, he looked to the west and planned his search. There was water there, a small lake, and a gorge. It would take at least a full day to reach the lake.

As long as I live, I have hope. He headed out as a suzuecu screamed overhead. He had never heard of one this far east. But since he had left the temple, he had heard one every day. That night he camped on the edge of the gorge. The sound of rushing water below acted like a lullaby, singing him to sleep.

The next day's cool, damp morning threatened rain. But the moist, heavy air brought the welcome scent of smoke. There was a fire nearby. He continued north along the gorge and came to a rock outcropping. He saw someone standing on top of the largest rock. Not wanting to appear threatening, he stepped out into the open and raised his hands high. He heard the alarm call from the boy on the rock, so he waited. Soon a band of warriors came through the rocks accompanied by two dogs.

He recognized the first of the dogs that ran ahead. "Toby!"

Toby ran and jumped on him, knocking him down. The dog stood over him and licked his face. The second dog came up and growled. It wasn't a dog but a manetoo with its teeth bared. He pushed Toby off so he could sit, but the dog would not leave him alone. The manetoo came over cautiously, and smelled him, then it licked him as well.

He heard a familiar voice. "Nanhin. You are alive." Wanika reached down to help him up. "Toby certainly recognized you, as did several of us, once we got a look at your grizzled face. Welcome home."

He accepted the hand and stood. "It is good to be home. I nearly lost hope when I found the village deserted."

"Yes. We moved to make it harder for the slavers to find us."

"I see you also set out a sentry." He pointed to the figure on the rock.

"We are trying to protect the village, though the enemies' weapons are too strong." He started back through the rocks. "Come. We will celebrate tonight, and you can tell us of your adventures."

Ryan and the rest of his warriors followed Wanika into the village. The entrance was through a narrow path between the rocks with a boma at the end. As they approached, the warriors inside opened the boma. The village layout was like what he remembered with a central firepit surrounded by huts. There wasn't a lake, but a spring ran from the rocks on the north end, creating a stream that flowed through the village before tumbling over the edge and down into the gorge.

The villagers crowded around him, and Zica ran up and jumped into his arms, throwing her arms around his neck and her legs around his waist. "I knew you would come back, Nanhin." She kissed his face and neck.

Others came and patted him on the back, greeting him and welcoming him back. He had to push Zica off so he could move.

She took his hand and led him from the others to a hut where she made him sit on the sleeping mat. She brought him water and stood, smiling.

After he rested a few minutes and finished his water, he said, "Why don't you show me around the village?"

"Leave your stuff and we can go out; I will show you." But the look in her eyes gave him the impression that she wanted to stay inside and make up for lost time.

That night at the feast, he told the village about the trek to the coast: being sold into slavery, the pirate attack, and being held by the Erotae.

"You saw the winged demons?" Niche shook his head. "Our legends tell of such creatures, but no one living has ever seen one. Tell me more about them."

"They are much like us. They are not demons, but simply people who can fly." He set his cup down. "In the world I came from, we would have called them angels because they resemble the legendary messengers of God. They struggle with people who live on land because the pirates hunt them and kill them for their wings. And just like you, they could not compete against the pirates' weapons."

Disbelief was etched into the warrior's face. "As a child, I was told they would eat little children, but you say they are not demons." Murmurs spread through the gathering. "How did you escape?"

"I didn't. They let me go. After I helped them defeat the pirates, they brought us back to dry land."

"They defeated the pirates?"

"Yes. I showed them how to make a weapon they could use to fight against the crossbows used by the pirates. I'll show you the weapon tomorrow in the daylight. You may not defeat the raiders, but you will make them pay dearly for each one they kill or capture."

Zica came to refill his cup of beer, but he refused.

The villagers asked him more questions about the Erotae and the people of the coast until Zica grabbed his hand and pulled him back to the hut. Lying in bed with him, she caressed his face. "I knew you would come back to me, Nanhin. I am happy you are home."

He gazed into her eyes. "I'm happy to be back. But you know I must still search to find my way back to my world."

"Will your other wife wait for you?"

"I hope so. Regardless, I must go back if it is possible."

She rolled over on top of him. "Don't I make you happy?"

"You make me very happy. If I cannot go back, I will stay with you." She smiled, then kissed him.

The next morning, he met with Wanika and the other warriors to show them how to use the bow and arrows. Then, after he explained the materials they needed, he sent them out to find suitable wood to make their own.

The warriors worked diligently at making the weapon, then practiced daily with it. While most practiced, Ryan and Wanika went around the perimeter of the village looking for defensive weaknesses. Ryan pointed out a couple of areas where they could install fences to slow attackers. He also had Wanika stockpile rocks near the edge of the cliff along the gorge. The warrior soon noticed areas that needed work on his own.

One evening, while Ryan sat at the fire he put his hand on Wanika's shoulder. "You picked an excellent location for the village. It should give you a chance to defeat the slavers, especially with the defenses you have added."

"True, but I chose it because it was hard to locate."

"That is the first step in defense." Ryan took a swig from his cup. "The next thing you could do is to teach your women how to use the bows. They are capable. I saw some fight the slavers during the raid when they captured me."

"Weeko has been asking me to teach her. I think you are right. We will start tomorrow."

"Speaking of Weeko, I noticed Toby is no longer my dog. He recognizes me and is happy to be around me, but he always returns to Weeko."

"She found him and nursed him back to health after they took you away. She spends most of her time with him and Namid, the injured manetoo she found."

"I remember her from the first day. She didn't seem friendly."

Wanika laughed and drank. "She is not. You are the first person she has approached and not bitten. Toby must have told her about you." They both laughed. "Have you heard the suzuecu screams? Since you arrived, one goes by every night. The people are worried."

"I have. It has followed me since I left the temple, though I don't think it is a threat. I wish I could talk to Wakakan."

"No one has told you. Wakakan is dead. He died not long after the raid. Paytah is the shaman now. He is away at the spirit cave, but should return soon."

Wakakan dead. Toby is no longer my dog. The suzuecu following me. Things are changing too fast. What does it all mean? Am I stuck here?

CHAPTER FORTY-TWO

PAYTAH RETURNS

A young warrior came up behind Ryan as he inspected the new fence across the gap in the rocks. "Nanhin, Paytah has arrived. He will wait for you at the firepit."

"Thank you. I will be there shortly." He continued his inspection. *Will he be able to help me get home? He is so young; I don't know if I trust him. But I need to find out.*

Paytah sat in the center of the village by the firepit, surrounded by villagers. As Ryan approached, he stood and greeted him. He waved the villagers away, telling them he would be back.

"Nanhin, I heard you had come back. It is good to see you, and I have things to tell you. Come with me."

"It is good to be back. I'm sorry for your loss, Paytah. I had hoped to speak with your father." He followed Paytah to the cave under the rock face, where the spring emerged. Apparently, the young shaman lived here when he stayed in the village. They sat on logs near his fire.

"I know you wanted him to help you return to your previous home. He passed along most of what he was doing, and I will help you if I can."

"Thank you."

Paytah took a stick and drew lines in the dirt. At first, the lines moved away from each other, then the slope on one line changed. It fell steeply toward the other line. He stopped drawing and put the end of the stick where the slope changed. "This happened two weeks ago. According to my father, this is the line that represents your presence in Almirosia. When I noticed the change, I believed you would return to the village."

"Your father told me when the lines on the spirit cave wall intersected, a portal would open that I could use to return to my home. Do you think that will happen soon?" He stared at the scratches in the dirt.

"Maybe. But as you can see, the lines change direction unexpectedly. However, other signs, like the suzuecu, could foretell a change." He drew another line that came at an even steeper slope toward the first two lines. "This is an older line that crossed the main one years ago. It looks like it is moving to the same intersection."

"What does it mean?"

"I don't know," Paytah said. "The line was moving steeply away from the first one until last week. Now it is moving almost perpendicular."

"Could it be someone else that came through a portal like I did?"

"Yes. That is the most logical explanation. But why the change?" He stood and walked to the entrance of the cave. "And why is that line related to your line?"

"I saw a man in Amut. He spoke in a language I understood from my world. His name is Yago, and he tried to have me killed." *Does he know I am alive? Is he coming for me?*

"Yago... Yago, yes. The priests say he is an evil man. He stayed at the temple and learned from the teachers there about the lines. Then, they say, he killed them all and tried to destroy the temple. Shortly after that time, the raids began on this village and other villages." He faced Ryan. "If Yago is coming here, we must warn Wanika."

That evening, the warriors met. Paytah repeated the warning he had given Wanika before the meeting. The tribal leader stood and raised his arms to silence their discussion. "Paytah believes this man, Yago, is coming to our village. We have two or three days until he arrives, if Paytah is correct. We must decide. Do we leave or do we fight?"

"How do we know he will find us?" a warrior asked. "We moved to make that harder."

"We cannot be certain he will. But Nanhin found us, so he may find us as well."

Another warrior stood.

"I say we fight. This is a good place for us. We have the new weapons Nanhin showed us how to make. We have lived in fear of the slavers our whole lives. I say we fight." There was a murmur of agreement from the warriors.

"Yago comes for me," Ryan said. "If I leave, he may not come at all."

Wanika faced him. "Do you believe that if he comes and you are not here, he will not harm our village?"

"No. He is an evil man, and if he finds you, he will try to destroy you."

"Nanhin is right," Paytah said. "I believe he is the one who killed the shamans in the temple years ago. He has brought evil to our land. He brought the weapons the raiders use, and he organizes the raids. We must fight."

In unison, the warriors echoed, "We must fight."

"Then we will prepare. Nanhin, will you help us like you helped the winged people?"

"I will, though you have already done most of what I would suggest."

After the council, Wanika sat beside Ryan and had the women bring food. A lot of nervous conversations ran through the assembly, now that the women had joined them. Zica came with a jar and cups for Wanika, Paytah, and him. She sat close to him and whispered, "I am afraid."

"You should be afraid. But we will fight together. Maybe the Creator will give us a victory. Only He knows what the outcome will be. But I believe we will survive."

She leaned on him for a while, then she took his hand and led him to their hut. "If we win, do you believe you will go home?"

"I do," he said. "The shaman at the temple told me I had to complete a task. Maybe this is the task I must complete."

Tears ran down her cheeks. "If we lose, they will kill you. I know you want to return to your home, but I do not want you to leave me."

"I don't want to leave you, but I must return to where I belong."

"You belong here." She drew him to her and kissed him. "I have already lost you once."

Later that night, he stared at her peaceful, sleeping face. *I will miss her. Maybe as much as I miss Emily. Is it possible to love two people so deeply? Have I sinned?*

CHAPTER FORTY-THREE

YAGO'S HUNT

Yago stood in the entrance to his tent. According to his sources, the village where they captured the white slave was nearby. Yet, he had heard nothing to indicate they had found it. His chief lieutenant, Balzer, came into camp, breathing hard. He met him halfway across the camp. "Did you find the village?"

"Yes." Balzer bent over, panting. "I came as quickly as I could. It was right where they told us it would be. But it appeared abandoned."

"Abandoned?"

"Yes."

Yago clenched his fists. *That is unexpected.* "How far is it to the village?"

"Three or four miles," Balzer said. "Less than two hours away."

"Order the men to break camp. I need to see it for myself." Yago turned back to his tent.

They broke camp and headed up the hill toward the village. Balzer led them while Yago went to the back of the column to check on their prisoner.

When he had returned to Amut, he learned that Maslic had left town. He had intended to eliminate him once things in town had settled down after the raid on Shera's estate. With Maslic gone, it would make it easier to take over the rest of the spice trade and solidify his position as the most powerful man on the coast.

When he heard Maslic was living on an isolated farm north of town, it provided an opportunity to eliminate him with no local repercussions. He had sent Balzer and several men to take care of it. But when Balzer returned with both Maslic and Shera, he exploded, throwing papers and furniture around his office. She was supposed to be dead. Hailama had assured him that there were no survivors on the ship after the winged demon's attack.

If Shera survived, the white slave may have survived as well. He had to find out. Maslic finally confessed that the white slave lived. It took two days of torture with no result. Then he brought Shera into the room. Once they began torturing her, Maslic told them everything.

Shera, tethered to the man in front of her, staggered. Her left eye had swollen shut and dried blood covered her mouth and chin. Ragged and torn, her clothing barely covered her bruised body. She looked nothing like the woman Yago had tried to woo not too long ago. Yet she held her head up and shoulders back, her matted hair hanging down past her shoulders.

Yago stepped up beside her. "We are almost to the village where we captured your white slave. It appears deserted. But they probably have not gone far. We will find them, and I will make you watch him die just as you watched Maslic die."

She stared straight ahead and didn't answer him.

Oh well, perhaps I will use her as a reward for the men once we have killed the white slave. She is more stubborn than an ox and less useful. Still, she might be of value once we find the village.

Yago walked up a mild grade through the thinning forest, which opened into a clearing around a small, clear lake. The remnants of the village sat along the shore. Long sections of the brush fence that surrounded it had fallen. The village itself lay in ruins. Piles of sticks and logs scattered around the perimeter of the village were all that remained of the huts. He found no pottery, tools, or other implements. They had apparently taken everything with them.

He sat on a log at what appeared to be a central firepit and waved Balzer over. "We will set up a base camp here. Once that is done, send scouts out to determine where the savages have gone."

"It will be done." He looked around before leaving. "What about the woman?"

"Tie her to a sturdy post in the middle of the camp."

While his men set up the camp, he explored the village. A layer of fine dust covered everything. The huts had earthen floors with dried pine boughs and reeds, probably used for sleeping, piled along the wall. These savages had even less than the Mexicas he fought while serving under Cortes in his other life. And there was no prospect of gold. But they were an excellent source of forced labor and had provided much of his wealth since he arrived. Even the Moors here were backward. Given enough time. He would be king.

Late the second day, Balzer came with his daily report. Yago motioned for him to sit. "We may have found the new village. One scout saw signs of a settlement northwest of here. He didn't get a good look at the village, but he saw smoke from several fires and savages in the distance."

"Have all the scouts returned?"

"They have."

"Good. Tell the men we leave at first light." Balzer left Yago alone in his tent.

The next day, they moved toward the suspected settlement. They reached the spot where the scout reported seeing smoke just before sunset.

He waved Balzer over. "Set up camp here. No fires tonight. We want to surprise them in the morning."

"As you wish. Shall I send out more scouts?"

"No." Yago put his hand on the lieutenant's shoulder. "You and I will go. I want to see it myself. We will plan our attack once I know the lay of the land and how to best approach the village."

"I will tell the men."

When Balzer returned, they moved through the forest, using the trees and darkness to cover their movements. The trees thinned as they neared the suspected entrance to the village. A narrow passage between large boulders looked well used and had a brush fence at the far end. The trail would limit the number of men that could go through at one time. Moving around the rocks, they searched for another entrance. It didn't take them long to find another gap through the rocks. Smaller and not as level, a narrow path wound up to the top of the boulder-strewn hill.

They watched for several minutes, then Yago said, "Let's head back. I think I have a plan."

Back at camp, his lieutenants gathered in Yago's tent. "Based on the accounts of those involved in the previous raid and the evidence provided by the abandoned village, I estimate there are only sixty individuals with maybe twenty warriors." He took his sword and drew on the ground in front of the men. "Hyrum, you will take fifteen men and attack through the main entrance here." He pointed to the diagram on the ground. "Stay close to the rocks until you reach the fence, then burn it and charge through. While you are attacking the front, Balzer will take ten men up the back entrance here."

He stabbed his sword into the ground and stood erect, looking at the faces of the men. "I will stay with the remaining five men to help if needed. Remember, take the white-skinned one alive. He is mine. I will give Shera to the one who brings him to me."

The men, except for Balzer, left the tent. "You must wait until you see the smoke from the burning fence before you head up the rocks. I want their warriors concentrating on the men there so you can surprise them from behind."

"I can do that. Do you think it will be necessary? Our weapons are superior. We have never needed many men to fight against the spears and clubs of the savages."

Yago sat. "I'm not concerned about getting into the village. But I want you to ensure they bring the white-skinned one to me. I don't want him killed. I need to talk to him and find out where he is from."

"Offering Shera as a reward should ensure the men will want to keep him alive for you." Balzer lifted his cup. "Success."

"Success." Yago lifted his cup. "Now prepare for tomorrow."

Later that night, the scream of the suzuecu woke Yago. The priests at the temple believed the dragon acted as an omen from their Creator. A portend of death and change. *Tomorrow, the white-skinned man will be mine and I will ensure he never returns to the other world. I can rule Almirosia. Their pagan god is no match for me.*

CHAPTER FORTY-FOUR

ATTACK ON THE VILLAGE

Ryan stood with Wanika and watched a boy, silhouetted by the orange glow of the sunrise, scamper across the rocks as he ran up to where they stood at the fire. Panting from the exertion, the boy stood and took two deep breaths. "Wanika, the raiders are coming. They formed into two groups. One group is coming through the main trail and a smaller group is moving through the forest toward the other trail."

Wanika turned to Ryan. "It is as you predicted. They will attack both paths leading to the village."

Ryan nodded his head in agreement. "You have your warriors in place?"

"Yes, some will die today. But for once, I feel like we can defend ourselves. Let's take our positions."

Ryan poked the fire with a stick, watching the sparks dance as they rose with the smoke. The heat felt good on this cool morning. "We must remind the warriors to be patient and allow the group on the main path to get close enough to the gate to make their retreat long and dangerous. We may not win the battle, but we will make them regret coming here."

Ryan picked up his weapons and the two men went to the rocks overlooking the trail that led to the main entrance to the village. Ryan went up the left side and Wanika went up along the right. The dim light of dawn made it difficult to see the stealthy figures below, but their movement gave them away. The warriors lay down flat against the top of the rocks and waited.

Ryan shivered as a cool breeze blew across the rocks. But he knew once the fighting started, he wouldn't feel the cold. His stomach churned, his tongue had barely enough spit to wet his lips. *Waiting is hard. I hope the warriors don't get impatient.*

The first of the raiders neared the fence on the far side of the path from where Ryan watched. He stopped there and lit a torch. Wanika shouted the signal for the attack. Ryan stood and shot at the raider below. The arrow pierced his side. He screamed and fell, dropping the torch. The next raider picked up the burning brand and threw it into the fence before he also fell with an arrow through his neck.

The once-still morning now echoed with shouts of the fighters and the screams of the wounded. Smoke from the burning fence filled the air and made it more difficult for the villagers to see the men below.

Tink! A crossbow bolt ricocheted off the rock at Ryan's feet barely missing his thigh. The battle quickly turned into a standoff with the raiders taking cover in the rocks below and the villagers keeping them pinned down from the top.

Toby's barking in the distance alerted Ryan that the raiders had begun their attack on the other entrance into the village. He waved to Wanika and left his position to go help the defenders there. He ran down the rocks, through the village, and up the rear path. As he neared the top of the trail, he slowed his breathing. He heard the shouts of the raiders and Toby's barks. When he reached the top, the raiders had hunkered down in the gully that cut across the path. A newly erected fence ran along the top on the nearside of the gully, and the arrows from the village defenders had stopped the raider's progress.

Toby and the manetoo worked together, keeping the raiders from moving along the bottom of the gully. After a while, the raiders scrambled up the far side and ran down the hill to escape the rain of arrows coming from the villagers. They left two dead and helped two wounded retreat with them. Ryan whistled to call Toby back. Once the raiders were out of sight, the villagers cheered. But he knew the battle was not over.

He sent scouts to follow and watch the raiders to ensure they didn't return. Then he checked on the villager's losses. One warrior, Enepay, was dead and two others wounded. Down in the gully, defenders gathered up the arrows littering the ground when he heard the cheers from the warriors at the main entrance. He guessed that the raiders there had also retreated.

When Ryan got back to the village, he met Wanika. "Today was a glorious victory," the chief said. "But you don't look happy. Your expression tells me it isn't over."

"No. It isn't over. I think Yago was a soldier. He knows how to fight, and he knows one defeat does not determine the outcome of the battle. We won the first skirmish with minimal losses. He will be more cautious now. We need to be alert."

"I will send out the young men to spy on them and report their movements." He waved a young man over and gave him instructions for the spies.

CHAPTER FORTY-FIVE

REGROUP

Back at the raider's encampment, Yago waited for word that his men had successfully taken the village. He expected the party going up the primary trail to face the most resistance, but once they burned through the fence, they should have easy access to the village. The Mexicas' spears and clubs would be no match for their crossbows and swords. Still, he paced around the fire, waiting.

He didn't have to wait long before he saw the column of smoke rising over the rocks. *It won't be long now.* But two hours passed and still no word came. *Surely they have taken the village by now.* After another hour, he was ready to send someone to check on the attack's progress when he saw his men running back to camp. He grabbed the arm of one man. "Where is Hyrum?"

"Back there." The man pointed back the way he had come. "He's wounded."

Yago ran to where two men helped another down the trail. As they got closer, Yago stopped wide-eyed, staring at the wounded man. Arrows protruded from his side and thigh. It was Hyrum. He stopped them. "What happened?"

"It was an ambush," the man on Hyrum's right answered. "As soon as we got to the fence, they started shooting these long arrows at us, trapping us between the rocks."

"But I saw the smoke."

"Yes. We lit the fence, but we couldn't go through."

More men came down from the village, helping the wounded. Most looked to have arrows in their legs or arms. Not serious, but the arrow in Hyrum's side could be fatal. *It makes little sense. They have never had these weapons. The white-skinned one must have helped them. I must kill him, or he could ruin my plans. Maybe Balzer's men got through.*

He went back to camp and waited for word from Balzer, knowing he had to change his tactics. The old way of assaulting the village might not work. He talked to the men that had returned so he could get an idea of how the villagers had set up their defenses. Yago began planning for the next attack if Balzer and his men returned unsuccessful in their attack. Yago went to his tent after leaving word for Balzer to join him there.

When his lieutenant joined him, Yago handed him a cup of ale. "What happened up there?"

Balzer gulped his ale. "They had built a fence across the top of the gully and trapped us there. They used manetoos to keep us there."

Yago got up and paced. "What are your thoughts on the village defenses?"

"If we want to go in through either of the entrances we scouted, we will need more men." He took another drink. "They have set up positions high on the rocks overlooking the trails, which are narrow and restrict the movement of our men at the bottom. The terrain also presented obstacles we could not see from our initial reconnaissance. Whoever is leading them knows what he is doing."

"It's that white-skinned outsider." Yago stood and paced. "He has brought weapons for them and knowledge from my world. He is trying to shift the balance of power. We need a way into the village."

Balzer finished his cup. "I can send small groups out to explore other ways in, but it will take time. More time for them to prepare."

"Still, it is a good idea. We can send them in groups of four or five to probe the rocks, looking for an entrance. Once we find one, we can trap them there. Though we don't have enough men for a full siege, we can harass them and spread their defenses."

For the next three days, his men kept probing the edges of the village defenses with little effect. Finally, Balzer came to him with another idea.

"The rocks on this side shelter the village, making it difficult to reach without using one of the two trails we tried earlier. A deep gorge surrounds the other three sides. However, we found a narrow path along the wall of the canyon that might lead us to a place below the village. If we can climb the wall from the path, it might provide a way in."

"Good. They won't expect that." Yago slapped his thigh. "They believe the gorge protects them. When do you propose we try?"

"Tomorrow morning, we can send a diversionary attack on the path I attacked to draw the defenders away. It is farther from the village and will give us more time to scale the wall. That way, they won't notice the men going along the gorge."

Yago put his hand on his lieutenant's shoulder. "You will lead the men in the gorge."

At dusk, Yago walked around the camp listening to the men talking. He had given them an extra ration of ale with their meal, but they still seemed discouraged.

"They have a shaman protecting them. Our weapons aren't effective," he heard one say as he listened from the shadows.

"Even the wild animals are helping," another said. "Did you see the size of the manetoo in the gully?" Hyenas chortled in the darkness. "Now the hyenas will help."

"I'm not afraid of the hyenas," a third man said. "But that monster that flies over at night, the suzuecu, scares me." The others nodded in agreement.

Yago headed back to his tent. *If we don't succeed soon, the men will desert.* He stopped to check on Shera.

She held her head high and sneered. "You will never take them; he is smarter than you. And his men will fight, to the death, for him. Will yours do the same for you?"

Yago grabbed her by the throat and pushed her against the pole to which they had tied her. "It won't matter to you, because you will die either way."

"I'm ready." Her voice was a raspy whisper through his choke hold.

"We will see about that." He released his hold. *I wonder if he is as willing to die for her as she is for him.*

The suzuecu screamed overhead.

The next morning, he watched the diversionary party leave camp, moving toward the second entrance. Their orders were to try a quick assault on the fence at the gully, but not to get pinned down there.

Balzer and his men gathered after they left. Yago walked to the gorge with them. "Send up a signal once you reach the village. I will have the men attack the main entrance."

"We will set the village ablaze once we get there. You will see the smoke." Balzer turned and followed his men along the narrow path.

When Yago got back to camp, he had the rest of his men gather for the assault on the main gate. They moved to the tree line and waited for the smoke to come from the village. Yago paced behind the men. After an hour, the diversionary forces came back and joined the main body of men waiting for Balzer's signal.

Two hours later, Balzer and only one other man came running to them.

"What happened?" Yago asked.

Balzer bent over, gasping for air. "They were ready for us. They pushed rocks down on us once we began climbing, knocking the rest of my men into the gorge." He continued to breathe hard. "What do we do now?"

"I have a plan. Keep the men here." Yago walked back to camp. Some men mumbled as he walked away. *If this doesn't work, I will lose the men.*

Chapter Forty-Six

Sacrifice

"Nanhin." Zica handed him a cup filled with warm tea. "You did not sleep well."

"No. The suzuecu kept waking me." Ryan drank the tea and picked up a piece of dried meat. "My dreams have also been troubling."

"The man who hunts you. What does he want?"

"He wants to kill me. He doesn't understand that I am from a different time than him, and even if I return to my time, I can't tell anyone about him. His life here in Almirosia is better than his former life. He doesn't want to return."

She sat next to him. "You still want to go back to your other life. Is it so much better than your life here?" She leaned into him, their skin sharing body heat, driving the morning chill away.

"My life here is not bad or even worse than my other life. It is just different. But I lived forty years in the other life and shared over twenty of those with Emily. We raised my son there and might one day see grandchildren." He put his arm around her. "Your people have treated me with respect and friendship. You have loved me unconditionally, even knowing I might leave. I love you, but I know I do not belong here and must return to where I belong."

She stayed next to him. They watched the flames dance up from the fire, curling and flashing. *Emily would not be happy if she could see me now. But I don't think I could have made it here this long without Zica.*

"Nanhin." A young man stood at the door. "The raiders have sent a detachment toward the back entrance. Wanika would like you to join him."

"I'll be right there." He gazed into Zica's dark eyes and kissed her. "Yago will never give up."

Wanika was standing on a boulder overlooking the main entrance when Ryan joined him. In the distance, a band of raiders moved through the trees toward the upper trail.

"What do you think, Nanhin?"

"I think it is a feint, a diversion. They want to draw our attention away from something else they want to try."

"They have not tested our defenses much lately," Wanika said. "I agree with you. The number of men is too small for a serious attack. I will put everyone on alert."

Wanika talked to the young warriors he used as messengers. They ran in different directions to alert the forces scattered around the perimeter. The two older men went down to the center of the village to wait for word on the attack. Toby came up to Ryan and nuzzled his hand.

"Hi, boy." He bent down and petted the shepherd's head and neck. Toby licked his face. "You're finally paying some attention to me. Since I got back, you've spent all your time with Weeko and the wolf." The dog's ears perked up, and he stared off toward the back gate. But he didn't move.

"The attack has started," he said to Wanika. The wolf came up to them and yelped at Toby, who stood for a few minutes, then sat beside Ryan. She came over to him and stood on his other side. He stroked the beast's head. *She is huge.*

Not long after, both animals relaxed and lay together. Toby's head lay against his stretched-out legs. The wolf lay on her side with her head against Toby's shoulder. Ryan figured the attack at the back gate had ended.

Both dogs jumped up and ran toward the gorge. There Toby looked over the lip, barking. The young men posted at the gorge shouted and threw rocks down the side of the cliff. Other warriors soon joined Wanika and Ryan at the precipice. Below them, several raiders scaled the rock face. Village warriors got behind rocks piled on the edge of the gorge, above the climbers, and pushed them over the cliff.

The men on the rock face screamed as the stones turned into a rockslide that carried all but two of them down in the bottom gorge. As the warriors continued to throw rocks down on them, the two remaining raiders scurried along the narrow ledge.

A messenger came to Wanika. "We have repelled the attack on the back gate. They did not try very hard. They didn't even enter the gully."

"Thank you. You can return to your post," Wanika said.

The messenger still stood in front of Wanika. "One more thing, the lookout at the main gate said the raiders have massed their forces just in the forest. They appear to be waiting for something." Wanika nodded and the young man ran back toward the rear gate.

Wanika turned to Ryan. "I think we know what they are waiting for. They will have to wait a long time. Do you think they will try another direct attack?"

"I don't know. Let's go see what they are doing."

The two men went back up to the top of the boulders to get a view of the forest. The raiders stood in the shelter of the trees. After a while, the raiders, who had gone to the back gate, came down the trail and joined the rest in the forest.

"Do you think they will attack again, Nanhin?"

"I don't think so. It looks to me like they don't have enough men for a direct assault." Ryan pointed to the men gathered in the trees. "They underestimated our strength and defenses. Now they don't know what to do. But Yago will not give up. They may try to wait us out, hoping we will run low on food and water."

"Hah!" The chief laughed. "They will wait a long time. We had a successful hunt before you got back. The three bison will provide enough food for months."

Ryan laughed. "Three bison. They will run out of food long before we do. We only need to use caution and not get careless. Without more men, they cannot defeat us."

The two leaders went back down to the village. Wanika went to see the warriors at the various sections of their defenses while Ryan went back into his hut. Zica had gone to take her shift at the main gate. She had become an excellent archer over the last few weeks. Maybe the best female archer in the village. Ryan even had the chance to take her hunting before the raiders came, and she killed a nice stag with one shot.

Tired from his restless night, he dozed on the mat until a warrior came into the hut. "Nanhin, we need you at the gate."

He sat up and cleared his head. "What's happening?"

"The leader of the slavers has a woman. He is asking for you. Come."

Ryan stood, grabbed his weapons, and followed the messenger to the top of the rocks overlooking the gate. Below, Yago stood with a woman on her knees in front of him, his sword point held to the back of her neck.

"Give me Nanhin!" Yago said. "I will release the woman and leave your village if you give me the one called Nanhin."

Wanika stood on top of the rock. "I do not know the woman. Why should I care what happens to her?"

"Nanhin knows her." Yago pulled Shera's hair so the villagers could see her face. "Ask him."

Wanika pointed to the woman when Ryan stepped up next to him. "Do you know the woman?"

"Yes. She is Shera, the woman who bought me in Amut."

"Do you care for her?"

"Yes."

Wanika shook his head and put his hand on Ryan's shoulder. "It is your decision. I do not trust him to leave. And, even if he does, I believe he will come back with more men."

Ryan saw Zica and motioned for her to join them. "Yago will kill her if we don't do something."

"If you go, he will kill you." Zica grabbed Ryan's arm. "Do not go, Nanhin. I need you."

"I know." He took her face in his hands. "But I promised to protect her. I cannot allow her to die for me." He kissed her, and she held him. He had to push her away.

"Yago." Ryan stood on top of the rock. "Let Shera go, and I will come down."

"You come down. Then I will let her go."

Ryan signaled for a warrior to throw down the rope ladder. Zica reached for him, tears streaming down her cheeks. "Why?"

"Because she is my friend. In the world I came from, there is a saying, 'Greater love has no man than this, that he would lay down his life for a friend.' I must do this. Yago will not kill me right away. He wants to find out what I know. Remember that while I live, there is hope."

He climbed down the ladder, carrying his weapons. When he got to the bottom, he walked out toward the raiders, but stopped about halfway. "Release her now," he said. "I will come the rest of the way once she has reached the ladder."

Yago stared at him, still holding his sword to her neck. "Throw down your weapons and I will release her."

Ryan dropped his bow and quiver and held his arms out. Yago finally released Shera with a push, sending her face down in the dirt. She got up and ran to Ryan. When she got near to him, he said, "Pick up the bow and arrows and run to the ladder. The villagers will help you. Don't stop and don't look back."

He watched until she reached the ladder before walking toward Yago. Three men ran out of the forest. Two grabbed his arms, and the third bound his hands behind him, giving him a push. "Move it." They followed Yago back into the trees.

Once in their camp, they tied him to a tree. "Yago wants to talk to you before he kills you," the raider who tied him said. "I remember you."

"Umph!" Ryan slumped from the punch to his gut. "Ugh!" The second blow took the wind out of him. He struggled to get his breath. His hands tied behind the tree held him up, straining his shoulders.

The raider grabbed his face with a rough, dirty hand. "You killed a friend of mine in that raid, and now two more friends have died. I want to watch you suffer while Yago questions you." Spit flew from his partially toothless mouth into Ryan's face. His sour breath made it harder for Ryan to recover his breath.

As the three men left, he heard one ask, "Will we go home now that Yago has the white-skinned stranger?"

"Not yet," the one who hit him said. "Yago doesn't like to leave things unfinished."

Alone, Ryan surveyed the camp. They had tied him to a tree that grew near the edge of the camp, close to the largest tent. He assumed it was Yago's. They had set up the remaining tents in a rough circle among the trees. In front of him was a fire with only a few embers remaining. The smell of pine smoke filled the air. The silence surprised him. All the raiders congregated at the edge of the forest a hundred yards away.

It would be dark in another hour, and he expected Yago's men to return to camp. *Heavenly Father, I don't know why you brought me here. The shaman says I am here for a purpose, but it looks to me like I will die. Forgive me, I am a sinful man and a slave to my flesh. Give me the courage to face my adversary with dignity. Help Emily know I love her and want to be with her. Help my friends to defeat the enemy that stands before them. In Jesus' name, amen.*

CHAPTER FORTY-SEVEN

YAGO'S CAMP

The raiders returned to camp in groups of three or four. One from the first group added logs to revive the fire, which warmed the chill evening air. Yago returned with the second group and went directly into the large tent near the tree where they tied Ryan. As it cooled, the men gathered around the fire. They ate dried meat with beer from a cask carried in the back of a two-wheeled hand cart. They didn't cook.

A raider Ryan recognized as the man who accompanied Yago to Shera's compound untied his hands while two other men held his arms. They took him into the tent. Yago sat on a bed, constructed from birch logs with fir boughs and blankets on top.

They kicked him in the back of the legs and forced him to his knees in front of Yago, who stood and came over to him. "Nanhin, that is what they call you? You have been quite troublesome to me. Apparently, no one has killed you. How do you explain that?"

"I have been lucky." Ryan looked him in the eye.

"Lucky, yes. Tell me, Nanhin, what is your birth name?" Yago stood with his hands on his hips.

"My name is Ryan."

"Well, Ryan, your luck is about to run out. Where are you from?"

"I'm from Colorado. Where are you from?" Ryan knew Yago would kill him, so he didn't try to hide the defiance in his voice.

"Malaga... But I will ask the questions. Did Cortes send you?" He picked his sword up from the bed, then walked around behind Ryan.

"Cortes? I don't know any Cortes!"

"Liar!" He poked Ryan in the back with the point of his sword. "Cortes hates deserters. Did he send you to find me? I know you came through the portal. Were you in the new world with him?"

Cortes, deserters, new world? Does he mean Cortes the conquistador? That would make sense with the crossbows and other weapons. "You mean Hernan Cortes, the conquistador? He is dead."

"Dead. The Mexicas killed him?" Yago stopped in front of Ryan.

"No, he conquered Mexico and returned to Spain, where he died over four hundred years ago. Were you one of his conquistadors?"

Yago hit Ryan in the face, knocking him over. "You lie!" The two guards helped him back to his knees. His nose bled, making it hard to breathe.

How can this be? According to the shaman at the temple, he has only been here a few years. He spit blood from his mouth and whispered, "Bastardo."

Yago hit him on the side of the head with the pommel of his sword, then kicked him in the stomach and ribs. He lay on the ground, barely conscious. Yago was yelling, but he couldn't understand what he was saying. The ringing in his ears and pounding of his head drowned out the words. Everything went black.

"Ooooh." Ryan opened his eyes. He could hear people talking, but it hurt too much to roll in that direction. Someone came over and stood at his head.

"Yago, he is regaining consciousness." The man pushed him over onto his back.

"Umph!" Sharp pain in his ribs forced the air out.

Yago came over and glared down at him. "Sit him up against the pole. We're not done talking."

They dragged Ryan over to the support pole in the center of the tent, near the small fire, and used it to brace his back. The fog was lifting from his mind.

Yago bent to stare into Ryan's eyes. "Now, you will tell me the truth."

"If I tell you the truth, you won't believe me." *I'm not sure I believe it myself.*

"How can I believe you when you tell me Cortes has been dead for four hundred years?" He stood with his hands on his hips. "I saw him the day I came here just a few years ago."

"I can't explain it. The shaman says it is magic. I don't know if it's magic or physics that makes the portals work. It transported me from Colorado to here, wherever here is, into a culture that is at least a thousand years behind the culture I know. Unlike you, I have a wife and a home I want to return to."

"You lie." He kicked Ryan again, knocking him over onto his side. "You want to send me back to hunger and thirst? To that tyrant, Cortes. You are just like the priests." He went and sat on the bed. "Balzer, take him out and kill him."

The two men picked him up and took him outside, his feet dragging as they carried him. Once they got beyond the circle of tents, one held a torch while the other tied him to a large pine tree. A third man with a crossbow joined them there. Ryan recognized him as the one who had treated him so roughly earlier.

"Balzer, can I kill him?" the third man asked.

"Yes."

A cruel smile creased his hate-filled face as he moved to stand a few paces in front of Ryan. He raised the crossbow. A suzue-cu screamed overhead. Its screams echoed through the trees. It sounded like it was right on top of them. The air moved around Ryan as it flapped its enormous wings. The man with the crossbow looked up at the enormous black shape, but another smaller black shape flew out of the trees and knocked the man down.

Toby, the German shepherd, had the man's throat in his jaws. Blood poured from the man's neck. He tried to get free, but with every move he made, Toby's grip tightened as he shook him and tore the man's windpipe out. Blood spurted over Toby's muzzle and the man's body lay limp, dead.

Ryan heard men yelling from the camp as Balzer ran at him with his sword. He got within two steps of Ryan before he fell to the ground with an arrow through his back. The third man was running back to camp when the manetoo pounced on his back.

"Nanhin." He recognized Wanika's voice behind him. "Can you stand?"

"I think so." The tension in his arms released, and he stumbled forward when Wanika cut the ropes holding him to the tree. "What's happening?"

"The woman, Shera, said Yago would not leave and if he did, he would return with more men." Wanika stood in front of him now. "We have more fighters than them and thought we could surprise them. So, we attacked." He put Ryan's arm around his shoulders so he could support him. "Now, let me get you back to the village."

When they got back to the main path to the village, Zica and Shera both ran out and got under his arms to support him into the village.

"I will see you once the battle is over," his friend said and went back toward the raider's camp.

The two women took him to his hut and laid him down on the mat. They began wiping the blood from his face and body. "Are you wounded?" Zica asked.

"No, just bruised. They beat me. Most of the blood is from my nose and mouth." He tried to move. "Ugh." He winced from the pain.

"They probably broke your ribs. Lie still. Let us tend to you," Shera said.

Zica continued to wipe blood off his swollen lips until Shera brought him a cup of cool water. "Drink this." She held the cup to his lips while Zica raised his head.

"How is he?" Weeko stood at the entrance.

"He will be fine, though they beat him severely." Zica let his head down. "It may take a day or two for him to be up and around."

"Good." Weeko moved and Toby came into the hut. The dog licked Ryan's swollen face and smeared it with blood.

"Ouch. That's enough boy." He put his arm around the dog and held him for a minute. "Thank you. You saved my life."

"Come, Toby. The warriors are returning. They defeated the raiders. My father will be in as soon as he returns." Weeko left the hut with Toby and the wolf at her side.

Shera was wrapping a leather sash around his chest when Wanika came to the hut. "How are you feeling, Nanhin?"

"I'm sore, but not too badly hurt. I think they broke my ribs, but I should recover." He tried to sit up straight, but pain shot through his chest, and he fell back onto his elbow. "Did you kill Yago?"

"No. He escaped with three men. We have trackers following them." The chief sat across the fire from him. "We will not let them get far."

"He will come back if he makes it to Amut or Jabyl."

"They will not get away. They have no food or water. The warriors that follow will attack if they get close to the cities. A runner reports on their location daily. When do you think you will move more freely? I would like you to be there when we attack."

"Maybe in two or three days. But they will have that long of a head start. How will we catch them?"

"Ha!" Wanika stood. "You are in capable hands. Let the women tend you. We have Yago and his men in the woods, and the trackers show themselves when they want them to change directions. We will catch them."

CHAPTER FORTY-EIGHT

SUZUECU

It took three days for the soreness in Ryan's ribs to subside enough for him to go with the war party after Yago. They didn't follow the raiders' tracks. Instead, they took a direct route to the scout's last reported location. Late on the first day, they crossed the stream where Ryan and Toby first caught fish. They camped there on the far side of the creek.

They ate dried thanka meat along with fresh berries picked along the trail and drank the cold water from the stream. As they sat by the fire, Ryan recounted his experience with the saber-tooth. They laughed at him, and one warrior said, "The shaman is right. You have magic. It is a miracle you survived out here at all."

Ryan went to his bed early. His ribs ached and made it difficult to get comfortable on the hard ground, but he dropped off to sleep only to have the scream of the suzuecu wake him. He stared up at the brightly shining stars in the clear night sky. A dark shadow passed between him and the stars. He recognized the shape of the suzuecu. It screamed again, sending chills down his back. *Why is that thing always around?*

He lay there for several minutes before drifting back to sleep as the cries of the dragon moved away from him.

The next morning, they traveled downstream toward the confluence of the stream and the river. He realized they would probably find Yago and his men trapped in difficult terrain with steep canyons on two sides.

Just after midday, a tracker joined them. "The raiders are just through the trees, huddled in the boulders at the top of the gorge."

The war party crept through the trees until they could see the slavers. Wanika spread his warriors out to surround them before he ordered the attack. The first volley of arrows killed one raider and wounded another. Yago and the unhurt man moved down toward the river under an overhanging boulder. The rocks made it difficult to get a clear shot, but after an hour, an arrow hit the man with Yago.

In the fading daylight, Yago jumped out from under the overhang and ran along the rim of the gorge, jumping from rock to rock. He ducked and veered to avoid being an easy target. Ryan was afraid they would lose him in the approaching darkness. Yago's run brought him close to Ryan. He climbed on top of a boulder to get a clear shot. Yago, unarmed, stopped and stared at him. Ryan raised his bow, ready to kill the conquistador, but the pain in his ribs prevented him from fully drawing the bow. *Kill him. He is evil.*

A suzuecu screamed above him. It swooped down and grabbed Yago with both feet, lifting him into the air. The monster curled its back and brought its feet to its mouth, like a bat bringing in a moth. It bit Yago in half, then flew toward the mountains. Ryan watched the suzuecu as it flew away. *I don't believe it. What just happened? Is Yago really gone?* The only thing he could see was the blood splatter on the boulders near where the monster had grabbed Yago.

"Nanhin." It was Wanika. "The suzuecu... how?"

"I don't know. I was ready to shoot, and it just took him. Like the one that took the manetoo when I went to the spirit caves." He shook his head, still unable to grasp what had just happened.

Wanika helped him climb down from the boulder. "We must move away from here before we camp. The scavengers will smell the blood and be here soon. We don't want to fight them in the dark."

"What about the other raiders?"

Wanika called for the rest of the party to join them. "We will leave them. They may live or die as the Creator wills."

They hiked up the small stream for two hours before setting up camp in the dark. None of the village warriors had even been wounded in the fight. Around the fire, all they could talk about was the suzuecu. Ryan didn't sit with them, but went to his bed as soon as it was ready. He listened to their excited chatter around the fire, and for the first time since he left the temple, no suzuecu screamed. He slept.

CHAPTER FORTY-NINE

ZICA AND SHERA

When Ryan got back to the village, Zica ran up and threw her arms around him.

"Oww!" He pushed her away.

"I forgot about your ribs." Her smile turned into a pout. "Come, Shera has everything ready in the hut. You can rest before you tell us what happened." Her smile returned as she took his hand and led him to the hut where Shera tended a pot over the fire.

Once on the mat, he watched the two women, talking and laughing like old friends or sisters. But the trip back to the village had been arduous, and the adrenaline of the chase and battle had worn off. Each breath produced a sharp, stabbing pain that made breathing difficult. Wanika and the others had helped him on the trip, giving him a supportive shoulder and maintaining a slow pace, but now he just wanted to sleep. The hum of the women's conversation helped him doze off.

He dreamed about the suzuecu, seeing it kill Yago. Then a second grabbed him in its clawed feet, carrying him up into the clouds. The pressure of the monster's grip on his ribs shot waves of pain through his chest. But he couldn't move. He struggled to free himself.

"Nanhin." Zica shook his shoulder. "You are dreaming."

He sat up with difficulty. The two women had him pinned between them. Both looked at him in the orange glow of the low fire. Sweat from the close bodily contact made the chill air seem colder. His ribs hurt, and he struggled to his feet.

Zica also stood. "Are you okay?"

"Yes, I just had a nightmare." He wrapped a pelt around himself. "I need to go out."

"Do you need help?" Shera still sat on the mat.

"No. I'm fine." He went outside. The stars sparkled brightly in the clear sky and a hint of pink on the eastern horizon augured the dawn.

When he returned to the hut, Zica was stirring a pot over the fire and Shera filled cups with water from a jar. He sat on a log and stared into the fire. "What is going on? Why are you both here?" He took the cup offered by Shera.

"Shera doesn't know anybody here but you." Zica spooned out stew from the pot into bowls. "She needed a place to stay, and I offered. I like her. She will stay with us until you leave. If you cannot leave, maybe we will share you."

"What makes you think I want to be shared? Nobody asked me."

"You like both of us, don't you? Besides, I know you will soon be leaving. I believe killing Yago was the reason the magic brought you here. Now you will leave, and we will be alone." She looked over at Shera.

"I will take Shera back to Amut as soon as I can arrange it," he said.

"No." Shera took his hand. "I don't want to return to Amut. There is nothing for me there. Yago killed Maslic and his family. I am alone, and I like it here. Zica is the sister I never had, and when you are gone, we will need each other."

Ryan sat in disbelief, eating his meal and staring into the fire. *Why do I feel like this makes things more complicated?*

Shera sat next to him and held his hand in her lap. "Why do you look so troubled? You showed me how to live with the Erotae. Living a simple life, like I had there and with Maslic, makes me happy. I made friends with Tatian and Maslic's mother. Now, Zica is my friend. We have a lot in common, including you. We will both miss you when you leave, or we will share you if you stay."

"Do you think two women can survive here without a man?" Ryan shook his head. "Who will hunt?"

"Hah." Shera laughed. "You taught us to use the bow and arrows. We have fought by your side. Who do you think killed the krolic (rabbit) you are eating?"

"You killed it?" Ryan stared at Shera.

"No, Zica did," Shera said. "I have not had time to learn about the creatures yet. But she is teaching me as is Weeko. The women here are not as helpless as you believe."

"I guess not. I apologize. Our time with the Erotae showed me your capabilities." Still holding her hand, he stood. "Now I need to find Paytah."

Before he got to the door, Zica stopped him. "Paytah has gone to the spirit caves. He left this morning before dawn." She led him back to the fire. "Sit. You still need time to heal. He will be back soon. Wanika saya Paytah must figure out why the suzuecu stays so close to you."

Ryan stayed in the village. The two women doted on him and practiced with their bows. Though he didn't go on hunts with the other warriors, he went out with Zica and Shera, looking for game near the village. Two weeks after Yago's death, while they hunted along the edge of the canyon north of the village, he spotted a stag just inside the trees. He put out his hand to signal a stop, but the two women had already seen it.

Shera had her bow up and drawn. She let the arrow fly. The stag jumped and turned as the arrow pierced its side. It took two bounds into the trees, then fell over dead. "Eeeeyaa!" Shera ran ahead of them to the animal. She got there, pulled her knife, and cut the stag's throat.

"Nice shot, sister," Zica said. "Right through the heart. Let's get it dressed."

The two women gutted and skinned the deer without letting him help, but they folded the hide and gave it to him to carry back. They tied the deer's legs to a pole and carried it between them back to camp. Ryan followed and watched as the two blood-smeared women walked, sang, and talked. *They are incredible. I don't think I could have made a better shot. They will be fine without me. Will I be fine without them?*

They returned to a commotion in the village. Paytah stood inside the gate, surrounded by the other villagers. He made eye contact with Ryan and nodded, but continued to take his time greeting those around him.

They went to the stream to clean the blood from their bodies. When they got back to the hut, Paytah was waiting for them.

"How are your ribs?" He put his hand on Ryan's shoulder. "You seem to move better than when I left."

"My ribs are healing, but it takes time for the bones to mend. Did you learn anything from your time at the spirit cave?" He watched the shaman's face for any sign. His heart sank when the young man looked down.

"The time provided some insights. I will tell you about it tomorrow. The journey back was exhausting, and the manetoo kept us awake." He removed his hand. "I heard the suzuecu last night. It is still nearby."

"Yes, but the villagers seem to have gotten used to it since it doesn't get too close. Are you sure we can't talk sooner?"

"No, there is too much to talk about." Paytah left, heading toward the spring.

"Come back inside, Nanhin." Zica took his arm and led him back into the hut.

He sat propped up against the wall while the women went about their chores. *What if I never see Emily again?* He fought back tears. He knew she would move on. She had a strength greater than her petite frame might show. And she had a strong support system that had been clear to him during their marital struggles.

"Ryan." Shera kneeled beside him. "You look troubled. Can I get you some water?"

"No, thank you. I am just trying to sort things out." He took her hand. The lines etched across her forehead showed her concern. "Paytah is back, and I'm not sure if he found a way for me to return to my other world. Even if I can, will my wife still take me back since I have been gone so long?"

She held his hand for several minutes. "As long as you live, there is hope. That is what you tell me."

He smiled. "Sit with me. You are right. You have changed since you first pulled me naked through Amut." She sat beside him, and he put his arm around her, wincing from the pain in his chest.

Zica came through the door. "The feast will be ready soon." She looked at them sitting together and turned to go back out.

"Come sit with us." He patted the mat next to his other side. "We should enjoy some time together."

She sat next to him, and he put his other arm around her. Both women leaned into him. The pressure on his ribs ached. But the warmth of their skin next to his and the comfort he found in their presence made him hold them there. Somehow, it just felt right, even if his mind told him it was wrong.

Later that night, Ryan went to Paytah. "I'm going to rest. When do you want to talk tomorrow?"

"If it looks like I'm up, come to my hut after you eat. Bring Zica and Shera with you. They will want to hear what I have to say. It affects them as well as you."

He went back to the hut still uncertain about Paytah's news, while the suzuecu screamed.

CHAPTER FIFTY

HOPE

The next day, Ryan, Zica, and Shera had to wait until midmorning for signs of activity from Paytah's hut.

He greeted them at the entrance. "Welcome, I am sorry it is so late. The last two days on the trail exhausted me. Thank you for your patience." He pointed to logs arranged as seats around his fire. He opened both entrances to allow as much light as possible into the hut.

A girl from the village came with a jar of water and poured cups for each of them while Paytah rummaged through several rolled-up pelts stacked along the wall. When he sat with his guests, he held a deer hide. "I know, Nanhin, you went to the spirit caves with my father. There, he explained the magic of the lines that appear and grow on the walls."

Ryan watched as the younger man unrolled the pelt. "I did. He told me the lines might show a way for me to return to my world."

Paytah put the skin on the ground in front of him. "This is a copy of the lines from the spirit cave." He took a stick and pointed to the pattern painted on the hide, tapping the end of the stick on one. "This is the line representing your presence here." He moved the stick to the place where two lines intersected. "The other line represents the appearance of another stranger who appeared years ago. The intersection was your meeting with him that ended in his death. Now, your line has moved directly toward the line representing Almirosia."

"Your father said if my line intersects Almirosia's line, it might open a portal to allow me to return to my world."

"Yes, that is what I believe as well. The magic of the lines brought you here to correct the balance in Almirosia. The other stranger had changed the world. He brought strange weapons and killed the priests. He did not want to return to his own world. The Creator built the magic you call the portal into Almirosia. The different peoples that populate this world came through the portal ages ago. A natural balance developed, and now, when something upsets it, a portal brings someone or something into our world to correct the imbalance."

"You're telling me Yago brought imbalance to the world and that his death will bring balance back?" Ryan shook his head. "It makes little sense to me. I brought imbalance to the world as well. I gave weapons to the Erotae and the villagers."

"You did, but it restored the balance by taking away the advantage the other weapons had given the coastal people. But you also made a fundamental change. You taught women to use the weapons and to fight. Our cultures will never be the same. Even now, they are more independent. My father gave Zica to you so you could protect and care for her. Now she believes she can take care of herself."

"I can. I can hunt, and I can fight." Zica held her head up. "I don't need a man to provide food for me."

"You see." Paytah slammed the stick down hard onto the skin. "If you stay, you may create a greater imbalance than the one Yago created. You must return."

"How?" Ryan asked.

"The lines should cross in two to three weeks. I suggest we go to the place where you arrived and wait for the portal to open." He picked up the pelt and rolled it back up. "Since we may have to wait for the portal to open, I will talk to Wanika. We need enough people to protect us from predators. He can make plans for a temporary village on the plains."

Ryan left with the two women. They went to the cliff edge and sat looking into the gorge below. It seemed either Zica or Shera had always been with him. Now both sat with him, one on each side.

"You seem sad, Nanhin." Shera leaned against him. "You should be happy."

"I am happy. I want to go home—but I want to stay." He hung his head. "I don't want to leave either of you. And I like it here. My other life is so different and complicated. How will my wife feel after over a year apart?"

"We don't know about your other wife. We don't want you to leave either," Zica said. "But Paytah said you could make the imbalance here worse if you stay."

"You need to go to protect our world. The Creator brought you here for a purpose that you have fulfilled." Shera squeezed his arm. "You have taught me so much."

They sat together for almost an hour before going back to the main part of the village. Wanika, Paytah, and several warriors sat at the firepit. Wanika waved Ryan over to join them. Shera and Zica went back to the hut.

"Nanhin," Paytah said. "Wanika agrees. We should take a large party to the plains."

"It is too dangerous to stay on the plains for very long." Wanika poked a stick into the coals. "Too many large predators hunt there: lions, hyenas, and saber-tooths. All can overcome a small party of two to six, especially if it remains in one place very long."

Ryan sat across from the chief. "What do you propose?"

"I think you need at least ten warriors or more to accompany you. A temporary village will need to be constructed with a large boma. We will need the women to set up shelters and cook while the warriors stand guard and hunt." The other warriors all nodded in agreement. "Paytah says we should be there in twelve days. It will take two days' travel, and at least two days to construct the village. I suggest we leave in seven days."

They sat and discussed Wanika's plan and what provisions they would need to take. Toby came up to Ryan. He petted the dog's neck and put his forehead against Toby's. "Are you ready to go home, boy?" The dog cocked his head and looked at him, then ran back toward Weeko's hut. Ryan wondered if the dog wanted to leave or stay. Ever since the slavers took him, Toby had lived with Weeko. Maybe he was her dog now. Would it change the balance if Toby stayed behind?

He left the other men and went to tell Zica and Shera about the plan. Though both said it was a good plan, their shoulders slumped and their eyes fell. Despite their assurances to the contrary, they were sad. The next few weeks would be difficult for them.

CHAPTER FIFTY-ONE

BACK TO THE PLAINS

Seven days later, Ryan, Zica, Shera, Paytah, Wanika, and Weeko, along with Toby and the manetoo, accompanied by nearly half the village left for the plains. They arrived at the stream at midmorning the first day. Ryan walked with Wanika at the head of the party. The chief nudged Ryan's arm and pointed to the left. There in the trees crouched a large saber-tooth.

"He has been following us for about a mile," Wanika said.

Ryan looked back at the band of villagers. "Do you think he will attack?"

"I don't think he will if we stay close together. The warriors around the perimeter will provide warning and defense if he does."

They kept walking. Occasionally, a warrior would alert Wanika of the big cat's location, but it never attacked and, after a couple more miles, it no longer followed them. They didn't stop until nearly sunset. Wanika had them camp in a clearing. The warriors built a thorny boma and brought in enough firewood to keep a large blaze going through the night.

Ryan lay on his back looking at the star-filled sky, nestled between Zica and Shera. No familiar constellations appeared, no matter how hard he searched. He remembered camping with his son and pointing out the various constellations, Ursa Major, Orion, and others, but here the sky was just a myriad of nameless stars. Even the moon was different, smaller. Zica put her arm across his chest and pressed into him. The seemingly ever-present suzuecu screamed as it soared above, blocking the sea of stars with a black shadow. Ryan drifted off to sleep.

The next morning, they broke camp before dawn, and headed up the long hill to the broad grassland plateau. When they cleared the trees, Wanika stopped them, calling the warriors to the front. "Here we will separate. I will leave half of the warriors with you and Paytah, while I take the other half ahead. We will set up a sturdier camp tonight with a larger boma. Lions and hyenas hunt in packs at night, and our numbers will not intimidate them." He put his hand on Ryan's shoulder. "Keep them close together. We don't want any stragglers ending up as dinner."

Ryan nodded to his friend. "I will keep them together."

Wanika and his band of warriors left at a trot to find a place for their camp. Ryan and the rest of the party followed at a steady walk. They easily followed the warrior's trail. Without the trees to shade them, the sun beat down, and the heat slowed their pace. They stopped frequently for water. As he understood the plan, Wanika knew of a spring near the place where Paytah expected the portal to open. Late that afternoon, the trail led up the tallest hill in sight. He could see Wanika's warriors working on the boma at the top of the hill.

Wanika greeted them when they entered the boma. "You made it safely, I see."

"Yes, everything went well except for the water. We are about out." Ryan held up an empty waterskin.

Wanika pointed to a small outcropping of rocks. "The spring comes out over there. Once you have rested for a few minutes, have the women set up the shelters. We will be here a while."

Ryan took his waterskin to the rocks, where a clear stream ran out into a muddy pool. He filled his skin and drank several handfuls from where the spring bubbled out and over the rocks before it entered the pool. He sat surveying the camp. Brush covered most of the top and two sides of the hill. Small trees grew along the stream bed as it ran down the north side and ended in a marshy pond. Wildlife had trampled down the grass around the pond, leaving mud banks around the dirty water. Herbivores crowded around the muddy banks, mastodons, camels, and large rhinoceros like beasts with broad flat horns.

Zica came and sat by him. "Nanhin, I don't want you to leave."

"I know. It will be hard for you." He held her close and kissed her forehead. "I will miss you too. But I must go when it is time. You go help set up the shelters and I will help with the boma."

He went and helped cut brush from the hillside for the fence and for firewood until the sun set. Back in the camp, deerskin tent-like shelters ringed the central firepit much like the village they had left behind. They had a quick meal and went to bed. He fell right to sleep until Wanika came to wake him for his watch. When he tried to get up, Shera held him. "Let me go. It is my time to stand watch."

She moaned, then let him up. Then she slid over and put her arm around Zica. Outside, the fire burned, lighting the camp. He took his position near the fence and walked along the section he guarded, holding his spear.

The night was still and clear, but not silent. Hyenas yipped and chortled in the distance. An occasional lion roared from the bottom of the hill, sending chills down his back, and the suzuecu screamed overhead. The dim light in the eastern sky portending the rising sun offered relief from the dark, lonely night. When it peaked over the horizon, he moved to wake the warrior taking his station, then went to catch a couple more hours of sleep before he had to get back to work on the boma.

He spent the rest of the day working, cutting, and hauling brush and wood. That night passed much like the previous one. The next day, with the boma completed, a small party of warriors left the enclosure to hunt. Ryan stayed in camp and sat with Paytah. "When do you think the portal will open?"

"Probably in the next three days, but it could be longer." The shaman held his hands out in front of his body and shrugged his shoulders.

"How will we know when it happens?"

"You should feel it. Do you remember how it felt the day you arrived?"

Ryan nodded. "Vaguely. I felt a tingling sensation and Toby barked frantically."

Almost on cue, Toby trotted up to him and sat beside him.

Paytah laughed. "Then he will alert you when the portal opens."

While Ryan sat and petted Toby, the manetoo came over and sat next to him as well. Since the battle, she had been friendlier to him. Now she let him stroke her neck and scratch behind her ears before she lay on her side. She was obviously pregnant. "Well, boy," he said to Toby. "It looks like you're about to be a father."

Two days passed without incident, then in the late afternoon on the third day, a pride of six lions attacked a flat-horned rhino near the water hole. The din of the rhino's high-pitched screams and the lions' roars put the camp on edge. It also attracted a large clan of over twenty hyenas that tried to steal the lions' kill. The ensuing battle lasted half an hour before the lions drove the hyenas up the hill away from the watering hole. The lions devoured the rhino while the hyenas watched. As darkness fell, they could still hear the cackling of the hyenas below.

That night, Ryan dreamed of the suzuecu swarming, like crows in the fall, their shrill screams replacing the caws and clicks as they clustered on a rock face looking down at him. Then someone called his name.

"Nanhin." An icy hand on his shoulder woke him. "It is time for your watch."

Sitting up, he tried to clear his head. With the air cooling his skin, he rubbed his eyes and focused on the fire outside the shelter before he crawled out. Once out of the shelter, he picked up his spear and went to his station.

"Stay alert, Nanhin," the warrior who woke him said. "The hyenas moved up the hill closer to camp."

Ryan nodded in assent, then walked to his section of the fence. He wished he could see over the top of the boma. The yips and chortles of the hyenas soon came from the other side as they circled the camp. Other warriors, including the one who woke him, gathered around the fire with their weapons.

Someone yelled an alarm from across the camp, and the warriors at the fire grabbed burning brands and ran to help. He stayed at his post, listening to the commotion, and watched for any movement within the camp. He heard the brush in the boma shifting.

"I need help here!" A hyena yelped and poked its head out through the brush. He ran and drove his spear into the animal's neck. It screamed and flailed, making the hole larger. Two more hyenas pushed through the hole. His spear was still in the neck of the first beast. He faced the two with only his knife. They stared at him snarling, saliva dripping from their mouths.

The whoosh of an arrow zipped by his ear. It stuck in the left shoulder of one hyena, causing it to yelp and jump toward him. He saw someone drive a spear into the animal's side as he dove to his right. From the ground, he saw Paytah, Shera, and Zica as the third hyena pounced on him. Arrows flew into the hyena's ribcage but didn't slow it down. The two women screamed when the hyena's drooling mouth went toward his face.

Then, the shrill cry of the suzuecu drowned out the noise of the battle. The weight of the hyena lifted off him as the suzuecu carried the animal into the dawn sky. More suzuecu screams accompanied by the rush of air from their wings filled the camp. Still on his back he saw at least two more dragons fly away, grasping hyenas in their feet. Zica kneeled at his head, wiping the saliva from his face, before she kissed him.

Shera and Paytah stood next to her. Wanika came over to them. "What just happened? I would not have believed it, if I had not seen it."

Paytah shook his head in apparent disbelief. "It is magic. Almirosia is protecting Nanhin. That is the only explanation that makes sense."

"Let me help you up." Wanika offered his hand to Ryan, who groaned as he stood. His ribs still had not completely healed.

"What about the rest of the hyenas?" Ryan asked.

"They fled down the hill to the east with two suzuecu chasing them."

"Let's get you to your shelter." Paytah got under Ryan's arm to give him some added support. "I will check your injuries, then you can rest."

When they got to the tent, Toby ran up, barking. "Where were you, boy?" The dog licked his face. "I could have used your help."

"He was protecting me." Weeko stood outside the tent entrance.

"You're a good dog." Ryan continued to pet Toby. "But I think you are Weeko's dog now."

"You need to rest," Paytah said. "You do not have any serious injuries, and others need my help. The women will see to you." He left, and Weeko called Toby away, leaving him with Zica and Shera.

CHAPTER FIFTY-TWO

THE PORTAL OPENS

After the hyena attack, the host of suzuecu stayed around Ryan's party. When resting, they encircled the top of the hill, sitting halfway between the camp and the watering hole. The sound of the resting beasts, a low rumble like the purring of giant cats, and their intermittent screams reminded humans and animals alike of their presence. A sense of safety settled over the camp.

On the morning of the third day, Ryan slept late after his shift on the watch. The piercing screams of the host of suzuecu jolted him awake. His whole body tingled with pins and needles. He sat up and shook his hands and squeezed his fingers, trying to get the normal feeling back.

Paytah came up to his tent. "Nanhin, get up. The suzuecu are leaving. I think the portal has opened and we need to follow them."

Ryan staggered when stood. "You may be right about the portal. My whole body is tingling."

Around the camp, villagers stood pointing to the sky where the suzuecu circled before they headed east. Paytah gathered Ryan, Shera, Zica, Wanika, and several warriors. They followed the suzuecu whose main body neared the eastern horizon. A second group of larger suzuecu circled over Ryan and the others. They encouraged the people forward with their low purring.

"Do you hear them, Nanhin?" Paytah said as they went down the hill. "I have never seen or heard of anything like this. They lead you, and they protect you."

"It seems so." The tingling still coursed through his body, but the feeling in his extremities had returned to normal.

They followed the suzuecu for two hours. The creatures had landed and formed a circle around an inconspicuous plot of grassland. There, they prevented the party from moving further. Only when Ryan approached did the animals move to open a narrow path between them.

Paytah put his hand on Ryan's shoulder. "The portal must be there." He pointed to the opening in the circle of suzuecu. "I think they want you to continue without us. You should say your goodbyes now."

He looked at the shaman. "I'm afraid. What if Emily doesn't take me back? How will I explain all of this to her?"

"I cannot answer your questions. I only know that you must leave, and I am uncertain that you have a choice. The suzuecu could force you to leave."

Ryan studied the circle of dragons. Paytah was right. The beasts could do anything they wanted. "You are right, my friend. I must finish this and go home." They clasped arms. Then Ryan went to the two women.

Zica threw her arms around him. "Don't go." Tears ran down her face.

"I must." He pushed her away so he could look into her eyes. "I love you, but I don't think I have any choice but to go home." He swallowed hard to push back his own tears. "Sometimes, God forces us into hard choices. This is the hardest choice I have ever made. I will miss waking up against your skin and watching you tend to the hut. You have brought joy and love into my time here."

He squeezed her to him, then kissed her deeply, before turning to Shera. "I am sorry that I couldn't give you more. I have loved you as well, and I will never forget the time we had together."

She held him and whispered in his ear, "I love you. You have saved my life multiple times and helped me to see who I am. I would be your wife if you let me, even if I share you with Zica. I know you must leave." She pushed herself away and put her arm around Zica. Tears ran down their faces. "Go," Shera said.

He left the two women. Wanika stepped up to him. "Nanhin, we will remember you in the tales of the prominent men from among our people. You taught us much and changed our way of life. You have been my friend. May your God go with you."

They hugged. "Goodbye, my friend. I will miss you and your people."

Ryan went to Weeko who was also crying. "You accepted me into the village before anyone else, and you took care of Toby after the raid. You even taught me your language and customs. I am forever in your debt." He hugged her, then turned and called Toby.

Toby ran to him, turning circles at his feet. "Sit." The dog obeyed. He stroked his neck, then said, "C'mon, boy." But Toby stayed. "Let's go home. Don't you want to see Emily?"

Toby cocked his head, wagged his tail, and stared at Ryan, but didn't come. He bent down on one knee and hugged the dog. He couldn't keep back the tears any longer. Grief gripped his heart. He knew Toby would stay behind. Looking up at Weeko, he said, "Toby is your dog now. Take care of him."

"You know I will, as he will take care of me. Goodbye, Nanhin."

He stood and walked through the rest of the party, clasping arms or hugging most of them. As he got close to the suzuecu circle, the closest animals still formed a gateway into the circle. He turned for one last wave, then walked through. The energy from the portal pulsed through his body, but when he reached the center of the circle, nothing happened. The pulses came from over his head. He stood, confused.

The pulsing slowed, and the energy in his body ebbed. The suzuecu became restless. Then a loud scream came from above and a giant suzuecu swooped into the circle. It grabbed him. With its feet wrapped around him, the monster took him high above the prairie. It circled once; he saw the villagers looking up in shock. Then it dove toward the circle where the other suzuecu still stood and released him. He plummeted to the ground, screaming.

CHAPTER FIFTY-THREE

HOSPITAL

Ryan woke up to mechanical noises, beeps, clicks, and whooshes. His body hurt. His mouth and throat felt dry. He wanted a drink. When he tried to sit, pain shot through his chest and up his arm. He opened his eyes. The dim light above his head and from the monitors beside him provided the only illumination in a darkened room. He was lying in bed with tubes connected to his arm and face.

A hospital... The suzuecu soaring away as he fell to earth was the last thing he remembered. How did he get here?

Light streamed through the door as a plump woman came into the room. He tried to turn to get a better look at her, but the stabbing pain in his side prevented him. She came over and looked down at him. "You're awake. How do you feel?"

"Thirsty," he rasped.

"Just a minute." He heard water running. She returned with a cup and put a straw to his lips. "Just take a couple of sips. I will bring cold water after I check your vitals. Close your eyes. I'm turning on the lights."

Even with his closed eyelids, the bright light momentarily stunned him. He blinked several times before his vision cleared. The nurse bent over him. "My name is Lisa, and I will be your shift nurse. Once I check your numbers, I will let the doctor know you're awake. She will be in as soon as she's available. Do you need anything for the pain?"

"I don't know. It only hurts when I try to sit."

She turned to the monitor and pressed a button. He felt the blood pressure cuff tighten on his arm. When it released, she noted the readings on his chart, then she checked his temperature. "Your vitals look good, considering your condition. I'll be back soon with ice water. Do you want the lights on or off?"

"Leave them on. Where am I?"

"UCHealth Memorial Hospital. Now you rest." She left, closing the door behind her.

He did a quick self-assessment. An oxygen line ran under his nose. He had an IV in his left arm and leads ran from his chest. Other than the pain from his ribs and a headache, he seemed fine.

Lisa returned with a large cup of ice water. "The doctor said she would be here shortly. She doesn't want you to have any pain medicine until she sees you." Lisa stood beside him again, her friendly round face smiling. "I'm going to raise the back of your bed a little. It should make you more comfortable." The vibrations from the motor surged through him as the back rose.

When he winced, she stopped. "Do I need to lower it a little?"

"Ooh. No, this is good for now. My wife—has anyone contacted my wife?"

"She is in the cafeteria. The doctor will let her know when she can see you. Now rest." She went through the bed controls, TV controls, and call button, then left him alone again.

"Emily is here. Thank you, Jesus." He closed his eyes. At least she still cared.

Over an hour had passed when an attractive brunette knocked on his door and entered. "I'm Dr. O'Donnell. How are you feeling?"

"Except for the pain in my ribs and a headache, I feel fine. How long have I been here?"

"The ambulance brought you down from Woodland Park three days ago. Your wife found you lying by the creek near your home. You have been unconscious until today. Can you tell me what happened? Your injuries are consistent with a significant fall or a beating. And there is an electrical burn on your chest. Do you remember how you got them?"

"The last thing I remember was walking with Toby, our dog, down by the creek after dinner. We came to a clearing. Toby was acting agitated, barking with his hackles up. I stepped out into the clearing, and the air felt charged. My hair stood on end. My hands tingled. The air crackled around me. That's the last I remember." He didn't know how much to tell her; she probably wouldn't believe him, anyway.

"Based on the burn on your chest and the description you gave, I believe you suffered from a lightning strike. But now, your vital signs are good. I'm going to order a couple of tests to check your brain functions. The nurses will get you some food. I will let your wife know she can come in. You're very lucky." She made some notes on the chart and went out.

A few minutes after the doctor left, Emily came into the room, moving slowly, looking unsure. Her long hair was down and her eyes bloodshot. When Ryan smiled, she ran to the bed, putting her arms around his neck.

"I thought I had lost you." She kissed him.

"Oomph." He winced as he tried to put his arms around her.

She released him and stepped back. "I'm sorry. Does it hurt bad?"

"No, it's just my ribs. You are so beautiful." Tears formed in his eyes. *I really am back.* "I didn't think I would ever see you again."

"This has been the longest three days of my life." She sat in the chair beside the bed, holding his hand. "The doctor said you had broken ribs and a possible concussion. She's going to run some tests but thinks you can come home in a day or two."

"It can't be soon enough. I need to be home with you." Then he asked a question to which he already knew the answer. "What about Toby? He was with me."

She looked down. "I'm sorry. Toby has disappeared. He wasn't there when I found you, and we haven't seen him since. It makes little sense. He always stayed so close."

"He might still turn up, and if not, we will get another dog." Though, he knew Toby was gone for good.

There was a knock on the door and a young man in scrubs came in. "I'm from Radiology. I will take Ryan up for a CT scan. You can wait here, but it will be an hour or more."

Emily stepped out of the room while the technician wheeled the bed out. "I'll be here when you get back."

The next day, the doctor came in while Ryan was still eating his lunch. "How are you feeling today, Ryan?"

"Better. The meds take the edge off the pain in my chest and the headache has eased." He continued to eat.

"I can see your appetite is back. The CT scan didn't show any bleeding or severe trauma to your head. But you have had a concussion. Because you were unconscious for three days, we are going to keep you another day to be sure you can go home safely. Will Emily be with you while you are there? I don't think you should be alone for any extended period over the next week."

"Yes. I will stay with him at the house. We should be fine," Emily said.

The doctor came over and checked his heart and lungs with a stethoscope. "I am a little puzzled by these old scars." She pointed to Ryan's shoulder and thigh. "They look like significant wounds, but there are no notes on them in your record."

"Hunting accidents," he lied. "They look worse on the surface than they were."

The doctor stared at him for a minute then said, "I will be by on my early rounds in the morning. If things go well tonight, you can go home."

CHAPTER FIFTY-FOUR

HOME

Two days later, Ryan sat in the passenger seat of their Subaru Outback while Emily drove them home. It had taken longer to get through the hospital bureaucracy than they had expected, so they didn't pull into the garage until late afternoon. She helped him out of the car and into the house. Some movements still caused him significant pain. She led him to the recliner and got him a glass of iced tea before she brought in the rest of his meager belongings.

While she fixed their dinner, he dozed in the chair and smiled. Relief flooded through him like a river, washing away the tension and fear of his ordeal. He was home with Emily. Tears ran down his cheeks.

"Thank you, Jesus. Thank you, Jesus. Lord, thank you for keeping my husband safe," he heard her pray out loud. Then she sang "What a Friend We Have in Jesus."

"That's an old song I haven't heard in a long time." He joined her from his chair, and they sang the rest of the song. After they finished, she continued to sing while she worked to finish preparing the fajitas.

"Do you want to eat in the recliner or at the table?" she asked.

"At the table." He stood. "Ugh." He kept a hand on the back of the recliner to let the dizziness pass, then he walked into the kitchen. The smell of the spiced meat, peppers, and onions caused his stomach to growl. He groaned as he sat. "That smells sooo good." A smile lit his face.

For a few minutes, they ate in silence. The food tasted much better than anything he had had since the incident. The thinly sliced, seasoned steak and vegetables wrapped in warm, home-made tortillas evoked sounds of pleasure from him as he ate.

"You're sure enjoying dinner," Emily said, laughing. "You act like I haven't fed you in ages."

"It feels like ages to me. Can I tell you something?"

"Sure, you can tell me anything." The smile left her face as she knit her dark eyebrows.

"You must listen to me with an open mind and let me finish before you say anything. Can you do that?"

"Yeah, I can do that, but you are worrying me."

He could see the concern in her eyes, and he watched her reactions as he told her of his ordeal in Almirosia. When he began, her face relaxed, her eyes widened, and she leaned forward toward him. She interrupted him when he told her about Zica and again when he first encountered the suzuecu, but he held up his hand. She sat back and let him continue.

But when he got to his time with the Erotae, she couldn't keep quiet. "Winged men. What did they look like?"

"The closest explanation is an artistic representation of an angel, but with more feathers. Beautiful and frightening at the same time." He gazed into her eyes and could tell she thought it was all a dream, but he continued. When he got to the part about leaving Toby, he stopped to keep from crying.

"Anyway, I know from your perspective, it has been just over a week since Toby and I walked out the door. But in my mind, it has been over a year." He leaned back.

"Wow. That was quite a dream. The doctor said you had some unusual brain activity while you were unconscious, but this is wild." She stared at him, wide-eyed, and shook her head. "It's late. Why don't you go shower while I clean up? We can talk more before bed."

"Okay." He knew she wouldn't believe him, but he had to tell her. Now he wasn't sure it had really happened. He got into the shower and let the hot water wash over him. It seemed like so long since he had bathed in hot water. As he washed, he felt the scar on his thigh and other reminders of the wounds he endured. It was real, even if nobody else believed him.

He walked out of the bathroom, and Emily was sitting on the bed. "You lost a lot of weight. You look different. Take off the towel."

He removed the towel from his waist and stood naked in front of her.

"Back in the bathroom. I want to see you in better light." They went into the bathroom. She eyed him up and down. "When did you get so tan?" She didn't wait for him to answer but ran her hands over his back. "You are a lot more muscular than I remember. Gosh, you're chiseled. Where did these scars come from? I don't remember these. Who are you?" She stepped back and stared at him.

"I can't explain it to you. I told you I was gone for over a year, living in primitive conditions, where I fought wild predators, hunted giant bison, and battled men. You think it was a dream, but I lived it. This is the scar from the crossbow bolt I received when the slavers attacked." He pointed to the scar on his thigh. "And the long scars on my back came from the lion that jumped on me after the bison hunt."

They went back to the bedroom. Emily sat on the bed quietly for a few minutes, then pulled a leather pouch out of the hospital bag. "The nurse said you wore this. It was in your tattered clothes. What is it?" She held up the necklace with the terror bird talons.

"Those are the talons from the tanwakua that attacked Weeko, the girl from the village. I killed them and they gave the necklace to me as a symbol of my status as a warrior."

She looked at them, turning the necklace in her hands. "I don't understand. You said Toby stayed back there."

"Yes, he didn't come with me when I went to the portal. He bonded to Weeko and the wolf that was pregnant with his pups." He finished putting on his pajamas and sat next to her. "I can't tell you for certain if it was real or a dream, but I believe it happened. Only God knows the truth."

She leaned into him. "It seems too impossible for you to be gone for three days and have all of that happen. It's crazy."

"Yes, crazy, a good way to describe it." They sat together without talking, then climbed into bed.

Several days later, he sat in the recliner, dozing. Emily had gone to Colorado Springs to run some errands. His ribs still hurt but were healing. He heard the door open through the haze of sleep as she came into the house.

"I have a surprise for you." He felt something cold and wet on his cheek. He sat up alert, looking into the deep brown eyes of a German shepherd puppy. "The breeder called me while I was in town. He said he had a couple of puppies that needed forever homes. So, I stopped by and got this beautiful girl." She put the puppy in his lap. It climbed up his chest and licked his face. "You can start training them while you recover."

"Them?" He held the pup away from his face.

"Yes. I named that one Lizzie. I have all her papers." She held up a manilla envelope. "Now sit still and I will go get the other surprise."

He held Lizzie in his lap, petting her and allowing her to chew on his fingers. Emily came back in with a smaller puppy. He could tell it wasn't a purebred German shepherd. It was too small, and it had too much white on its face. But its markings nearly matched Lizzie's. She brought the pup over and put it in his lap and picked up Lizzie.

"This is Bailey. She is a German shepherd and an Australian cattle dog mix. Apparently, one of his males got with the neighbor's female heeler. She doesn't have any papers, but I fell in love with her the moment I saw her."

He pulled Bailey up to his face and looked at her. She was beautiful, but shy. She didn't lick his face. Emily took Bailey from Ryan and set both puppies on the floor. Lizzie ran right over to Bailey and jumped on her. They wrestled on the floor while Emily went out and brought in the rest of the things she had bought in town.

They spent the rest of the afternoon playing with the puppies until they were tired and slept cuddled next to each other. Emily went to the kitchen and started dinner. "You know, I had another idea while I was out. I think we should go see Pastor Glenn for some counseling. I can't reconcile the fact that you were only gone for three days with all that you have told me. Some of it disturbs me. You said you had a wife, uh..."

"Zica."

"Yes. I know it can't be true, but given your past infidelity, I worry it is still on your mind. I think the pastor can help."

"You're probably right. I know the guilt is real even if the relationship was a dream. But you must know I wanted to get back to you more than anything. It was the only reason I survived. Can you forgive me?"

THE END

CHAPTER FIFTY-FIVE

EPILOGUE

"Well, Ryan." Pastor Glenn sat across the table from Ryan in the church coffee shop. It was Tuesday morning, and they had been meeting for the past three months. "You have told me the most incredible story. I don't know what I can do to help you. I know you are still attending Celebrate Recovery and another recovery group. You're taking the right approach. How is your relationship with Emily?"

Ryan set his cup down. "Right now, it is as good or better than it has ever been. We are communicating better than at any time in our marriage. Though she still shakes her head at the changes in my body."

"Do you blame her?" Pastor Glenn reached across the table and put his hand on Ryan's arm. "One last question. How is your relationship with God?"

"I would say it's the same as with Emily. I am communicating better, and I feel like He answers especially when I pray about my feelings of guilt and shame. He reminds me He took care of everything."

The pastor held out his hands. "Let's pray that God continues to work in your life."

They prayed, then Ryan took their cups to the sink and got ready to leave. As they shook hands, the pastor held on for a minute. "You have an amazing story. I think you should write a book about all the adventures you had, real or imagined."

"You think I should?"

"Yes, it could be like *A Princess of Mars* by Edgar Rice Burroughs, or something. I enjoyed reading those when I was younger." He looked serious. "I am not kidding. I think you should."

Ryan shook his head and turned to leave. "If I do. I'll sign a copy for you."

ABOUT THE AUTHOR

C. Buck Jones writes science fiction and fantasy novels with a Christian perspective. When he retired as an engineer, he started writing to occupy his time and keep out of his wife's hair. When not at his computer writing or editing, he fishes with his grandkids or his dog in the Colorado streams and lakes near his home. He enjoys soccer, walks with his wife, and spending time in God's infinitely beautiful creation.

If you enjoyed reading this, you can get a copy of his debut novel, <u>Salvation and Doom: The Cathardi Prophecy</u> at Amazon or order a copy through your local bookstore, or on my website. Please leave a review on Amazon or Goodreads. Reader reviews are critical to the success of books.

For more about C. Buck Jones visit his website: https://www.cbuckjones.com

Acknowledgements

I started this novel while my first novel was going through the editing process. I have always enjoyed reading adventure science fiction about a hero thrust into a new world or situation unexpectedly. I thought it would be fun to write something along the lines of <u>A Princess of Mars</u> by Edgar Rice Burroughs, <u>The Lost World</u> by Arthur Conan Doyle, or <u>Out of the Silent Planet</u> by C.S. Lewis. This is the result of that process. I hope it is a fun read.

Many people helped me along the way making important tangible and intangible contributions. I thank God for leading me in the development of the story, and my wife Carol for the patience to put up with the hours of writing, the endless videos on publishing, marketing, and creating a following, and the money spent on editors, software, and a cover design. She may not realize how important her constant support and encouragement are to my writing.

One thing I learned during the process is that I don't write as well as I might think. Fortunately, other people helped me hone the book into a final product. Rachel Swanson provided the final copy edit and some much-needed encouragement. Belle Manuel from Fiverr did the final proofreading to polish the text. Being retired and having a limited budget, they were perfect for me.

As a new writer, having other people read your work is frightening. What if they don't like it? Thankfully, I found support and help at the Colorado Springs ACFW chapter. The critique group provided early insights and support, offering suggestions for improvement, and encouraging me to keep working.

I also received a lot of encouragement from my Beta readers, Mikayla Steiger, Jens Pedersen, Eileen Hickman, Elle R at Fiverr, and my wife Carol. They let me know the story was something people would read. I also owe thanks to many friends and co-workers who supported me.

www.ingramcontent.com/pod-product-compliance
Lightning Source LLC
Chambersburg PA
CBHW051307300726
48976CB00002B/301